A Most Unusual Señorita

By

Joseph R. Costa

ISBN-13:9798525237803

Contents

Note: For the convenience of readers, distances are expressed in English units rather than the Spanish units of the time.

- JRC

Pronunciation
Guadalquivir (gwa-DAL-ki-veer)
Andalusia (an-da-loo-SEE-a)
Guillermo (gee-YAIR-mo)
Mencía (men-SEE-a)

Foreword

In *Along the Guadalquivir*, our two true friends were first introduced. This book tells of the further adventures of Mateo and Guillermo. A most unusual señorita named Mencía joined them in earlier adventures and is their true friend now as well. Like Mateo and Guillermo, she is brave and skilled with the weapons of their time.

The setting is the late sixteenth century along the Guadalquivir River in Andalusia, an ancient section of southern Spain still heavily influenced by its Moorish past. In those times, Spain was the richest and most powerful kingdom in Europe. Yet, in his quest to be the champion and defender of the Catholic faith, the king spent the huge amounts of silver and riches from the Indies as fast as they arrived on the treasure fleets, so Spain was not a flourishing country. Banditry, crime, and poverty were commonplace.

The Spanish kingdom was dominated by the Catholic Church, which was intolerant of all other religions. Many years before, royal edicts had expelled from Spain all Jews and Moors who refused to convert to Christianity. The converted Jews (conversos) and converted Moors (moriscos) who remained in Spain were of particular interest to the Spanish Inquisition, which sought to rid Spain of all heretics such as Jews and Moors only posing to be converted to Christianity.

Fortunately, the above information is merely backdrop, and this story is not about kings or religious struggles. With that good news, the further adventures of our three true friends begins.

Main Characters

Mateo, Guillermo & Mencía - the true friends
Luisa - Mateo's wife
Don Lorenzo & Doña Antonia - Mateo's father & mother
Miguel - Guillermo's father, Don Lorenzo's overseer
María - Guillermo's mother
Pascual - local highwayman, Don Lorenzo's friend
Sebastian - one of Pascual's men, friend of the true friends

Don Francisco & Doña Isabel - Luisa's father & mother
Domingo & Gabriel - Luisa's younger brothers
Don Carlos & Doña Catalina - Mateo's cousins

Don Diego - Mateo's uncle, Guillermo's natural father
Floriana - Don Diego's love, Guillermo's natural mother
Andrés & Agustin - Don Diego's sons
Beatriz - Rescued girl adopted by Don Diego
Martín - Mencía's devotee

Note: "Don" and "Doña" are titles of respect of the time for wealthy estate owners and their wives, as well as other people of importance. In the story, these titles are included in the conversations with estate owners. However, the titles are used sparingly at other times to help reduce confusion from seeing "Don" so many times.

1. Kidnapped

"WE BROUGHT YOU some company!" announced the swarthy villain as he shoved the bound and gagged Mencía to the floor. Then with a malicious laugh, he slammed the door.

Mencía could hear the wooden drop bar being put in place to secure it. Now in the dark, Mencía could see nothing at first. She was sore from her rough treatment but immediately wiggled up close to the door to listen. She could hear the men on the other side talking carelessly.

"What do we do with the other one?" asked one voice.

"He might be worth some ransom, I think, maybe?" said a second voice.

"Yes, they have family north of here somewhere, and a ransom note delivered to the merchant will get to them. Tie him up and put him in another room," said a third voice.

Mencía gasped quietly in surprise, recognizing the voice of the merchant's wagon driver named Pablo.

With a laugh, he added, "The old Jew may even send me to deliver the ransom note to them."

"So *he* is behind Rachel's kidnapping," Mencía thought to herself. "Guillermo and I should have suspected as much and been more careful."

This Pablo villain had supposedly been leading Guillermo and Mencía to where he had seen kidnappers bring Rachel, the merchant's daughter. But instead, he had led them into an ambush. Mencía, Guillermo, and Pablo had been walking along a narrow alleyway when several men suddenly and unexpectedly attacked them from several close-by doorways.

The first attacker had clubbed Guillermo over the head from behind, knocking him unconscious to the ground. When Mencía turned and saw Guillermo struck, two other attackers had grabbed her from behind and cupped a hand over her mouth. With her arms held tightly, they dragged her inside a door and bound her as she struggled. It had all happened so fast.

1

She had initially thought the merchant's driver had suffered a fate like theirs, but now she knew better. The one bit of good news she had just learned was that Guillermo was still alive. But he was injured and bound up in another room, so it would be up to her to get them out.

Thanks to the light coming from the gap beneath the door, she could now make out objects in the dark room. When flung into the room, she had seen the young girl sitting against one wall with hands tied behind her back, ankles bound, and scarf tied across her mouth. Now in the dim light, she could again make her out, in much the same position.

Mencía could taste blood in her mouth from the blows the men had given her as she struggled with them. She was wearing her riding outfit with her arms bound behind her back and her legs bound by ropes tied tightly around her riding boots. She raised herself up onto her knees and worked her way across to the girl who watched her in resigned silence.

"Rachel?" Mencía managed to quietly ask despite the gag tied across her mouth.

Coming out of her despair, the young girl nodded in surprise. "I Mencía, you remember me."

After eyeing her for a moment in the dark, she recognized her.

"You and Guillermo. He save us?" Rachel whispered through her gag.

She knew Guillermo from his business dealings with her father and greatly admired the fearless young man. Mencía had accompanied him once several months ago.

"No, tied up here too."

"Oh," grunted Rachel dejectedly.

"Stay here," whispered Mencía.

Rachel watched as Mencía scooted silently back over to the door and listened. She could hear the banter of the men. They were playing cards and talking about how much money the new captives might bring.

She again heard the voice of Pablo say, "I am going back to the merchant to dramatically and pathetically inform him that we were viciously attacked in these dangerous alleys of Cordoba. The man and woman were regrettably taken while I, coward that I am, ran and got away. I will need some visible signs of having been attacked. Angulo, hit me across the face."

She heard a loud smack and then a crash of furniture.

After a quiet moment, Pablo said with mock satisfaction, "Very good, Angulo. A nice bloody nose and mouth. Yes, very good."

"I am happy that you like it, Señor."

Then they heard another punch and more furniture crashing.

"I liked it so much I thought I would share. Damn you!"

After more moments of silence, Pablo said gruffly, "All right, I am going now and will be back later. Stay alert. No food or water for any of them."

She heard an outer door slammed and bolted. Afterward, she heard a banter among the men about what had happened and finally more card playing. They seemed to have no concern or thoughts of their captives. From the different voices, Mencía concluded there were three men on the other side of their barred door.

Mencía already knew what she had to do. She scooted back across and got close to Rachel's ear.

"Rachel, we escape."

"How?"

"Knives inside pockets of my jacket," Mencía struggled to say through the gag.

Having no reason to suspect that a young attractive Spanish girl in a handsome riding outfit would be carrying weapons, the kidnappers had not bothered to search her. Always prepared, Mencía had two throwing knives concealed inside her short jacket. Fortunately, their kidnappers had not noticed them while tying her up.

"I lie down. You get knife out with hands. Then I cut ropes," Mencía managed to whisper.

3

Saying this, Mencía lowered herself again to the floor as Rachel turned with a worried look and crept backward until her hands could feel Mencía's jacket. After a minute of probing and pulling, she succeeded in getting a knife out.

Mencía sat up, turned, and grasped the knife on the floor with her hands behind her back. Coming together back-to-back, Mencía felt the ropes with one hand as she held the knife with the other. After a minute of sawing, she was able to cut through a rope to free Rachel's hands. Soon they were both free of their bindings and had their gags removed.

Coming together, Rachel whispered, "Now what?"

"Three men are in the next room, guarding us. They are playing cards and not paying attention," whispered Mencía.

"But how can we escape with them outside?" whispered Rachel incredulously.

"I have two knives. I saw several cutlasses against the wall and a pistol on the table. I am skilled with weapons and have a plan. I will beat on the door to get them to unbar and open it. When they do, I will rush out and kill the first two with my knives. Before the third one recovers from his surprise, I will get to the pistol or a cutlass to kill him."

"Can you really do that?"

"Yes. These knives are designed for throwing, and I am good at it. You should follow me into the room and try to help if you can. Maybe you could get to the pistol first. Shoot him with it or just hit it away, out of reach. Do you know how to use one?"

"Yes, my father showed me how to use the one in his desk."

"Good."

"With luck, your help will not be necessary. Once the guards are subdued, we will find Guillermo and escape with him back to your father's."

Rachel, a young and pretty girl of fifteen, could only look at her in amazement and nod.

After a few moments getting her knives out and ready, Mencía quietly asked, "Are you ready, Rachel?"

"Yes, I think so."

"Remember, come out behind me. See if you can get to the pistol while they are busy with me."

Rachel nodded nervously.

Mencía turned and went to the door. She banged on it several times with her knee and then stood back, poised to attack.

She could hear the card playing and conversation stop in the other room, but she got no response.

She banged again on the door with her knee several times.

"Quiet in there!" one of them hollered.

She banged on the door again only louder.

"I said quiet! If you bang on that door again, I am going to come in there! You do *not* want me to do that!"

She banged on the door again loudly.

"Ramír! Someone in there needs to be taught a lesson. Do not break any bones though. The slave traders will not pay as much for damaged goods. Angulo, keep dealing."

Mencía could hear a chair noisily thrown aside and heavy stomping toward the door. The door was unbarred noisily and swung open to reveal the large figure of a man, who angrily declared, "We warned you and now…"

He stopped short in surprise, maybe at seeing the figure of Mencía standing unbound in front of him or maybe at the realization that a knife now penetrated his throat, and he was spewing blood.

He stumbled backward clutching his throat and crashed into the table where the other two jumped up in surprise. Mencía was close behind him and soon the man on the left discovered a knife in his throat. He grasped at the knife as he staggered wide-eyed forward and past Mencía.

When the first man crashed into the table, the cards, money, food, drink, and pistol on it were scattered wildly about. Mencía looked quickly for the pistol without seeing it. The third man had now regained his senses and was climbing and stumbling over furniture and the body of the first man to make a lunge at her. Seeing a cutlass resting nearby against the wall to her left, she sprang to get it and then made a vicious slash with it to her right, a slashing move she had practiced many times before during cutlass training sessions with Don Tomás. Her cutlass caught the man in the throat and nearly decapitated him as blood spurted from his neck.

Already thinking of Guillermo, she had started for an open door to other rooms when she heard Rachel scream, "Mencía! Watch out! Behind you!"

Apparently, the knife in the throat of the second man had not been immediately fatal. He had pulled it out of his own bloody neck and was aiming to return it to its owner. Now close behind her with the knife raised, he was about to strike her in the back.

At Rachel's scream, Mencía wheeled around with her cutlass, slashing his arm and deflecting the knife. She immediately followed up her slash with a thrust of her cutlass into the belly of the man. This slash and thrust was again another move she had practiced many times before.

The arms of the man now fell to his sides dropping the knife as his eyes rolled back and his face glazed over. Putting her boot on his belly, she pulled her cutlass blade from it and gave him a shove backward with her boot. He fell to the floor with a crash like a fallen tree.

Mencía looked at Rachel who looked back with surprise.

"Thank you, Rachel. See if you can find the pistol," she said hurriedly as she reached down to pick up her knife.

Soon she had both her knives retrieved and the blood on them quickly wiped off on the shirt of one of the men. Seeing Rachel now with the pistol in her hand, Mencía motioned toward the door. They stepped their way across the bodies, blood, and debris to the open door where Mencía stopped to look and listen.

She saw a corridor with several doors along it. At the far end looked to be the barred exterior door.

"Quickly, we must find Guillermo!" said Mencía.

They rushed into a corridor and to the first door, the only one with a drop bar securing it. They quickly got the drop bar off, the door opened, and found Guillermo tied up and lying motionless on the floor of the filthy room.

"Oh, dear God, is he dead?" asked Rachel anxiously.

Mencía rushed to him and examined him quickly.

"He is not dead, only unconscious. I will cut him loose. Rachel, see if you can find some water!"

She rapidly had his ropes cut and removed. Seeing a ragged cloak lying nearby, she put it under his bloody head as she turned him onto his back.

"I only found this wine," said Rachel, returning and handing her a bottle.

"It will have to do," said Mencía, taking it.

"Rachel, check the other rooms to see if other captives are here."

Mencía began splashing wine onto Guillermo's face as Rachel disappeared again.

The wine was working. He was soon gasping for breath, spitting out wine, and looking about with bleary eyes.

"Guillermo, can you walk? I have killed the men who kidnapped us. We must leave quickly before any others come."

Moaning at his terrible headache, his eyes finally focused on Mencía.

"Mencía," he said drowsily.

"Guillermo, we need to escape! Can you walk?"

"Yes, I think so."

When he saw Rachel's face appear behind Mencía, he said in surprise, "Rachel, you are safe."

"Yes, Guillermo," said Mencía, raising him and wiping the blood and wine from his face with the cloak, "but we must get away from here. We will help you on your feet."

Bending to help, Rachel reported, "I found no others here."

After getting Guillermo up with difficulty, they started out into the corridor with one girl on each side of him for support. As Rachel supported an unsteady Guillermo, Mencía unbarred the sturdy wooden exterior door, opened it a bit, and cautiously peered into a narrow alleyway.

"It looks clear," said Mencía.

They emerged from the hideout, closing the door behind them, then staggered along the alleyway until they finally reached a street where they rested for a moment.

Mencía had quickly wiped his face and placed his hat loosely on his head to hide the bloody hair underneath. Still, they were a curious sight to others as they walked along unsteadily with Mencía and Rachel helping support him on each side.

As they walked, Mencía filled in Guillermo on what had happened. Although groggy and in pain from the bang on his head, he seemed to grasp what she said. Rachel was surprised to hear her father's new wagon driver was involved. She herself had not heard his voice there.

Expecting to find the villain Pablo with the merchant, Mencía was determined not to let him escape. She and Guillermo did not take kindly to being ambushed and kidnapped. They also wanted to find out who else was involved.

When they arrived at the front of the merchant's business and its attached residence, they paused outside and Mencía got her knives out.

In a low voice, Mencía said, "Rachel, when we go inside, you help support Guillermo while I keep Pablo from getting away."

Rachel nodded.

"I am stronger now and will try to help as well," said Guillermo.

"Very good. Let's go in," said Mencía with resolve.

2. Pablo

WITH THE LARGE WOODEN DOORS for wagons closed, they entered through the door beside them. They scanned quickly about inside without seeing Pablo. Seeing a small shovel inside by the door, Guillermo picked it up.

"I'll stay by the door. Mencía, you keep looking," he said in a low voice.

They saw the merchant slumped in a cushioned armchair near his desk. He was facing away from them with his head resting on one hand.

At hearing someone come in, the merchant gave a deep sigh and said sadly without looking around, "I am sorry, but we are closed. Please come back tomorrow."

"Papa, it is me! Mencía and Guillermo rescued me!"

The merchant jolted in the chair, whirled around, and gaped at them in utter surprise.

"Rachel, my child!"

She ran to him as he rose from the chair, and they hugged in teary happiness.

"Oh, my little lamb, I thought I had lost you," he said as they hugged. "My child, are you hurt?"

"No, Papa. I am fine."

"Señor Cruz, there is still danger," interrupted Mencía as she continued looking about. "Where is your wagon driver Pablo? He is one of the kidnappers."

"What? Can it be true?" exclaimed the merchant, staring at her in disbelief.

"Yes, he led Guillermo and me into an ambush, and we were abducted too. I heard him there with our kidnappers. After he left, we killed three of them to escape. Now we want him."

"He's not here! He told me you were attacked and you two had been seized, possibly killed, but he had gotten away. He told his tale most convincingly! That's why I sat in such utter misery as you found me. My Rachel's rescue had failed, and

9

now you both probably killed. It was a tremendous, yes, a terrible blow," the merchant stammered.

"The villain!" hissed Guillermo. "He shall pay."

Now noticing Guillermo by the door, the merchant started again excitedly, "Guillermo, Mencía, he left fifteen minutes ago to see to his bruised face, or so he said. I expect him back shortly. Oh, the evil ungrateful blackheart! And I pay him a fair wage too!"

"We must prepare to seize the scoundrel when he returns," stated Guillermo, coming closer.

"Guillermo! You are *hurt*!" the merchant said anxiously when he saw blood running down the side of his face.

"I am well enough for the time being. Seizing this scoundrel Pablo is our immediate concern. Señor Cruz, you should resume your position in the chair, and we will…"

Guillermo stopped midsentence with a start as they heard the door suddenly open. They turned in surprise to see Pablo take a casual unsuspecting step inside.

Looking up and stunned at seeing them, he stopped and stood staring, with his hand still on the door. Then with a sudden look of alarm, he jerked back out the door as a knife thumped in the wall behind where he had just stood.

He was running fast, already twenty yards down the narrow street when Mencía made it outside. She started to chase after him although he was much faster. He pushed his way past several people walking and raced past others lounging along the walls.

"Stop that man, he is a kidnapper!" called out Mencía.

The people, looking up at the excitement of running people, only watched as he ran by. Except for one thin young man who leaped at him as he passed, knocking him down. When the young man went to jump on him, Pablo brandished a knife and slashed at him several times as the young man backed away. Looking for some defense, the young man took several rushed steps to get a bench by a nearby doorway. He grabbed it and swung it around, but by then, Pablo was running again and away.

In a moment, Mencía arrived and seeing the futility of further chase, she pulled to a stop by the young man.

"Thank you, Señor, for your brave attempt to stop him."

"When I heard your calls of distress, I thought perhaps a little chivalry was in order, but I had no idea I was helping such a lovely damsel." Grasping her hand and kissing it quickly, he said with determination, "I will chase and catch him even if it costs me my life."

"No, it is not necessary, Señor," Mencía said grabbing his arm to stop him as he turned. "He has gotten away."

Looking back up the street, she saw Guillermo halfway to them. The merchant and his daughter were outside their door watching.

The merchant was waving for them to come back and called, "Bring the young man with you!"

"Señor, would you care to join us?" asked Mencía.

"It would please me greatly."

Up the street they met Guillermo, who had tried to join the chase but had been hampered by his pounding, bleeding head.

"He may have escaped us today," Guillermo told them, "but we will find the villain. Thank you, Señor, for trying to help. Come, let us go back inside. Perhaps when we get inside, someone can attend to this scratch on my head."

The merchant was still affectionately hugging his daughter when they reached them.

Patting the young man on the back, the merchant told him, "We saw what you did, my brave young man. You do not look well fed. Come inside and join us for some food and wine."

"I will not offend you by declining your most gracious offer, Señor," the young man replied with a slight bow, which caused Mencía and Guillermo to exchange an amused glance.

Coming inside, they locked the door and made their way to the living area in back. There they found the housekeeper who was surprised and happy to see Rachel safe. After she tearfully hugged the young girl, the merchant asked the housekeeper to bring some food and wine.

Still overjoyed at her rescue, he now clung to his daughter as he beckoned the young man to sit down at their table, "Please, my brave young friend, have a seat."

Then turning, he said, "Mencía, Guillermo, how can I ever repay you for bringing back my beloved child? I greatly desire to hear how you accomplished it, but first, Guillermo, we must see to your wound. Fortunately, my lamb Rachel is excellent at dressing wounds and will take care of it."

While food and wine were being brought out, Rachel and Mencía helped Guillermo clean up. Rachel made an herbal balm for his head wound and wrapped a dressing over it. After the three of them washed up a bit and brushed off the dirt of their captivity, they made their appearance again at the table.

The young man named Antonio had been telling the merchant that he was the son of an affluent family. After growing up, he had concluded that working for a living was not something that appealed to him. So he and his friend had joined the many young men idly living day to day in cities like Seville and Cordoba. Sometimes they were able to live in an apartment and other times they lived on the streets. Depending on the good nature and charity of others, they were usually hungry. Yet, they regarded themselves as gentlemen of a sort, and kept up their gentleman airs as much as possible. Their time was spent lazing in the streets, going to church, paying compliments to ladies, and seeking acquaintances who might support their lifestyle.

After telling his history, Antonio mused, "I cannot now, in full conscience, claim that decisions made in the freshness of youth stand the test of time. My friend recently fell ill and died. An unhappy event for both of us since it has caused me to reflect with brutal honesty upon my present and future circumstances."

"But your family can surely assist you, can they not?" asked the merchant.

"They have previously attempted it on a number of occasions without success and have washed their hands of me, rightfully so."

Their conversation was interrupted when the other three returned, and the merchant and visitor rose to greet them.

"My dear sweet girl, I am so happy you are safe," he said, hugging his daughter.

"Come, let us have some food and wine to celebrate," he said, directing them to the table.

The young man, still standing, cordially stated, "Ladies, gentlemen, I have imposed upon your kind hospitality long enough and must take my leave. I add that it has been my distinct honor and pleasure to have met you and to have rendered what little assistance I may have."

"You must not leave on our account, please stay. We have not had a chance to thank you," said Guillermo.

"My gracious host, Señor Cruz, has already thanked me more than my paltry efforts merit."

"Well, if you must go, Antonio, goodbye and best of luck to you," said the merchant, coming over and shaking his hand.

To the others, Antonio gave a bow and left. In the next room, the housekeeper gave him a sack of food and bottle of wine, which he respectfully declined to take. But she insisted and forced it into his hands.

"Well, if you insist, kind lady, thank you and God bless you," he said, taking the sack and leaving.

The housekeeper had been previously watching Antonio at the table as he nibbled food and sipped wine like an aristocrat, despite the fact that he must have been terribly hungry.

Meanwhile back at the table, Mencía and Rachel were telling the merchant how they had escaped and what they had heard. Mencía told them the kidnappers had no intention of delivering his daughter up after getting ransom money. They planned to sell her at a slave auction, probably in a city on

Spain's southern coast where she would be bought for the pleasure of a Muslim sultan and smuggled to the Barbary Coast of North Africa. It pained the merchant to even think of it.

Rachel described with awe how Mencía had gotten them free and then dispatched the kidnappers with such speed and skill. She had been frightened the entire time and barely able to shriek her warning to Mencía.

"He may have killed me if you had not called out, Rachel. You deserve credit for the escape as well," said Mencía with a pat to her nearby arm.

"Bravo! A daring and skillful feat of arms!" said Guillermo, much impressed. "Meanwhile, I lay in slumber in another room. After performing the dirty work, they then had to revive and carry me out. I regret that I was unable to do my part in the action and can only offer my sincere thanks to these two valiant young ladies for my rescue."

"I am so happy to have my little lamb back. Again, I do not know how I can ever repay you for rescuing my Rachel."

"Señor Cruz, the work is unfinished. We still must find this Pablo wretch and any others involved!" stated Guillermo.

"Yes, he still poses a danger to my lamb. I will ask a few of my workers to come and help guard us tonight."

"Has this Pablo worked long for you?"

"No, only about three weeks. When one of my drivers did not show up for work one morning, I sent someone to find him and was told he had disappeared. He had apparently left town, and I had a good many deliveries to make. I cursed the missing man as an irresponsible, ungrateful lout. This Pablo showed up the same day looking for work, so I hired him on a trial basis.

"He carried out his work dependably, and I began to think the disappearance of my last driver was a blessing in disguise. What unfortunate and poor judgement on my part. I suspect the miscreant Pablo may have abducted and killed my driver to create an opening. I now regret my ill thoughts toward the unfortunate man and my misplaced trust in this fiend Pablo."

"Rachel checked all the rooms before we escaped their hideout, without finding anyone," said Mencía.

"Most regrettable," said the merchant sadly.

"It appears to be a deliberate plot of kidnap and ransom directed at you in particular," pondered Guillermo.

"Yes, it would seem so."

"Do you have enemies who would stoop to such crime?"

"Just the normal business rivals. On the other hand, I am a prosperous converso, which might be considered ripe pickings to the bad elements of this Catholic society."

"Señor Cruz, do you want to report this crime to the authorities?" asked Mencía.

"Please, I wish you would call me Gonzalo, which is more pleasant to my ears."

"If that is what you desire."

"Yes, it is. Alas, many years ago, I believe the same year that Columbus found the Indies, my Jewish grandfather was given the choice of converting to Christianity or being expelled from Spain. He was a prosperous businessman and chose to stay, assuming the name Cruz as part of his so-called religious conversion. Can you imagine a Jew assuming the last name Cruz (cross)? It is all part of this converso game we play for the sake of appearances."

"Señor Cruz, you should be more guarded in what you say," cautioned Guillermo with concern, looking around.

With a startled look, the merchant replied, "Truly I have been quite careless! Alas, with my recent distress, I forget myself. Rachel's life and mine are again in your hands. Our inquisition tribunal would consider such words heresy. I am quite certain that they would love to have it reported to them so they could put me and my Rachel on trial as heretics and non-believers. They would surely feel the need to torture us to confess and then burn us at the stake for freely admitting our guilt. They could then finish up their handiwork by confiscating all my property and belongings for themselves and the church, all-in-all, a neat piece of work and tidy profit for them. I must trust you, my friends, not to repeat my words."

"You have no need for worry."

"I thank you, my friends," he said with a sigh. "In answer to your question, Mencía, I do not think it wise to report it to our authorities. We should wait to see what results from the discovery of the kidnapper's bodies. Even then, we may want to stay quiet. Conversos, such as myself, would rather avoid any dealings with authorities if possible. So let us not say anything for now."

"However," said Guillermo, deep in thought, "the task of finding this villain Pablo still exists. Do you know where he lives or what friends he might have?"

"No, but we can ask the others here."

"I suggest we watch their hideout to see if we might spot him there," offered Mencía.

"He seems to operate freely. I wonder if a constable* or city official might be involved with this ring," asked Guillermo.

"No, I think it unlikely. Such ruffians and kidnappers tend to operate boldly without need for connections," said the merchant.

"Gonzalo, you may want to close your business for a time," suggested Guillermo. "You and your daughter are not safe until we have found and eliminated this kidnapping gang. You can question your workers to see what they know of him. After a day of rest to allow my head to recover, I will also be able to participate in the search for the wretch."

"It will be a severe financial burden for me, but I agree, for my Rachel's sake," said the merchant, patting her hand.

* A constable was an officer of the local court, who executed the orders and judgements decreed by judges and magistrates. Not allowed to hold any other offices or have a business, he received a portion of the judgements he executed. He wore a cape and carried a staff as a sign of his office, as well as pistol and sword when needed in the course of this duties. He and his assistants were the civil law and order of the time.

3. Hunted

THE NEXT DAY, they began their efforts. The workers were called in and questioned by the merchant and Mencía. None of the workers had liked Pablo or knew any personal information about him. While they did not suspect beforehand that he would do such a dastardly thing, they were not surprised after the fact to learn that he had been involved.

Only one had ever spotted him outside of work. While driving a wagon of goods late one evening, he had noticed Pablo and several other men eating outside a bar on the south side of town. They would have to watch this place.

To their surprise, the young man, Antonio, returned that morning. The incident and his time with them on the previous day had made an impression on him. After further reflection, he had decided that a change in his lifestyle might be in order, so he came to ask the merchant for work.

Such loafers would surely be poor workers, and he would normally never consider hiring one. Yet, he thought this particular one might be different and deserved a chance.

"Your gentleman airs are out of place here. You will be expected to work as the others do. Can you do that?"

"Yes, I will endeavor to do so."

"Well then, we will give it a try. You can stay in one of the equipment rooms in the stable."

Listening nearby, Mencía had an idea and said, "But before he begins his work here, Gonzalo, we have an important assignment for him."

The merchant looked at her curiously.

"Antonio, do you think you can recognize the villain with whom you tangled yesterday?" she asked.

"Yes, I vividly remember him and his knife."

"Good. We are after him. A worker here has previously seen him at a bar on the south side of town. We will give you a different cloak and hat so he will not recognize you. You will sit along the street as you normally do. If you see him, follow him to see where he goes, and let us know."

"Good thinking," said the merchant.

"We are going soon to find the bar," continued Mencía. "Get some food and drink here and then come with us."

"As you wish. I will do my best," said Antonio with a bow.

Without much trouble, they found the bar and left Antonio there to watch. That night, Mencía and one of the merchant's workers watched the hideout for a time. Guillermo remained at the merchant's and slept to help heal his head.

They saw nothing that night and heard nothing the next day from Antonio. During the next days and nights, Guillermo joined them in the watches. They began to watch other bars in the same area as well, all without success.

By the end of a week, they had heard and seen nothing of Pablo and had heard no news about authorities finding the three dead kidnappers.

Frustrated that nothing had turned up, Guillermo, Mencía, and the merchant considered what to do next. They speculated that Rachel was probably not the gang's first victim. Others must have come before her. Clues to Pablo's whereabouts might be found in those cases. They inquired at local businesses without success. The merchant inquired within his converso community and was surprised to find one such crime had occurred six months before.

Guillermo, Mencía, and the merchant went to see the crime victim, a converso money lender named Ramirez. At their knock, the man excitedly opened the door, ushered them inside into a lavishly decorated parlor. Quickly closing the door behind them, he asked with bated breath, "Please tell me. I cannot wait. My friend said you wanted to talk about my kidnapped children. Do you have news of my two dear little ones?"

Their sad, uncomfortable glances at one another told him the answer, and he collapsed down into a chair in misery.

"Regrettably, we cannot, Señor Ramirez. I am very sorry if our request to talk to you about the kidnapping might have led you to believe so," the merchant told him with remorse.

Rising from the chair, the man demanded, "Then why are you here torturing me! For that is what it is to talk of it!"

"I am very sorry, Señor, for your loss and grief," said Guillermo with resolve, "but we are looking for a kidnapper who may have been involved in the kidnapping of your children as well. Our intention is to put him and his partners out of their kidnapping business for good!"

"You mean *justice*? Send them to *prison*? Unlikely! Even so, it is too late to be of any good for my darlings!"

"We are not constables," replied Guillermo.

The man studied Guillermo and the girl in the riding outfit beside him for a time.

"So what is it you want from me then! How can I *possibly* help you find this man!"

"We hope for a possible clue to his whereabouts in the details of his crimes. It is perhaps only a slim chance, and it will require you to tell us details about it. If it is too painful for you, we understand. We will leave now and bother you no more."

"And what makes you think *you* will have better success than our constable who failed so miserably?"

"We have already killed three of the gang and want the rest," said Mencía firmly.

The man looked at Mencía with astonishment.

"Could it be true?" he pondered. "This young man and woman exude such strength and competence that it gives me hope. It is too late for my poor dear ones, but they might be able to bring some level of justice to their kidnappers. Oh, it is too much to hope for."

After a few moments of contemplation, he said, "Yes, I will tell you about it, and if there is a God in heaven, these men will experience His wrath."

"That is exactly our intent," said Guillermo.

After sitting them down and giving them a glass of wine, he began to tell them about it as they listened intently.

"I really do not know how I can be of any assistance. There is so little to tell. My little Fernando was only eight years old, and my little Consuela was ten. One afternoon, they were at play in our backyard with its high masonry wall. Their nanny was with them but went inside momentarily to get them a snack. Suddenly she heard cries for help. When she raced outside, my two darlings were gone, and two large men were just climbing back over the walls. She grasped one by the foot, but he kicked her away and was gone. It broke her heart to hear their muffled cries as they were carried away.

"She ran inside to get help, but my wife was grief-stricken at the news and collapsed. I was away at the time. My housekeeper ran to tell the constable, who came promptly, but too late to do anything about it. The nanny could only describe the men as large dark hairy men dressed like everyone else. The constable looked in the backyard for clues but found nothing. I suspect he did not consider two stolen converso children worth much of his time and wrote it off as some random unsolvable crime soon after."

"The neighbors saw nothing?" asked Guillermo.

"No."

"Did you pay a ransom?" asked the merchant.

"Yes," he replied painfully. "We found a ransom note at our doorstep two days later telling us how much money and where to leave it. It was a great deal of money, but of course, we paid it. We waited for their return but never got them back."

"Do you still have the ransom note?" asked Mencía.

"No, I burned it in anger one night."

"Do you think the kidnapping could have been planned at a time when you would be gone?" asked Guillermo.

"Possibly," he said thoughtfully. "I was lunching with a group of friends as I do every Tuesday afternoon."

"Then it may have been pre-planned and not random."

"Yes, I suppose it is possible."

"My daughter's kidnapping was perpetrated by a gang, whose leader inserted himself into my business beforehand," related the merchant. "He was a young man of average height, strong build, brown hair, narrow face with a scar on his left cheek, thin beard, intelligent, and well spoken. Do you recall any dealing with such a young man before the crime took place?"

With a look of surprise, the man stammered, "Yes, yes, there was such a man! I loaned him money. He gave me a diamond ring as collateral. He came to this very room several times to make partial payments! Oh my God! Yes! My wife said he was admiring our things, and she showed him around a bit. I told her at the time that it was unwise to have done so, that he might try to steal something. Oh my God. I was worried about some urn or statue, and he stole my children!"

"He was probably seeing how wealthy you were and set his ransom amount accordingly."

"God in Heaven, I now remember telling him one time that I could not meet him on a Tuesday afternoon because I lunch with friends," he said with terrible realization.

"Señor Ramirez, can you tell us anything about him that might help us?" asked Guillermo.

"Let me think. I do remember there was something about him. What was it? Let me think."

Sitting up, he said, "I must ask my wife. I believe she was the one who commented something about him."

He rose, rushed to the closed door, and then suddenly stopped. Turning, he said, "Please do not tell my wife the reason for your visit. If she were to think that her showing the young man around contributed to their kidnapping, it would devastate her."

"I will say he owes me money," said the merchant.

Señor Ramirez left and soon returned with his wife. After introductions, he asked her, "My dear, as I just mentioned, these two gentlemen and this young lady are interested in the young man with the diamond who borrowed money about six months ago. You recall him, do you not?"

"The housekeeper certainly recalls him," she replied. "She would complain to me each time he was here about the mud he left on the carpets. We have nice carpets that show dirt easily."

"What color was the mud?" asked Mencía.

A little surprised by the question, the wife nonchalantly replied, "The mud was plain, not particularly light or dark, just plain brown mud. Not particularly sandy or gravelly either, I suppose, just plain brown mud."

After a pause, she continued, "I also remember a slight smell of fish on him."

"Like he had been eating fish?" asked Guillermo.

"No, more as if the smell was on his clothes."

"Could it only have been body odor?" asked Mencía.

"No, it smelled like fish."

"Is there anything else about him that you can recall? Any kind of dirt, or hair, or debris on his clothing?" asked Guillermo.

"I remember that he had a scar on his cheek. Have you already told them, dear?"

Her husband nodded.

"No, nothing else comes to mind. I suppose that is all I can tell you. Why are you looking for him?"

The merchant calmly replied, "I sell goods, and he owes me a great deal of money. I want to find the shirker and be paid. Thank you very much for the information. It may aid us in finding him."

"I hope I have been of help. You should be more careful with whom you conduct business, Señor Cruz. One must be careful," she told the merchant. Then turning to her husband, she added, "Is that not so, dear?"

"Yes, dear, quite so."

With that, she nodded to her visitors, excused herself, and left the room.

After closing the door behind her, the money lender turned and asked hopefully, "Is it true what you say, that this information may be of help?"

"Possibly, we shall see."

4. Captured

BACK AT THE MERCHANT'S, they sat together and considered this new information. A fish smell must mean some kind of fish market. Such markets are normally located on cobbled streets or in market plazas, not normally places to get mud on shoes. Guillermo and Mencía went to visit them, dressed to conceal their identity, not wanting to alert their prey that he was being hunted. They only found one with noticeable muddy places, the riverside fish market.

Thinking it was a better location for spotting the kidnapper, Guillermo went to see Antonio who he found dutifully seated in the street near the bar. Casually walking past, he discreetly got the young man's attention. On their way back to the merchant's, Guillermo told him what new information had been learned and that he was now to watch the area near the riverside fish market. After a little food and drink, he was off to his new assignment.

The merchant, after thinking about it, recalled he had also smelled fish on Pablo a few times. But with all the smells of the goods in his business, it had not been as noticeable.

The next day, they heard reports of three murdered men found in an apartment. The neighbors had hesitated to complain to their rough neighbors about the growing awful smell. But when it became horrible, they contacted the constable who entered the apartment and found the bodies. Their investigation had no leads or suspects. The neighbors claimed they heard and saw nothing.

Two days later, Guillermo, Mencía, and Señor Cruz sat in the evening, discussing the next day's efforts, when they heard a pounding on the door of the business.

Looking at each other in surprise, Guillermo said, "Maybe Antonio has found him!"

As they hurried to answer it, they heard more pounding and a voice outside call, "Señor Cruz! Señor Cruz! Please open up!"

"That is Mateo!" said Mencía, recognizing the voice. "We are overdue in returning, and he has come to look for us."

Opening the door, Guillermo saw two friends outside and said with surprise, "Mateo, Sebastian, my friends."

"Guillermo, Mencía, thank goodness, you had us worried," said Mateo, coming inside and feeling relieved at the sight of them both. "You expected to be gone a few days, and it has been two weeks. Your families were worried, so we came to find you."

"I am very sorry to have caused worry," said Guillermo.

"Yes, me too," said Mencía as the four friends embraced.

"I am afraid that I am to blame, Mateo," said the merchant. "I got your friends wrapped up in my difficulties here."

"I thought you might be in some kind of trouble and need help, so Sebastian came too," said Mateo.

"Pascual almost came as well," said Sebastian, "but happily, we see now that it was not necessary."

As they all walked back to the merchant's living area, Guillermo told them, laughing, "It was most kind of you both to come, thinking to rescue us. Only, my friends, you are about two weeks too late!"

Mateo and Sebastian looked puzzled.

"When we arrived here to deliver potato seed to our merchant friend," explained Guillermo, "we found him in the depths of despair and at wit's end. He had just learned that his daughter Rachel had been kidnapped. One of his wagon drivers named Pablo was here expressing his condolences and saying that he had seen several suspicious men lurking about earlier but had no idea that they were planning such a heinous crime. The driver listened as the merchant lamented her loss and then left. He returned a short time later and excitedly told us that he had seen the same suspicious men and had followed them to their place. He offered to take us there.

"Mencía and I went with him, but this scoundrel Pablo was part of the crime and led us into a trap. I was knocked unconscious from behind while Mencía was seized, bound, and gagged. He must have admired Mencía and thought that she might fetch him a pretty penny at the slave market as well. They also planned to ransom me, so they bound and gagged me while unconscious, instead of killing me."

"How did you escape?" asked Mateo, listening with amazement.

"The ruffians made the fatal mistake of thinking Mencía was just another pretty face and not a warrior princess as Don Tomás likes to call her," he said, pointing to Mencía.

"She still had her throwing knives in her riding jacket. She and Rachel used them to cut their bonds and then Mencía with the help of Rachel killed the three villains and brought me away with them. She saved our lives. Unfortunately, the villain Pablo got away, and we are still searching for him."

Mateo went over to Mencía and gave her a hug, "Well done, Mencía, my heartfelt thanks."

To the merchant, he said, "I am so glad you got your daughter back safely. I know how you cherish her."

"Yes, indeed. Thank you, Mateo."

Meanwhile, Sebastian had gone over to Mencía. Smiling broadly, he bowed to her, took her hand and kissed it, saying, "Bravo, Mencía, you were amazing as usual."

"Thank you, Sebastian," she said, smiling.

Turning to the rest of them, Mateo declared, "I want to hear all the details later, but first, let us put our horses away in your stable, and then we want to know what we can do to help find this villain Pablo."

When they returned from the stables, they all sat and had food and wine as Guillermo filled them in on their efforts to find Pablo. Mateo concurred with their efforts thus far and suggested that finding more kidnapping cases might yield further clues. The two known cases so far were both conversos, which they suspected were targeted because the Christian authorities put less effort into investigating crimes against them. That might also be true of moriscos. Sebastian said that he had a morisco acquaintance in town, the brother of one of Pascual's men. Sebastian would visit him first thing in the morning to ask him about kidnappings within the morisco community.

With the added resources, they began to discreetly watch the other fish markets the next day, without luck. On the following day, however, Antonio gave them the electrifying news that he found Pablo staying in an outbuilding next to the fish market by the river.

He had seen a man and woman exit and enter the decrepit outbuilding once a day before but had not recognized the man to be Pablo because his face had been concealed by his hat and bandana. But on this day, a gust of wind blew off his hat, and Antonio got a good look at his face.

They immediately commenced a watch on the place from a rooftop perch. The merchant found a spyglass for them to use.

The next day, they watched as the couple warily exited their hideout and walked across a dirt area to the riverfront street, as Antonio had previously seen them do. With the spyglass, they were able to confirm the man was Pablo. They could not identify the woman.

After crossing the street, they walked up a narrow alleyway leading to a marketplace. There, they shopped quickly and returned via the same route. The man looked to be keeping the woman close, never letting her beyond arm's reach.

Based on their observations, they made preparations to capture the wretch when he next emerged from the outbuilding.

The next morning, the door of the hideout opened slightly as Pablo scanned the area outside. Satisfied that all looked normal and safe, he and the woman came out. He looked about nervously while he locked a padlock on the door.

As he had before, Pablo wore his hat low and bandana high to conceal his face as much as possible. He kept one arm concealed in his coat as if clutching a weapon. She was carrying a bag as they walked rapidly to the alleyway and along it to the marketplace where they hurriedly bought various foods and wine. Pablo got impatient with his woman companion for taking too long with one vendor.

After finishing their shopping, she brought out a water bag that she filled at a nearby fountain, and then they started back to the hideout. They wasted no time as they walked down the alleyway with Pablo warily looking back several times and in alcoves as they passed.

They were about fifty feet from the end of the alleyway when two people suddenly sprang into view there and stood with cutlasses drawn, blocking the way.

Pablo recognized Guillermo and Mencía with surprise and dismay. Furious at being discovered and trapped, he cursed. Starting to pull the pistol from his coat, he looked back to see if the other end of the alleyway was also blocked. All he saw was a brief glimpse of Sebastian bringing a club down on his head.

During that brief glimpse, he did not see Mateo emerging from a doorway on the other side of the alley to grab the woman. Mateo pressed her against a wall with his hand cupped over her mouth. He told her to be calm, cooperate, and she would not be hurt. She nodded her head nervously in wide-eyed agreement.

Mencía now arrived to quickly tie her hands behind her back. As she hustled the woman down to an awaiting covered wagon at the end of the alleyway, she reassured her several times that she would not be harmed.

When being dragged along the alleyway with his hands tied behind his back, Pablo briefly came to, raising his head and snarling at his abductors, only to have his head slammed against the road surface to knock him out again.

He had half-conscious recollections of a bumpy ride in a wagon, lying blindfolded and gagged with hands and feet bound. He quickly learned not to move or say anything during the ride, since it always resulted in a vicious slap to his head. He could hear someone talking with the woman who was telling them her name was Alonza.

Finally, the wagon came to a stop, and Pablo heard heavy wooden doors open. The wagon pulled into a building and stopped. Recognizing the smells of the place, he knew he was back at the merchant's business. He was roughly carried from the wagon, thrown on the floor of a room, and locked inside.

Upon arrival, Mencía took the woman to a separate, locked room where she sat her down on a chair. The operation had gone smoothly and according to plan. Only one man and woman, entering the far end of the alley, had stopped in surprise when they saw Pablo being thrown in the back of the wagon just before it quickly rolled off. So it had been nearly flawless.

Now began the effort to find out more information. The first thing to do seemed to be the interrogation of the woman. Mencía and Guillermo brought chairs into her room. They readily noticed the fish smell on the woman as they untied her. They gave her food and wine and a washcloth to clean off a bit. Next, they sat down with her and told her at the beginning, that based on their observations, they suspected she was a victim of the criminal gang and not a participant. They wanted to interrogate her only to find out as much as possible about the gang before releasing her. This soothed the frazzled nerves of the woman, and she freely answered their questions.

She confirmed their observations were correct. She was not of the upper-class world of respectability, proprieties, and duennas. She had been a waitress in a Cordoba bar, where she met Pablo and went home with him one night only to find that she had become his captive. She was forced to serve him and gratify his needs. He beat her frequently and fed her little. Sometimes, he left her there for days by herself. Whenever he left, he locked her inside and threatened to slit her throat if she tried to escape.

"Alonza, how long have you been held there?"

"About eight months, I think."

"Who do you know are members of his crime gang?"

"Besides Pablo, I only saw and heard three other men named Rodrigo, Angulo, and Ramír. They would meet sometimes at the hideout but normally stayed at another location. But I have not seen them lately."

"Did you ever see or hear talk of any city officials being involved with the gang?"

"No, they had a low opinion of officials and constables."

"Is there anyone inside the hideout right now?"

"No, just us two were there. Lately, he seemed nervous about being caught and would not leave the hideout except with me to get supplies at the market. He was fearful of someone and paced like a hunted animal. He talked about having to lie low for a time before trying to slip away. I do not know why."

"He probably feared us and rightfully so," said Guillermo. "Mencía here killed the other three members of his gang that you just mentioned."

Alonza gasped in surprise, saying, "So that is why."

"Did anyone besides those three ever visit the hideout?"

"Only the two children they kidnapped some time ago. My job was to take care of them during the few days they were there."

Both Guillermo and Mencía stiffened at the mention of the children.

"A boy of eight and a girl of ten?" asked Mencía.

"Yes, I believe so. They sold them to a priest in a small town to the south."

"What! To a *priest!*" exclaimed Guillermo, outraged.

"Yes, they thought it was a great joke," she said grimly. "Apparently, they could sell young children themselves in this area, without having to deal with a nasty slave trader to the south, like with the rest," she said sadly.

"Do you recall the name of the town?" asked Guillermo with intense interest.

"It was a short funny name, but I do not remember it."

"Think a moment. Try to remember."

After a time in thought, she said with a sigh, "I am sorry. It was six months ago. I cannot remember the name of the town."

Though greatly disappointed, Guillermo continued, "What else did they do besides kidnapping?"

"They may have committed other crimes, but their main source of money was from kidnapping. After each one, they spent their dirty money like sailors back from the Indies, on women and wine. I heard them tell of it when they came to the shack. They have been living for the last six months on the big ransom they got from kidnapping the children. When the money begins to run low, they plan another kidnapping."

"It sounds like there is no cache of hidden money to speak of," concluded Guillermo.

"Pablo kept the money from the children's ransom and sale in a cigar box buried in a corner of the shack. It is their spending money between kidnappings. There is no other cache of money that I know of."

"So with the ransom money from the children getting low, they kidnapped the merchant's daughter."

"Yes, I heard them plotting it."

"And what did he intend to do with the merchant's daughter, once kidnapped?"

"Collect a ransom and sell her to the slave trader."

"And you, in effect, were kidnapped too?"

"Yes. He threatened me regularly that if I caused him any trouble, I would soon find myself on the way to the slave trader too."

"It sounds like you have been through quite an ordeal. Do you have family? Can we take you to them?"

"Yes," she said as she began to cry. "My poor parents, they must have searched for me and think they have lost me."

"They must be distraught. We will take you to them tomorrow. I believe that we are about done now. If you reflect back and remember anything else, please let us know?" said Guillermo.

"Reflect, reflect, reflect," muttered Alonza, staring vacantly for a moment.

Suddenly her eyes widened, and she burst out, "Reflejo!"

"What?"

"Reflejo is the name of the town."

"Fantastic!" said Guillermo with intense delight. "We may soon pay a visit to that priest! Such things make my blood boil!"

"Alonza, thank you for all the information. You have been most helpful," Mencía told her.

"Yes, Alonza. I thank you too. If you think of anything else, let us know. We will get you a basin to clean up and find a bed for you tonight. As I said, we will take you home tomorrow. So now, you are free to come out and join the rest of us," said Guillermo, getting up.

At hearing this, Alonza seemed to realize that her terrible ordeal was finally over. She began to sob and gave Mencía a hug of gratitude.

They went out to join the others in a toast to the success of their operation. Guillermo announced to them the gist of what had been learned from Alonza and how she was now their welcome guest. After only a small bite of bread, Alonza wanted badly to clean up, so she went back with Rachel and the housekeeper to wash her hair and begin to remove the stink of her months of captivity.

5. The Children

WITH NO ONE INSIDE the locked hideout, there seemed to be no hurry to search it. Pablo was securely bound up, and his interrogation could also wait. After a brief time of celebration, food and drink, Guillermo gathered up Mencía, Mateo, and Sebastian. He had a burning desire to rescue the two kidnapped children of Señor Ramirez and his wife. He thought that they owed it to them since their information had led to the capture of the ringleader Pablo.

The merchant found a map of their area, which they spread out on a table. Huddling around it, they located the town of Reflejo, south of the city.

"It looks to be about a three-hour ride," said Mencía.

"Bandits may be in that country. We should all go and bring our archery gear with us," advised Sebastian.

"Sebastian, you are probably right, but I want to slip into the town, grab the children, and get away quickly without notice, if possible. Four of us riding into the town might be too conspicuous."

"I take it that you and Mencía want to do this," said Mateo to Guillermo. "You met with the parents and are closer to it."

"Yes, do you agree, Mencía?"

"I do."

"Well, Sebastian and I can stay outside the town and wait for you to bring them out," offered Mateo.

"That should be fine. I am guessing it is just a sleepy small town. Mencía and I can manage this. Dealing with wayward priests seems to be our lot in life. We will get the children and meet you outside the town again for the ride back."

"If we leave early enough, we could get to the town after their morning mass and before the midday mass at noon. Less people should be in and about the church at that time."

"Good thinking, Mencía. I cannot think of anything else. We ride early tomorrow," said Guillermo with a determined look.

The four of them left early the next day as planned. Hours later in the late morning, the town loomed ahead as they pulled their horses to a stop. Looking up at the sun, they estimated the time was about an hour before midday. On the way, they had encountered no bandits, or at least, none had shown their faces when their well-armed party rode past.

"We will wait here for you to return. Leave your archery gear here with us, unless you plan to shoot arrows in this priest," said Mateo with a smile.

"No, they will not be necessary. I hope to whisk the children away before he knows it," said Guillermo, as he and Mencía lowered their archery gear to the ground.

"Shall we proceed, Mencía?"

"Yes, I am ready," she replied calmly, and they both started for the town at an easy gait, so as not to draw attention.

Upon entering the town, they could see the church's bell tower and rode to a nearby alleyway behind it without seeing any townspeople. They dismounted and tied their horses to a post. Going around to the back of the church, Guillermo climbed up and peered over a six-foot high masonry wall and saw a boy and a girl working in a garden behind the church. The two children they saw appeared to fit the ages of the kidnapped children. One was carrying a water bucket, and the other was hoeing around rows of sprouting vegetables. No priest or other adults were in sight.

"Mencía, stay here behind this wall out of sight while I find out if they are the Ramirez children. If so, I will hand them over to you."

Guillermo climbed over and jumped down behind a nearby shed. Then emerging from the shed, he approached them, and they shrank away when they saw him.

"Are your names Fernando and Consuela?" he asked them in a quiet voice.

"Yes, are you here to help us?" asked the girl with emotion.

"Yes, I am here to take you back to your parents."

Bursting with joy and tears, they dropped their things and rushed to him, hugging him around the waist as he eyed the side door of the church.

"Are there any other children here?"

"No, just us two."

Ushering them back toward the wall, he said, "Quickly, we must get you out of…"

He stopped mid-sentence, hearing a shout from behind.

"Here, here, who are you? Take your hands off those children!"

Guillermo turned and saw a priest in a dark cassock angrily hastening out to stop him. The frightened children sought protection behind Guillermo as he faced the priest.

"Leave those children alone and be gone, I say!"

"Are these your children?"

"Certainly not, I am a priest. They belong to the church. What is it of your business!"

"Is it normal church policy to buy children?"

Now the priest stood directly in front of Guillermo with an angry expression and his finger pointing.

"Why, you vile sinner! I warn you. You are in serious risk of eternal damnation!" he threatened. "Who are you to question me or the church in that way? I have taken them into God's care."

"Is that what you call slavery?"

"How dare you! I recently returned from New Spain. We took the natives into God's care there too. This is no different. God permits it so that they may be saved. So why should *you* question it?"

"They were kidnapped from their parents. Did they tell you that?"

"They are not allowed to speak. Besides, I had nothing to do with it. It concerns me not. They belong to the church now. So be gone! And do not bother me with your worldly concerns! I have higher concerns. I am a man of God," declared the priest haughtily and defiantly.

"And a poor one at that. I am taking them back to their parents," said Guillermo firmly.

"You shall do no such thing! That is robbery. I will call for help! I will get the constable!" sputtered the priest, flabbergasted at such disrespect.

The priest turned and opened his mouth to shout, but before he could do so, Guillermo smacked him hard on the side of the head knocking him to the ground unconscious.

"God forgive me for striking a priest, but this one deserved it," said Guillermo, looking down at him.

At this point, Mencía peered over the wall and said, "Guillermo, pass the children to me."

Guillermo quickly did so. Then turning and looking back at the church, he saw no one coming out or shouting for help. Apparently, no one had seen the deed. Beside him was a row of green bean plants with stakes and twine along them for the shoots to climb on.

"Mencía, I must keep this one quiet for a while. I will tie him up and be out shortly."

"Be quick, Guillermo. We will be by the horses."

Guillermo hurriedly dragged the priest behind the nearby shed. He quickly cut twine from the garden stakes with his knife, tied the priest's hands behind his back, tied his legs together, and then gagged and blindfolded him with material cut from the bottom of the priest's cassock. Afterward, he peered out from behind the shed and still saw no people or alarm. He looked down momentarily at the priest who was beginning to come to, moving his head and moaning.

"He is unharmed, but he will not be praying for my sole when he wakes up," thought Guillermo to himself.

He leaped up and was over the wall in an instant. When he raced up to Mencía and the children at the horses, Mencía had to laugh at the excited grin on his face. They speedily mounted with the girl behind Mencía and the boy behind Guillermo. Soon they were away from the town and its priest.

"Bravo, you were successful!" shouted Mateo and Sebastian gleefully when they saw them coming with the children.

"Yes, my friends," said Guillermo, laughing, "but we must hurry. I had to tie up the priest in the garden, so the midday mass worshipers are in for a shock!"

Surprised and chuckling, Mateo and Sebastian jumped on their horses, and they all rode away at top speed.

After their initial high-speed exit, they rode at a steady pace back to Cordoba. As they rode, Guillermo kept thinking that he was going to burn in hell if he did not confess his deed. But what would his own parish priest Father Giraldo think of him when he confessed what he had just done? At every Sunday mass afterward, he would look up when receiving communion and imagine Father Giraldo was thinking, "Why am I giving the body of Christ to this sinner who slaps and hog-ties priests?"

No, that would not do. He decided that he must confess the deed to a priest in Cordoba, where he was not known.

"But then again," he thought, "if God had not wanted it to happen, He would have allowed them to rescue the children without the priest noticing. Apparently, God thought the priest needed a slap."

It made him feel better to think of it in that light. Even so, he would have to confess it.

In the afternoon, they arrived tired and hungry in Cordoba. They left their sweaty horses in the merchant's stable and brought the children inside. When the merchant and the others saw the children, they erupted into cheering and clapping. They rushed happily to the rescuers, giving them jubilant congratulations and ushering the children to a table for some milk and food. The children were overwhelmed by the joyful celebration and all the hugs from strangers.

"Has anything been said to the parents?" asked Guillermo over the uproar.

"No," said the delighted merchant, beaming. "They are about to receive a most pleasant surprise."

"And is all the same with our friend Pablo?" asked Mateo.

"Yes, he is still uncomfortably bound, and probably hungry and thirsty too."

"Good. He can wait until tomorrow."

Seeing the young man from the streets, Guillermo went to him saying, "Antonio, we celebrate now thanks to you and your watchful eye, which deserves a good deal of the credit."

"My efforts in no way deserve such praise, yet I confess that I am gratified that my small part contributed to the villain's capture and this most agreeable scene."

"Antonio, my friend, I hope things work well for you here," said Guillermo, giving him a pat on the back.

"Thank you, Guillermo."

Guillermo now rejoined the merchant, and they hugged in celebration. Mateo joined them, saying, "What a glorious day, certainly one for celebration. I do not see Alonza here. Did you take her home?"

"Yes," replied the merchant, "one of my drivers took her in a carriage to her parents, about one and a half hours from here. He described the scene of their reunion as very touching."

"Yes, I can imagine," said Mateo.

When Mencía joined them, the merchant said with a wink, "Mencía, I hope that slaying the priest with your cutlass was not necessary in this latest endeavor."

"No," she laughed, "but I believe that Guillermo considered it. Instead, he only tied him up, and left him in the garden."

"Oooh," moaned the converso merchant longingly. "Oooh, how I *wish* I could have seen it."

One of the merchant's men from the stable now came in and reported something to him.

"Ah, thank you, Manuel."

Then he announced to everyone, "A carriage and horses to take the children home are ready."

6. Villain's End

THE HOUSEKEEPER AND RACHEL had been cleaning up the children a bit as they sat and ate at the table. Having been fed little by the priest, they looked thin and worn. After their six months of captivity, they were now as cleaned up and presentable as they could be made on short notice.

The merchant wanted all the principal participants to come along to see the joy of the children's return. A covered carriage and horses were ready and waiting. He and his daughter ushered the children outside and into the covered carriage. Antonio joined them in it, the others mounted horses, and they began the short ride across the city to the money lender's residence.

As their little cavalcade passed along the streets, the riders tipped their hats to people who turned to look. Their procession slowed to a walk as they passed along a narrow alleyway to the residence. In the small open area in front of it, they pulled to a stop, only a dozen feet from the front door.

They quickly disembarked and made ready for the children's joyous return. The children stayed concealed in the covered carriage as Antonio, Mateo, Sebastian, and Rachel stood together beside it. Hearing the noise outside, someone peered from a nearby barred window and another peered through curtains of a second-floor window. With the merchant standing on one side of the door and Guillermo and Mencía standing on the other side, the merchant banged the door knocker.

In a moment, a maid opened the door, but before they could ask for Señor Ramirez, he appeared and looked with wonder upon the scene of carriage, horses, and people. He recognized and nodded to Mencía, Guillermo, and the merchant, but looked uncertainly at the others.

"Señor Cruz, what *is* all of this?"

His wife now appeared beside him, and she too looked perplexed by the scene.

"Señor Ramirez, you may recall that when we concluded our visit, you asked if your information may be of help, and I replied, 'Possibly, we shall see.' I am happy to inform you that it was. And with the assistance of the people you see here," said the merchant, pointing, "we have found and captured the villain."

The father considered this sudden news, looking upset and apprehensive, while his wife did not see how it affected them.

"Congratulations, Señor Cruz," said the wife. "I hope you will get the money he owes you, but what is all this?"

"Señor Cruz, please tell me. Were you able to find out something of value from him?" asked Señor Ramirez with a pained look.

The merchant continued, "No, Señor, not from him, but from a kidnap victim rescued during his capture, we were able to learn the location of your children."

The parents stiffened in frozen wide-eyed shock.

"Señor, Señora Ramirez," said Guillermo, "since the information you provided was instrumental in our capture of the kidnapper we sought, we considered it only fitting that we should attempt a rescue of your children."

The parents gasped and stared, unable to breathe.

"Señor, Señora, early this morning, we set out to do so, and I am happy to report that we were successful. Here they are!"

With a sweep of his arm back toward the carriage, the four standing before it parted, and the children burst from the carriage, flushed with emotion and crying as they dashed to their parents who hugged them and sobbed, unable to speak.

Needless to say, a great deal of happiness and thankfulness ensued in the Ramirez residence as the ecstatic parents invited the rescuers of their children inside.

The very next day, the grateful parents sent a generous reward to the merchant to be shared by the participants in the rescue. Mateo, Guillermo, Mencía, and Sebastian declined their parts. Antonio told the merchant that he had no use for money.

"Antonio, you have not learned yet to appreciate money that is earned. I will set aside a portion to give to you later when you may better understand such things," the merchant told him.

"As you wish, Señor," said Antonio with a shrug.

As a result, the lion's share of the reward was delivered to Alonza, which was fitting since her information had led to the recovery of the children, and she had suffered a great deal herself at the hands of the gang's leader.

The next morning, Mateo, Guillermo, Sebastian, and Mencía went to the dilapidated wooden shack by the fish market. With the key taken from Pablo's pocket, they unlocked the padlock on the hideout door. Guillermo then swung it open and cautiously stepped inside.

"It reeks of fish in here. No wonder he had the smell on him. Fish must have been stored or sold in here in the past."

With his throwing knife ready, he slowly moved forward. Sebastian remained to guard outside as Mateo and Mencía followed Guillermo inside where they found a single open room with dirt floors and no windows. They began to search it, looking for anything new they might learn about Pablo and his gang.

The room contained wooden crates used as furniture, a crude bed with ratty blankets strewn on top, a cooking grill with pile of old firewood, a pile of clothes, a waste bucket in one corner, crude shelves on one wall, and wine bottles and trash scattered freely about. On the shelves, they found a few cooking and eating utensils, a small lantern, used candles, and a satchel containing flint, powder, and ball for his pistol. That was it.

Guillermo kicked at the dirt in one corner and found the buried cigar box. He opened it to find a pouch containing a dozen coins, the diamond ring, and several other pieces of jewelry. He returned them to the pouch and tossed the cigar box on the ground. After one more careful look around and seeing nothing else of use, they left with the pouch and satchel, glad to be out of the smelly place.

When they got back, Guillermo showed the merchant what they had found and said, "These few dozen coins are the only money we found. From what Alonza described, they lived on their money from kidnapping to kidnapping. I doubt that he has any other cache of money, and I certainly had no desire to stay in the awful-smelling place to hunt for one."

"Perhaps it is time to talk with our friend Pablo."

They went to the locked room where he lay bound, gagged, and hooded on the floor. They hoisted him up and put him in a chair, then tied his upper body to the chair back and his bound legs to the front legs of the chair. When they removed his hood, he glared at them with his mouth still gagged. Guillermo and Sebastian eyed him up close as Mateo and Mencía stood back watching.

"Pablo, or whatever your name is," Guillermo told him calmly, "we already know all about your gang. Alonza has told us about you and your three friends, your kidnapping activities, about the children you kidnapped six months ago, and how you operated. You really are of little or no use to us now. Yet, we are still interested to learn if any others were perhaps involved in your activities. If you cooperate and answer our questions, we might consider sparing your life."

Pablo only glared at them.

"Perhaps you are thirsty and in need of a little water."

Sebastian untied his gag and Guillermo put a wet rag to his mouth, which he sucked on momentarily.

Taking the rag away, Guillermo continued, "Is it true that no others were involved besides you, Rodrigo, Angulo, and Ramír?"

Pablo continued to glare at them in silence.

Sebastian got in his face and said loudly in a threatening voice, "Talk! You scum!"

Turning to Sebastian, Pablo said with a sneer, "I *spit* on your grandmother's shadow."

In a rage, Sebastian gave him a terrific smash in the face with his fist, sending him and the chair flying backward across the room. In a second, Sebastian was on top of him again giving him another terrific punch to the face. Guillermo and Mateo had to pull Sebastian off and calm him down. They uprighted Pablo in the chair as he spit out blood and one or two teeth.

Sebastian brandished his knife in Pablo's face and threatened, "If you insult me like that again, I will cut your tongue out!"

Pablo looked at him and said nothing.

Guillermo began again, "Pablo, as I previously said, Alonza has already told us everything. We are only…"

Pablo interrupted, grinning and laughing, "So she told you about the children, did she? I bet she did not tell you where the poor dears are!"

With an evil grin, he added, "Maybe if you untie me and promise to let me go, I will take you to them."

"And why should we let you go after what you have done?"

"Because! That is my price for telling you where the little sweethearts are! Take it or leave it. I know your type. You want to get them back to their poor broken-hearted parents. Well, you will never get it out of me! Their poor parents will never see their little dears ever again. Aaaah, that is so sad. If you want to know where they are, then untie me right now! Or else you will never find them!" he declared with a smug, malevolent sneer.

"Do you mean the priest in Reflejo?"

The sneer suddenly went slack as he flinched and gaped in surprise and disappointment.

"The whore!" he hissed, grimacing.

"It is actually most fortunate for you, Señor, that she remembered," said Guillermo matter-of-factly. "For I assure you that I would have stopped at nothing to get their location out of your miserable hide."

Pablo scoffed and said with renewed defiance, "I *know* she did not tell you about the money. Did she! She probably told you about the cigar box, but the whore does not know about the money! There is lots of it. More than you can imagine. If you turn me loose, I will take you to it and give half to you. *If* you promise to turn me loose!"

At this, Sebastian swelled with rage. As he and his knife got into Pablo's face, he asked urgently, "Guillermo, let me kill him right now and be done with it!"

"Sebastian, I certainly share your feelings. I loathe the vile creature and want to kill him myself, but perhaps we should give him a little time to reconsider his situation and his unwillingness to answer a few questions."

Pablo scoffed, and Guillermo said with a sigh, "I believe I have had enough of this for now. Let us put his gag and hood back on and leave him. Maybe by tomorrow or the next day or the next, he will be hungry and thirsty enough to be more cooperative."

Back at the table, they had a glass of wine to ease their aroused feelings as they talked about the interrogation.

"I do not see any benefit derived from it," said Mateo.

"The talk of money was probably just a ruse in hopes of escaping," speculated Mencía.

"I have seen his kind before, Guillermo, and we will get nothing from him," said Sebastian.

"Well, then what should we do with him? Turn him over to the authorities?" asked Guillermo.

"I am fine with letting him rot in there," muttered Sebastian.

They all pondered the question as they gazed at their wine glasses, not having a ready answer.

As they sat, a worker entered and told them, "Sebastian, Señor, someone at the front door wishes to speak with you."

Sebastian got up and went out.

Several minutes later, he came back in with a serious looking, dark young man about twenty years of age. Everyone watched with curiosity as Sebastian brought him to the table.

"You recall that I asked my morisco acquaintance about kidnappings in the morisco community," explained Sebastian. "This is Jaime Sánchez whose sister was kidnapped a year ago."

"We are very sorry to hear it, Jaime," said Guillermo, rising.

"Thank you," said the young man.

"My name is Guillermo, and these are my friends Mateo, Mencía, and Señor Cruz. Please sit down and join us."

"Thank you," he said, nodding and sitting.

"I heard you want to talk to people about kidnappings in hopes of finding the men responsible for yours. One year ago, when my sister was thirteen and my little brother was nine, they were walking to work in the fields one morning when several men passed in a wagon. They stopped ahead of them and then seemed to be waiting. My brother and sister got scared and started to run. They caught my little sister, threw her in the wagon, and drove off. My little brother was too fast for them and got away."

"How awful," said Mencía.

"Yes, especially for my little brother who was greatly affected by it. Sebastian has just told me that you have been successful in capturing the kidnapper you sought, so you no longer need information. I congratulate you."

"Thank you," replied Guillermo. "We have him tied up here in a room now.

The calm young man straightened with interest at this news.

"We are questioning him," continued Guillermo, "to find out what we can about his gang. He is uncooperative so far."

"I have a very great favor to ask if I may," said the young man with great sincerity. "I would like to look at him and see if he is one of the men who took my sister."

The request caught Guillermo by surprise. He blinked several times and looked around at the others.

"I certainly have no objection to it," said Señor Cruz.

The others nodded in agreement, and Guillermo replied, "Yes, of course, Jaime. We can do it now if you wish."

"Yes, please."

They all went back into the room where their prisoner sat tied in his chair. As the young man stood stoically in front of Pablo, they lifted the hood from his head. The young man looked him over for a long time. Meanwhile Pablo became desperate and alarmed, and excitedly muttered through his gag, "Who is this? What does he want? I do not know him!"

Finally, the young man said, "This may be one of the men. His face is bruised, but I see a scar on his cheek, and he fits my little brother's description of one. I wish to bring my little brother here to see him."

At hearing this, Pablo began to squirm violently in the chair with bulging, frantic eyes. Sebastian had to hold him down.

After a quick glance around at the others, Guillermo told Jaime, "Yes, certainly, if you wish."

"Thank you. I will go now and be back in one hour."

"He will be here," said Sebastian, putting the hood back on the squirming Pablo. "I will personally stay here to ensure it."

In an hour, the young man returned with his younger brother who looked a little pale and nervous. They took the boy into the room. Everyone followed in behind him and stood back along the walls to watch. Inside the room, the young man spoke to his little brother.

"Juan, there is no need to be nervous. They are going to lift the hood from this man, and I want you to tell us whether he is one of the men that took Marina. Do you understand?"

The boy nodded his head and looked about nervously at the other people. Pablo who had also heard started to squirm violently and make tortured muffled sounds through his gag. The young man brought the boy over to stand in front of the sitting, squirming, hooded captive. The young man gave a nod to Sebastian who raised the captive's hood.

Pablo immediately stopped squirming and stared anxiously and silently at the boy. The boy stared back intently without moving or saying anything. There was complete silence in the room as everyone held their breath awaiting the verdict.

Suddenly, the boy burst forward in a tearful violent rage, attacking Pablo. Screaming wildly, he hit him repeatedly with his fists, screaming and sobbing as he did so. After a struggle, the young man and Mateo were able to get the boy off the stunned Pablo.

"Yes," said the boy, sobbing, "he was one of them."

Everyone in the room stood stunned and speechless as the young man took his little brother out of the room.

Suddenly, Pablo recovered from his shock and made frantic muffled pleas through his gag, "Please, do not let them have me! You can have all the money! You'll be rich beyond your wildest dreams. Do not let them have me! They are morisco! They will kill me! The boy is wrong! It was not me! Please!"

"Shut up!" commanded Sebastian as he put the hood back down over his head.

"No, please! I beg of you! They are morisco! They will kill me! Please!" he pleaded through the hood as they left the room.

Outside the room, the young man requested that they give Pablo to his family who would render justice upon the kidnapper of their daughter. After a glance at the others, Guillermo consented, and the young man thanked him most sincerely.

"Jaime," added Guillermo, "it might also provide you and your family some comfort to know that the other three members of his kidnapping gang are also dead. During our own escape from the kidnapper's hideout, Mencía killed them. They were, most likely, the others involved in your sister's kidnapping."

He listened and stood like a stone for a time. Then his tears began to flow as he expressed his gratitude for all they had done. Wanting very much to get back to his family to tell them, he asked to be excused and hurried out with his little brother.

An hour later, Jaime, his father, an uncle, and several older brothers arrived with a donkey-drawn wagon. They were grim and unsmiling as they carried Pablo, still tied in his chair and pleading, from the room and loaded him flat into the wagon.

Leaving one behind in the wagon with Pablo, the men then came back inside and expressed their deepest gratitude to the merchant and the others for finding the man. The grateful morisco family bowed and kissed their hands with great affection and sincerity. After this genuine demonstration of thanks, they begged to be excused, went back out to the wagon, and drove off.

7. Time To Return

BACK INSIDE, they looked at one another in stunned silence, and Mateo said, "I think we have seen the last of our vile friend Pablo."

"Gonzalo, my friend, our work here is done," said Guillermo. "The threat of kidnapping from these villains is over."

"Guillermo, Mencía, Mateo, Sebastian, I am overwhelmed. How am I ever to thank you all. My Rachel is safe again," said the merchant, shedding tears of relief.

He and his daughter began to embrace each one of them. Rachel went to Mencía and gave her a long tearful hug, saying, "Thank you again, Mencía, for saving me. I will always remember seeing you attacking those hardened men. They did not stand a chance."

"You saved me in return. We did it together."

That night, they seemed too emotionally drained to celebrate. After dinner, Guillermo was talking with the merchant.

"Gonzalo," said Guillermo, "we have overstayed and are much overdue at home. We will be leaving tomorrow. My fifteen-minute delivery of potato seed pods turned into weeks. Say, did you ever pay me for those pods? I do not even remember what happened to them."

"You left the bag of them by the door when you came in. I found them and put money in one of your saddle bags for them. I paid you a fair price too. Yes, a fair price. Much better than what my competitors would have given. I fear I will not be able to sell them for what I paid and will lose money. I have lost much business and money during these weeks. My finances are now in jeopardy. I do not know if I will survive."

"Those lines sound very familiar. You are up to your usual trickery. I suppose you have an overstock of potato seeds too and are buying them only to help us out."

The merchant laughed and said, "I forgot that you know me too well. Such poses and exaggerations do not work on you."

"Well, it is good to see you are back to your old self," said Guillermo with a laugh. "I look forward to seeing you again on the next delivery of our estate's goods. Based on our efforts last year, we have high hopes for growing the new plants from the Indies this year. There should be good profit in it for us and for you."

"Such talk is music to my ears, Guillermo," said the merchant, beaming. "I hope to someday visit the estate. I have known Mateo's father and your father, his overseer, for many years. Not only will I be able to see these new plants from the Indies growing, but I also will tell them how grateful I am to you all for saving my Rachel."

"I believe they would welcome such a visit. Don Lorenzo will undoubtedly want to show you his oak meadows and black pigs."

"Yes, as I recall, he is quite enamored with them," said the merchant with a laugh. "And I am quite enamored with the profits to be made from the cured hams of those wonderful creatures. I may try to talk him into selling me his extra hams instead of selling them to those ham dealers who rob him. Yes, they rob him, the same as with a pistol!"

Just then, Mateo, Mencía, and Sebastian joined them.

"All right, what are you two plotting?" joked Mateo. "No, wait. I do not want to hear it. Gonzalo, we came in to say goodbye. We are much overdue at home, so we are departing very early in the morning."

"We also came to thank you for your hospitality," added Mencía.

"Hospitality?" said the merchant with a sigh. "I usually do not have my visitors clubbed over the head, bound, and gagged."

"No, I suppose not," said Guillermo, amused. "Even so, it turned out well."

"Yes, it did, and I am extremely grateful," said the merchant as he shook hands and hugged them.

They were off at dawn the next morning and rode steadily all day. They stopped several times to rest the horses, stretch their legs, and have a bite to eat. In the late afternoon, Mateo looked up at the sun and judged from it that they should arrive at his family's estate well before dark.

But before that was Pascual's camp where Sebastian lived. Pascual and his men were not really bandits or highwaymen who rob travelers. They merely charged for passage on the main road to Cordoba, much like a toll. Pascual had informally arranged it with the nearby town's constable in exchange for his assistance should the constable require it.

When the foursome approached the camp early that evening, the man stationed along the road to collect money was sitting half asleep on a large rock. Seeing a group of travelers coming, he rose from his rock and stood by the road. Eyeing them as they approached, he suddenly perked up smiling. He waved to them and then ran back along the path to the camp.

"Pascual! Pascual! Sebastian and Mateo are coming! And they have Guillermo and Mencía with them!"

Soon, the entire camp was excitedly rushing out to the road in a hubbub of talk, cheering, and noise. Pascual was there too, smiling and expectant, standing along the road with the crowd of his followers behind him watching.

Pascual was happy to see that Sebastian and Mateo had found his two missing friends. And all, thankfully, looked well and uninjured. He too had been worried when Guillermo and Mencía had not returned from their brief trip to Cordoba. Pascual happily greeted them as they rode up and dismounted.

"Welcome back, all of you! Guillermo, Mencía, you had us worried."

Walking stiffly after a long ride, Guillermo approached Pascual and, giving him a hug, said, "It has been an eventful trip, Pascual. It is very good to see you again, very good to be back."

Several people in the crowd chimed in, "Welcome back. God bless your safe return."

49

Looking beyond Pascual to the crowd, Guillermo smiled and waved. "Thank you, my friends. It is good to see you all again too."

Taking Mencía's hand and kissing it, Pascual said, "Mencía, my dear, you look very becoming as usual, only perhaps a little tired."

After examining her for a moment, he added, "Something tells me that you have been at it again on this trip. Some villains are wishing they had not tangled with our lioness."

She just smiled back at him.

"I knew it," he said.

Then clapping the other two on the back, Pascual said, "Mateo, Sebastian, congratulations, you were successful in bringing them back. I want to hear all about it. But the three of you should be on your way. Your families have been concerned for your safety and will be greatly relieved to see you. I hope to see you back soon to tell us about it, but now, please, you should be going, my friends."

Mateo, Guillermo, and Mencía remounted and waved as the whole camp cheered and waved back. After a tip of their hats, they reined around and rode off.

Once they were away, the crowd was abuzz with talk as they sauntered back to their camp. As Pascual walked with Sebastian, he asked, "So, Sebastian, there *was* trouble, then."

"Only for the ones foolish enough to cross Mencía and Guillermo."

"Oh, I must hear it. Let us get you some food and wine. Then you can tell the whole camp about it."

"Mencía was amazing as usual. One less gang of kidnappers now roams the streets of Cordoba. There is much to tell, but the authorities in Cordoba would also like to hear it, so we must be careful about it."

"Yes, yes, we must be careful. Come, Sebastian, let us hurry," said Pascual excitedly. "I am dying to hear it."

Then to the crowd, he shouted, "Everyone! Let us hurry! Sebastian has much to tell!"

8. Home Again

"MATEO, YOU ARE BACK!" exclaimed his father with surprise, rising from his chair at the table. "And what of Guillermo and Mencía? Were you able to find them?"

Turning around and seeing him, Mateo's mother and his wife Luisa were now also up to greet him.

Coming in from a side door out to the sables, Mateo looked tired after a day of riding. Getting to him first, Luisa kissed and hugged him. Moving then aside, she gave his eager parents a chance to come forward to embrace him.

"Mateo, I see you are tired, but tell us, did you find them?"

"Yes, he did," said Guillermo as he came through the door, also looking tired but smiling. Mencía was right behind him. Seeing them, the concerned looks of Don Lorenzo and Doña Antonia changed into happy smiles.

"Oh, such a relief," said Lorenzo with a sigh. Looking around and seeing the housekeeper, he said, "Rosa, please send someone to tell Miguel and Maria. Have them come here so we can celebrate."

"Yes, Don Lorenzo. Praise God, they have returned safely," she said, disappearing.

"Thank you, Rosa," called Guillermo.

As the Don and Doña welcomed Guillermo and Mencía, Mateo hugged his wife again and asked, "So, my sweet, how are you and our little one."

"We are fine. Little Santiago is asleep."

Motioning, Lorenzo said, "Come and sit down at the table with us. Or perhaps you would prefer to stand for a moment after your ride. Someone will be out shortly with a basin so you can clean up. Then you can join us. We were just having a late dinner."

"I believe I will stand for a moment," said Mateo. "We rode from Cordoba today."

"Quite a long day in the saddle. Here, let me get you some wine," said Lorenzo, going over and pouring glasses of wine.

"Cordoba? So that is where Guillermo and Mencía have been hiding," said Antonia, only half in jest.

"Do not be critical, Antonia," said Lorenzo. "I am sure that much has happened to keep them away, and they were not hiding, as you say."

"Yes, the trip was eventful, and we became preoccupied," said Guillermo. "I deeply regret that we gave you cause to worry."

"We look forward to hearing about it," said Antonia.

The Doña had never been comfortable with Mencía's friendship and comradery with Mateo and Guillermo. It was most unusual in their Spanish upper-class culture of men formally courting women as wives, not having them as friends. Normally, an unmarried young woman would not be together with an unmarried young man without a nearby escorting matron called a duenna.

"Mencía, my dear," said Lorenzo, "you must be quite tired. You will spend the night here, of course. We will send a messenger very shortly to inform your parents that you are safely back. I am certain they will want to come in the morning to see you."

"Thank you, Don Lorenzo, you are most kind."

By now, a servant had brought a basin of water, soap, wash cloths, and towels into the next room for them. They left to wash up a bit and were soon back.

"So, what was it that preoccupied you?" asked Antonia with a look.

"When first arriving, we found…" Guillermo started to reply, but stopped when his parents, Miguel and María, arrived and rushed over to the newcomers.

As they were hugging, Lorenzo announced, "Miguel, María, as you see, I am pleased to inform you that your wayward son Guillermo and dear Mencía have been located and brought back into our fold."

"Yes, it is a happy day, Don Lorenzo," said Miguel, smiling and examining his son and Mencía.

"And thank God they appear to be intact and unharmed," he added.

Going to Mateo, María told him, "Thank you, Mateo, for bringing back our dear little boy."

Hugging her with a laugh, Mateo said, "Dear mother of my true friend, I do not believe that I should claim any credit for bringing back your dear little boy, as you say."

"Guillermo was about to tell us what kept him and Mencía away for so long," said Antonio.

"I believe, Mother," said Mateo in defense of his friend, "that Guillermo was about to say that upon arrival there, they found Señor Cruz, our merchant friend, in deep despair. His daughter Rachel had just been kidnapped."

"God forbid," said Lorenzo as they all inhaled with surprise.

"And when they went to rescue her, they managed to get themselves kidnapped as well," added Mateo.

"Good heavens," said Maria.

"You should not jest about such things, Mateo," his mother admonished.

"No, Mateo does not jest. It is all quite true!" Guillermo chimed in. "We were kidnapped, in mortal danger, and saved by a daring rescue."

They all stared in wonder at hearing this.

"But Mateo," asked Miguel, confused, "If *you* claim no credit, then who was it that rescued them?"

"It was Mencía," announced Mateo.

The listeners were stunned and dumbstruck as they turned to look over at her.

"Mencía was tied up and thrown into the same room as Rachel," explained Mateo. "They used Mencía's hidden throwing knives to get free. With her knives and a cutlass, Mencía overpowered their three captors. Then she and Rachel carried Guillermo off to safety."

53

"I had been knocked over the head, unconscious, and tied up in a separate room," interjected Guillermo.

Maria with a wobbly hand felt a nearby chair and sat down. After a moment, the surprised listeners regained their senses and came forward to thank and hug Mencía who smiled broadly.

"We returned only after tracking down and putting an end to the remaining kidnapper, who was the ringleader. But we have had a long ride," declared Mateo, "and will say no more until we are properly fed and wined."

"Yes," agreed Lorenzo, "let us all sit down at the table to enjoy some food and drink. We must get these adventurers fed so we may hear more about it."

Mateo excused himself momentarily while he and Luisa went back to see little six-month-old Santiago, who was fortunately back with a nanny in a distant room, away from the noise.

Upon return, Mateo and Luisa found the dinner table astir with excited talk and speculation as food was brought out and wine served.

The din was broken only momentarily when Lorenzo asked for everyone to quiet down for a moment of prayer, thanking God for their food and for bringing their adventurers home safely. After "amen," the noise and laughter instantly resumed as they enjoyed a memorable celebration of their safe return.

On their ride from Cordoba, the foursome had discussed it and thought it best to say that Mencía had "overpowered" the men rather than "killed" them. They worried that her killing them might be too much for the sensibilities of the women at home. Doña Antonia was already uncomfortable with her lack of traditional Spanish lady-like qualities. Besides, they knew the women would not want to hear about blood and gore, and the men could separately be told the bloody details of the escape.

Their families listened that night with wonder as the story of their adventure was told. The listeners marveled at their escape with Rachel from the kidnappers. They beamed with pride as they heard the story of finding and rescuing the money lender's children. Guillermo left out the part about striking and tying up the priest. The parents seemed especially touched by the story of the morisco family. After several hours, the travelers were looking tired, and Lorenzo suggested that they all turn in for the night.

Mencía's parents and sisters came the next day and happily rushed to her, thankful for her safe return. The story of their adventure was retold in the morning for their benefit as everyone sat around the table snacking and sipping wine.

As their story spread from the main house staff around to the families of the estate, it naturally became embellished. When Mencía, Guillermo, Mateo, Luisa, and Mencía's family came outside that afternoon for a walk, one of the little boys of the estate ran up to her.

"Señorita Mencía, is it true you killed ten men and carried Guillermo from a burning building to save him?" he asked excitedly, which caused them all to laugh.

"Manuelito, where did you hear *that*?" asked Guillermo.

"I heard it from Paco, who heard it from Jorge, who heard it from Pedrito, who heard it from his mother, who heard it from Señora Rosa," replied the little boy.

"He forgot to tell you about the one-eyed giant."

"Really?"

"No, Manuelito, but Señorita Mencía did save me. That part is true."

With a smile, Guillermo asked him, "Manuelito, I suppose I should keep her around. What do you think?"

Grinning, Manuelito eagerly nodded 'yes' several times, causing more laughter.

Later as their group was returning to the main house, Luisa looked up and saw her best friend Ana and her family arriving in a carriage. Ana excitedly waved, and she waved back.

9. Luisa's Friend Ana

IT WAS LATE LAST AUGUST when Luisa was still pregnant with little Santiago that she first met Ana, who was the daughter of Lorenzo's friend and neighbor Don Felipe. One morning, he came to visit and brought her along. She had been living with her aunt for several years and had recently returned to live again with her father.

After their introduction, Luisa and Ana were soon chatting away. Luisa was happy to meet another girl her age with whom she might become friends. She was close with Mencía, of course, because of Mencía's closeness with Mateo and Guillermo. But Mencía was not a girlfriend with whom she could talk about normal feminine interests, such as marriage, having babies, raising children, dresses, jewelry, and so on.

Luisa was six months older than Ana, and they shared many interests. She was an intelligent young girl with a good figure and pleasant looks who Luisa found to be affectionate and unpretentious. They became good friends and began to visit each other regularly.

During these visits, Ana told Luisa about herself. Ana was Felipe's only living offspring. An older brother had been killed in the bullring, and a younger sister had died in childhood. When Ana was eight, her mother tragically died in childbirth along with the baby. So Ana was the sole heir to Felipe's estate, which was a great deal to bring to a marriage.

"When I was fourteen years old, I went to stay with an aunt who was to help me through my developing years and with the responsibilities of courtship and marriage. While she was good to me and paid attention to my education, she lacked the motherly affection I had enjoyed before."

"I understand your aunt found a prospective husband for you, but it did not work out?" asked Luisa, having previously heard Felipe mention it.

"Yes, when it came time for courtship, my aunt arranged for a duenna and took me to various social events. Several initial encounters proved unsuccessful, a young man who did not appeal to me, and a couple young men to whom I did not appeal."

"Ah, too bad," said Luisa.

"My aunt then became acquainted with a family with four sons and one daughter living on an estate in her area. The eldest son was to inherit the family estate, as is the normal custom. Therefore, the second oldest son was proposed as a suitor. The parents and son were invited to a dinner party at my aunt's home, and my father came to attend as well."

"What was he like?"

"He seemed nice enough and was cordial to me. After our second dinner together, it was decided that the next dinner should be at my father's estate. The parents and son came down and took great interest in looking over the estate which their son and I would inherit with time."

"Did you love him, or he love you? It sounds like a purely arranged marriage," asked Luisa, feeling bad for her friend.

"The family impressed me as being more interested in marrying the estate than me," she said with a smile.

"Oh, dear. But you do not seem upset by it? What happened?" asked Luisa.

"After their visit, they accepted the proposed marriage, which was to take place three months later. However, a week before the wedding, my husband-to-be died in a riding accident. His horse tripped on something, and he fell hitting his head."

"Oh, I am so sorry," said Luisa.

"That was about the extent of my feelings toward it too," said Ana with a frown.

"Oh, my," said Luisa with a laugh.

"Fortunately, we were not yet married, so a year in black mourning attire was not required. Well, the family still wanted to marry my father's estate, so to speak, so they offered up the third son. I found him similar in character to his brother, only he drank a great deal more."

"My poor Ana! And what happened to him?"

The wedding date was set for three months again. Two weeks before the wedding, the brothers were planning a hunting trip into the hills to hunt wild boar. I was visiting and watching as they practiced beforehand with crossbows. They had been drinking and the oldest brother managed to accidentally discharge his crossbow bolt into the leg of my husband-to-be.

"Oh!" said Luisa in surprise.

"He was rolling around on the ground in pain when I rushed over to him. When he saw me, he told me to get away saying, 'It is all your fault! You are bad luck! I do not wish to marry you. Please go away!'

"What an unfair, cruel thing to say! I hope you were not too hurt by it."

"I suspect not. Seeing my reaction, he gave me a strange look and said, 'Well, you need not look so happy about it, just go!' The fourth brother too young for me besides being unwilling to risk becoming my next husband-to-be."

They both laughed, and Ana continued, "A few more unsuccessful courtship attempts were made afterward, but by then, I needed a break from the rigors of finding a husband. I thanked my aunt for her efforts and came home to be with my father. I may tempt fate again someday but am in no hurry."

"Good! I am glad you came to live with your father. Now we can visit and be friends."

After the birth of Santiago, Ana visited with Luisa often and made a great fuss over the beautiful new baby.

"We must see about getting one for you," Luisa told her with determination. "It is now my mission, as Mateo would say. You are a dear sweet girl, and I see no reason why you should not have one of your own."

"Oh, Luisa."

"You must try to look your best and soon the young men will come beating at your door."

Luisa began working on her during her visits. She gave her make-up and hair suggestions, loaned her pretty dresses, coached her on walking more erectly and confidently, and most important of all, to smile more. Luisa knew how pretty she was when she smiled, since she was always smiling with her. She just needed to smile more when with men.

"You must have had girlfriends when you were growing up. Why would you and they not have talked about and worked at looking pretty for young men?"

"No, I had no close friends. When I went to my aunt's, I was a stranger, and the local girls already had their groups of friends. They were not very friendly to the outsider who was there to compete with them for their men."

"Oh, What a shame. Well, you have a close friend now," Luisa said with a smile.

During Ana's visits, Mencía sometimes joined them and gave encouragement as well. Periodically, the three of them would ride into town and presented an attractive sight to the passersby who stopped to watch and tip their hats.

In early November, Ana told her with excitement, "Luisa, do you remember the young man riding his horse the other day who tipped his hat to us?"

"Yes, I think so."

"Well, he came to our estate yesterday to pay me a social call. He said he had seen us riding and was interested in better knowing me. We sat and talked for a time. Our housekeeper sat with us to act as my duenna."

"See, I told you. Did you smile?"

"Yes, I hope not too much. He is to visit again tomorrow afternoon. I want you to meet him. Can you come?"

"Yes, of course."

The next afternoon, Ana and Luisa sat in a sitting room and rose when the young man named Lope entered with the housekeeper.

"Good afternoon, Lope. I would like to introduce you to my best friend, la Señora Luisa de Cordoba, who is married to the son of our neighbor Don Lorenzo." Then turning to Luisa, "And this is el Señor Lope Alvarado."

The young man seemed very taken by the sight of Luisa and came eagerly forward to take her hand, saying, "The greatest of pleasure."

Luisa thought he was kissing her hand too long and looking up at her with desirous eyes as he did so. Feeling uneasy, she glanced at Ana who glanced back with embarrassment. When Lope saw this, he abruptly stopped and shifted his attention to Ana, kissing her hand.

After this uncomfortable introduction, they sat and talked about the weather, the roads, horses, and other small talk.

After about fifteen minutes of this, Luisa said, "Well, I should be going so you may talk. It was a pleasure to meet you, Señor Alvarado."

"I wish you would call me Lope and that I might call you Luisa."

With a look at Ana, Luisa said, "Perhaps in time, but now I must go."

"Could I have the honor of accompanying you on your ride home?"

"No, it is not necessary. Good day, Señor. Goodbye, Ana."

On the ride home, she could not get over how he had fawned over her, even though he knew she was married.

"Who is this young man?" she wondered.

At dinner that night, she told the others about Lope's visit. Without making any accusations, she asked what was known about him.

"We know the family," said Lorenzo. "He is a son of Don Cosme Alvarado, who has an estate with oak meadows, raising pigs and cattle as we do. He is a friend, living only a half hour west of here, who I have been remiss in not visiting for quite some time. Why do you ask?"

"I am not sure Lope is right for my friend Ana. It might be useful to find out more about him."

"Well, it is almost time for the start of La Matanza. I have been wanting to visit my friend Cosme to see his meadows and pigs again. I could see how his preparations for the slaughter are coming," offered Lorenzo. "Perhaps Antonia and I should pay them an overdue visit and take Miguel and Maria along. Maria is friends with the overseer's wife, and you know how these wives of overseers love to gossip. I suspect she knows a great deal about the young man."

"Thank you, Father. I would appreciate it," said Luisa.

"Well, it is no great sacrifice for me. I am always happy to visit with neighbors to talk pigs and the curing of hams."

At hearing this, his wife rolled her eyes and shook her head.

Mateo had listened with interest and when alone with Luisa later, asked her what happened. She told him, and he considered it for a moment.

"Perhaps we should watch this man and see what his habits are. I am sure Guillermo and Mencía would be willing to help."

"Let us first hear what is learned by your father's visit."

The next day, Ana came to visit and told Luisa that after she left, Lope apologized for his behavior, saying he was carried away by thoughts that he knew Luisa. He had been very attentive and complimentary to Ana afterward. They were on good terms when he departed.

"No harm done, Ana. I can assure you that I have never met him before. I am happy to hear he felt the need for an apology. What is his situation?"

"He has two older brothers and a sister. He acted surprised when I told him that I had no living siblings. I am fond of him, Luisa. I hope he will work out."

"I just want you to be happy, Ana," said Luisa, hugging her.

The day after Ana's visit, Lorenzo and his wife paid a call to the Alvarado estate. With them went his overseer Miguel and Miguel's wife María. After they returned, Lorenzo sat down in private with Mateo and Luisa.

"Oh, you should have seen it," gushed Lorenzo. "His meadows are green from the rains, and his acorns have been falling for some weeks. His pigs are already starting to fatten, although his pigs look leaner than mine, I think. Our acorns began falling sooner than his. He is busy with preparations for the slaughter and gave me a nice tour of his curing cellar. Oh, Mateo, I told him about you bringing seeds from the Indies, and he was quite astounded to hear of it."

"Father, what about his son Lope?" asked Mateo.

"Ah, yes, Lope. Well, his son was not there when we called, so we did not see him ourselves, but the overseer's wife had much to tell Maria about the son Lope. The family wants him to strike out on his own in a new place, but he has shown little desire to leave the estate. Perhaps, she said, it is because he would miss the young woman he sees regularly in a nearby town."

Both Mateo and Luisa frowned at hearing this.

"Now that he has found Ana, possibly he has given up seeing the other woman," suggested Mateo with doubt.

"It is hard to say. I asked Cosme what was new with his sons, and he made no mention of Ana. I believe he knows nothing of Lope seeing her. He talked more about his second son who is returning very soon from a military tour in the Netherlands."

With an uneasy look, Lorenzo added, "Miguel also heard from their overseer that Lope has bragged to a stableman about having found a young woman with a nice estate to marry."

"Oh, dear," said Luisa with concern.

"That does not sound good. We must learn more about him and the truth of him and this woman. And the sooner the better," suggested Mateo. "Guillermo and I will take turns watching him. Mencía will want to help. Perhaps Sebastian and José from Pascual's camp can help. I will ride to see them now."

"I think it best," agreed Lorenzo. "He may prove to be less than honorable."

"I appreciate you visiting them for me, Father," said Luisa. "Now I am concerned more than ever for my friend."

"Rightfully so," he replied with a sad smile.

A week later, Luisa, Mateo, Guillermo, and Mencía sat with Don Lorenzo to discuss what they had learned from watching Lope.

"Well, as I suspected the news is not good," said Mateo. "We have followed his movements for a week and have confirmed that he continues to visit a young woman in the nearby town, during which time he visited Ana three times. But we were surprised to find he also visits a second woman in a separate nearby town."

"Are they perhaps just friends?" asked Lorenzo.

"No, these are not young girls with family and duennas. He usually only stays for an hour or two. When we inquired about the women, they were described to be less than reputable. We saw one kiss him sensually at the door when leaving."

With a heavy sigh, Luisa said, "Now that we know he is contemptable, what can we do? I suppose I should tell her."

"Does Ana suspect anything herself?" asked Mencía.

"No, I think not. I hope she is not in love with him."

"Other options might be confronting the man himself or informing her father or his father. All such options will cause your friend pain and may create hard feelings. The worst outcome would be for her to deny the truth of it and rush to marry him," said Mateo.

"Oh, that would be so terrible. I do not want to risk doing or saying anything yet. I believe we should wait to see what further happens," suggested Luisa.

Ana came to see Luisa the next day and told her about her latest visit from Lope. She seemed very happy. It was hard for Luisa to maintain a happy outward appearance and not tell Ana what she knew. Luisa finally had to pretend to suffer from a headache and cut Ana's visit short.

Two days later, Ana visited Luisa again and seemed troubled. They went into a sitting room and closed the door.

"Ana, you look unhappy today."

She started crying, and Luisa gave her a hug.

"Ana, what is the matter? What has happened?"

"Lope visited me earlier. When he came forward to kiss my hand, I could smell a woman's perfume on him and saw several long fine red hairs on his jacket. He seemed careless in his manner as if he had been drinking. When he saw me looking at his coat, he brushed the hair off and dismissed it as that darned dog of his."

Luisa listened without speaking as she continued.

"He looked at me and said, 'Ana, where is your pretty smile? It means the world to me.' I told him that I was not feeling well.

"Our housekeeper, who was nearby acting as my duenna, told him, 'Perhaps you should come back, Señor Alvarado, when Señorita Ana is feeling better.'

"At first, he looked perturbed by her intrusion, but then he recovered his manners, smiled at her, and told me, 'Yes, I am sorry to hear you feel ill, my dear. I shall call upon you perhaps tomorrow when you may feel better.'

"He bowed and left. Luisa, I do not know what to think. I asked our housekeeper if she had also noticed the perfume and she said yes. I suspect him of having been with another woman. I needed to talk to someone, so I came right away to see you."

Luisa gave her another hug and took a deep breath.

"I am so glad you did. Ana, I wanted to tell you before but could not."

Ana looked at her in surprise.

Holding her hands, Luisa told her directly, "Ana, I regret to tell you this, but Lope does not merit your esteem, and you deserve much better."

"So my suspicions are true? You know something, Luisa?" Luisa nodded.

"What is it you know? Please tell me."

Just then, the door opened, and Mateo looked in, saying, "I am sorry to interrupt but must speak to Luisa for a moment."

Luisa rose and went out as Ana sat sadly, patting her teary eyes with a handkerchief.

In a moment, Luisa returned and informed her, "I am sorry to tell you this, Ana, but Mateo has just told me that after Lope left your estate, he returned to the apartment of the red-haired woman."

Ana gasped in shock. After collecting herself, she asked for a glass of wine.

"So you have suspected and have been watching him?" asked Ana as Luisa poured it.

"Yes, I am sorry to say that I felt very uncomfortable about him from the very first. You saw how he kissed my hand and his attraction to me even though he knew I was married."

"Luisa, please ask Mateo to join us."

When Luisa came back with Mateo, Ana asked, "So Lope is back with the woman?"

"Yes, I intruded because I thought that you and Luisa would want to know."

"And how long will he stay? Is there a chance of seeing it now for myself?"

"Yes, possibly if we leave now," replied Mateo in a serious tone.

"Are you sure you want to do this, Ana?" asked Luisa.

"Yes, I wish to see the rogue in action myself," she said finishing her wine.

With that, the three of them left to get their horses and were soon galloping off.

Walking furtively along the street in the town, Mateo led them to an alcove where they found Mencía and Guillermo who were surprised at seeing Ana and Luisa with Mateo.

"Is he still with her?" asked Mateo.

"Yes, they had been drinking together down the street in the bar," said Mencía.

"Since he does not know me," said Guillermo, "I took the liberty of going into the bar and having a glass of wine nearby so I might listen as they talked. Lope, it seems, is unhappy with the return this week of his brother from soldier duty and the attention being paid him. He sarcastically called him his 'brave, honorable, and esteemed brother,' which they most likely do not say about *him*. He drinks to sooth his jealousy."

"His jealousy and drinking have made him quite reckless," said Mateo.

"Ana, you are here to see for yourself?" asked Mencía.

"Yes."

"I would probably do the same in your place. Believe us though when we tell you that he does not deserve your regard."

"I do believe you all, but it is something one must see firsthand to fully appreciate. Which doorway is it? Does he walk by this way when he leaves?"

"That one," said Guillermo, pointing. "He normally walks to get his horse in the other direction, but the bar is this way if they return there. We all should not stay here in this small alcove. I can stay here with Ana while the rest of you wait farther down the street. If he walks in this direction, she can hide behind me and watch."

"That will be fine. We will wait down the street a bit by the marketplace," said Mateo.

"Ana, I know you are angry, but you should avoid making a scene here in town," Luisa said earnestly to her.

"Yes, I can see that. Thank you, Luisa."

About fifteen minutes later, Lope and the red-haired woman emerged from the doorway and walked unsteadily along the opposite side of the street back toward the bar. They talked and laughed as they walked and stopped for a drunken kiss before continuing. When Lope burped aloud, he and the woman giggled. Lope only glanced over in Guillermo's direction momentarily as they passed. Ana saw their whole display for herself as she peered from behind Guillermo. She continued to observe the high-spirited couple as they entered the bar with Lope chuckling and taking a deep bow as he opened the door for the red-haired woman.

Afterward, Ana and Guillermo rejoined the others, and they left town. There was no further need for watching Lope. Luisa and Mencía went with Ana back to her estate to sit with and comfort her for a time. They also told her about the second woman, and Ana could only shake her head. Mencía gladly noted that Ana no longer shed tears over him and was instead angry at having been so deceived.

The next day, Lope returned to call on Ana and, upon entering the room, said, "Ana, my dear, I hope you are feeling better. I am so sorry about what happened yesterday. I was not myself just as you were not yourself. We must forget it, my sweet. Yes, we must put it from our minds."

When he came forward and reached for her hand to kiss, he instead got a fierce slap across the face. Turned around by the blow, he turned back again to her, held his hand to his smarting cheek, and looked at her in surprise.

"How dare you come here and call me 'your sweet.' I know about you and your two lovers!" she told him angrily. "I watched you myself last night staggering down the street with that red-haired hussy!"

"But, my sweet? I, I can explain?" he stammered.

"Get out! And never come back! I never want to see you again!"

Then with a note of defiance, he said, "But that is not fair. You do not let me explain. I have a perfectly good explanation. I think you owe me an apology!"

"I said get out!"

"No, not until you let me explain!"

He then heard the cocking of a pistol and turned in surprise to see the housekeeper with a pistol aimed at him.

"She said to get out, Señor, so leave," the housekeeper told him in a threatening manner.

"This is absurd! A duenna with a pistol! This is a madhouse! I am leaving and shall *never* return!" he declared arrogantly and then stormed out.

Coincidently, Lope's father had also heard reports from friends in town about his son's carousing and cavorting with the woman that night. He was not pleased and confronted his son when he came home later that day. Not at all satisfied with his son's excuses, his father called Lope an embarrassment to the family. Within days, he was to pack up and be on his way to Seville to stay with a cousin while awaiting passage on a treasure fleet ship to the Indies. A relative there had been asking for nephews to come help with his business, and his father was offering up his wayward son Lope.

When Ana told Luisa and the others about Lope's visit, they all expressed regret at not having had someone there to support her. She told them her father was also in the next room with a pistol, so it was not required.

Luisa and the others felt great relief that she had gotten over Lope so nicely. When they heard he was gone and was to be shipped off to the Indies, they all toasted to his voyage. Mateo observed that during his time in the Indies, he had seen many scoundrels in the ports, much like Lope. He would have much company there and fit right in.

With Lope gone, so ended the drama of Ana's courtship. She seemed to have become stronger and more confident as a result of it. The added confidence gave her a very becoming look. Ana and Luisa were even closer now and continued to visit regularly.

One day in early December while visiting, Ana was holding and playing with little three-month-old Santiago. He was cooing and staring at colorful little things that Ana and Luisa dangled in front of him. After a few more smiles at the baby who squirmed and smiled back, they gave him to the nanny and left the nursery to talk in a sitting room.

On the way, they heard guests being announced. Lorenzo came out and seeing his friend Don Cosme and another young man, he enthusiastically welcomed them.

"Cosme, my friend, I am so happy you have come for a visit. How nice to see you again. My pigs happen to be in the nearby meadows. What good timing. Ah, and who is this?"

"Lorenzo, my friend, we were traveling by, and I thought we might stop in to see how your pigs are doing and to let you meet my son who has recently returned from the king's service in the Netherlands."

"Cosme, I am so pleased that you have," he said, looking with admiration at the son.

"Lorenzo, this is my son Bernardino, of whom I am exceedingly proud. Bernardino, this is my friend, el Señor Don Lorenzo de Cordoba."

The young man, whose left arm looked to be unusable and was in a sling, bowed and said, "An honor."

"An honor, Bernardino, truly an honor," said Lorenzo with some emotion. "Perhaps your father has told you that two of my sons died in service in the Netherlands. I am so delighted for my friend Cosme that God has returned you to him."

"I thank you, Don Lorenzo, for your kind words," said Bernardino with a bow.

"And who are these two lovely young ladies?" asked Cosme, looking past Lorenzo.

Turning and seeing them, Lorenzo called cheerily, "Luisa, Ana, please come to meet my friend and his son."

Turning back to his visitors, he said glowingly, "Gentlemen, this lovely young lady is Lisa who I proudly say is the wife of my son Mateo and the mother of my grandson Santiago. And this second lovely young lady is her dear friend Ana, the daughter of my neighbor Felipe."

Then to Luisa and Ana, "And this is my good friend, el Señor Don Cosme Alvarado, and his son Bernardino."

The two men came forward, bowed, and kissed their hands, saying, "Charmed."

In doing so, Luisa thought she had noticed a look pass between Ana and Bernardino.

"My friend Cosme and I share a great interest in our oak meadows and black pigs. I visited him a few weeks back and saw his pigs. Now I want to show him mine. Let us have a glass of wine and then we will go out to see them. Why do you not come along, Luisa, Ana? I am sure Bernardino would not mind the company of two pretty ladies. We can find Mateo, and he can come too."

Luisa and Ana both nodded, smiling. Mateo was soon found and introduced. The wine glasses were emptied, and they went outside to see the black pigs. As Mateo and Luisa walked together, Ana walked beside Bernardino.

Lorenzo excitedly pointed, saying, "Look, I see a group of pigs now!"

They approached the pigs and watched them as they rooted around in the green grass.

"Look how they are eating. A good many acorns are down, and our pig tenders have been taking the pigs to the various meadows to get them all. Look at that young one there. Oh, look at the nice shape of his hams already."

"Yes, yes, very nice indeed," agreed Cosme.

"He might be big enough for slaughter next year. See the big one there. He will get even bigger by the time of our slaughter in January. Ah, those lovely acorns, each one is a little dose of sweetness for the meat. When cured, their luscious hams become the delicacy for which we here are so famous."

The others were greatly amused at his exuberance and passion for the pigs.

"You must forgive my father's enthusiasm for his pigs," said Mateo, chuckling. "He does drive my mother crazy sometimes with it."

Ana and Bernardino seemed to be getting along well, exchanging small talk and smiling at each other. Luisa thought him a fine gentleman and a rugged kind of handsome.

Later, Mateo and Bernardino were together in his father's den as Mateo showed him a saber mounted on the wall. After telling how it had been used in battle by an ancestor, Mateo noticed how much Bernardino was admiring it and seemed to be remembering his own military past.

"Bernardino, how was your arm injured?"

"In battle. Many were killed and injured that day when we stormed across a bridge to attack the Dutch rebel defenders."

"Is it hurt badly? Do you have any use of it?"

"No, I have no use of it, and fortunately, it is not painful."

"I am sorry to hear it."

"You need not feel sorry. I am proud of it. My withered arm is my badge of courage, earned in battle, the same as a fine ornate medal pinned to my chest. Luckily, it is my left arm, and I am right-handed. I still can do a great many things I have always done."

"Bernardino, it is a privilege to have met you, and I look forward to getting to know you better and talking of things of interest over wine. I was a soldier on a treasure fleet galleon and saw battle as well."

"I would like that very much."

"By the way, you and Ana seem to have gotten on well. She is a lovely, sweet girl."

"Yes, I must admit that I am already quite fond of her," he replied with a grin.

10. Morisco Gardener

WE NOW RETURN three months later to the afternoon walk on the estate. Mencía, her family, Luisa, Mateo, and Guillermo were out getting some air after spending the morning hearing about their unexpected run-in with kidnappers in Cordoba.

As they strolled along, Mencía's younger sister, Margarita, came over to hug Mencía, saying, "I am so glad you are back. We were worried about you when you were away for so long."

"You should know by now not to worry about me, Margarita," said Mencía affectionately.

"We still do," said her other younger sister, Cristina, coming up to hug her too. "But you were with Guillermo, so we were not too worried."

Guillermo, walking nearby, smiled.

"Only, should he not have saved you, instead of the other way around?" asked Margarita with a grin at Guillermo.

Guillermo stopped abruptly with his hands on his hips with a mock expression of being offended.

"I beg your pardon," he said, and they laughed.

Then walking on with a smile, he added, "Besides, I have saved Mencía so many times in the past, that it was her turn to save me for a change."

"I'm just glad that you made it back safely," said Luisa.

Little Manuelito ran up at this point and asked his question about Mencía's rescue of Guillermo. Afterward, the group continued along in high spirits, laughing about the wild rumors spreading on the estate. Soon Mencía would be a legend, Mateo told them.

As they approached the house, Luisa saw her best friend Ana and her family coming up the drive in a carriage. Ana excitedly waved and Luisa waved back. She also appeared to be very happy to hear that Guillermo and Mencía were back.

Their carriage pulled up at the front door as Luisa and the others walked up. Lorenzo came from the house to greet his neighbors as Don Felipe, his daughter and his new son-in-law climbed from the carriage.

Yes, Bernardino and Ana were now married. After meeting in early December, they were so taken with each other that a whirlwind romance and courtship ensued. Dinners and after dinner walks in patios with a duenna were nearly nightly. Within two weeks, Bernardino had proposed, and Ana had happily accepted. The two families were delighted and saw no reason for a lengthy time before a wedding. They were married in late January by Father Giraldo in the local parish church. All, especially Luisa, were ecstatically happy for them.

Now, Ana and her husband Bernardino came forward from the carriage, warmly greeted Guillermo and Mencía, and expressed their happiness at seeing them again. They had been worried like everyone else.

Amidst the hubbub of greetings, Lorenzo called for everyone to come inside, ushering them in.

Right away, Ana took Luisa aside and embraced her friend. She seemed to be bursting with joy. Luisa sensed that it was more than just her happiness at the safe return of her friends. Luisa guessed the reason.

"Ana, it has been almost two months since you were married. Could it be?"

"Yes!" said Ana gleefully.

"How wonderful!"

"Luisa, I have you to thank. You were the one who took an interest in me, helped me to be better, saved me from a big mistake. Thank you, you sweetheart."

"I just helped my friend. And now you are expecting. What wonderful news!"

Only a few minutes later, Ana and Bernardino made the announcement. Everyone began congratulating them and celebrating. Meanwhile, Felipe was shedding tears of happiness amidst the hubbub.

A week later after all the excitement of kidnappings and baby news, life on the estate was returning to normal. Pedro, the gardener in charge of growing the new plants from the Indies, had not been as distracted by events as the others. He had been concerned about potato seeds.

When serving as a soldier on a treasure fleet galleon, Mateo had brought back seeds from the Indies for growing peppers, potatoes, tomatoes, beans, and maize (corn). These vegetables, native to the Indies, were still largely unknown to people in Spain and therefore the rest of Europe. Last year, Pedro had successfully grown sample amounts of the new plants, which when tasted for the first time had caused great interest.

Over the fall and winter, Pedro had planted more potatoes since they seemed to be a winter crop in their hot climate. From these plants, he harvested both seeds and potatoes. When he tried to grow new plants from the seeds, he experienced only limited success.

Pedro was concerned and uncertain how to do better. He was also concerned that he would need more help growing larger amounts of the new plants when summer came. He passed on his concerns to Miguel who listened intently.

A few days later after much consideration, Miguel had a recommendation for addressing it. After he and Lorenzo visited Pedro in the garden, they talked on their walk back to the main house.

"Don Lorenzo, I have been considering how to help Pedro and have even discussed it with friends who are overseers on surrounding estates."

"Yes, it is a difficulty. We must be confident that our potato seeds can grow potato plants reliably if we are to sell them. And here, we have already sold some to our merchant, Señor Cruz."

After a pause in thought, he pondered, "I wonder if my cousin Carlos or Luisa's father down south are having better results."

"I have not heard from them but believe I know what may help our efforts."

"I am eager to hear it, Miguel."

"As I am sure you are aware, moriscos are skilled at growing things. The gardens, parks, and orchards of Moorish times are said to have been far better than any present ones. They seem to have more skill at it, or it is in their blood, or something. I have talked with my friend Hernán, Don Alejandro's overseer. They have three morisco families on their estate and can spare one to come here to work for a time."

Lorenzo had been listening intently as they walked and now stopped to ask with concern, "A family of moriscos here, Miguel? Is that really such a good notion? I am aware of their skills at agriculture. They may be sober and hardworking, but there is such a question about their sincerity as true Christian converts and their stubborn clinging to their Oriental roots and customs."

Miguel was about to respond when Lorenzo continued, "Many suspect they only pose as Christians while they plot with the Turks to take back Spain and return it to Moorish rule."

To this Miguel replied, "These morisco families have not been a problem on Don Alejandro's estate. Quite the opposite, they are excellent gardeners and such hard workers that Hernán can spare one family. He said that Don Alejandro is agreeable to let a family come here to work, if you desire it."

"And what do you know about this family?"

"I have met the man and his family. They impress me as good people."

"I have read," began Lorenzo, "that decades of our efforts to make them 'good and faithful Christians' have thus far been in vain. They continue their beliefs and customs in private and breed like rabbits, four children in three years! In time, they will outnumber us. Our clergy say the moriscos only attend church when forced, that some show great boredom in it, while to others, it appears to be torture.

Lorenzo paused abruptly, looking awkwardly at Miguel who said nothing.

"You need not say it, Miguel. I, myself, have been bored and tortured at times in church. I suppose that is no meaningful criticism," he confessed. "Alas, perhaps my military service suppressing the morisco rebellion in Granada, not so many years ago, has colored my opinion of them. It was a nasty affair, with which I was glad to be done and in which it was no great honor to have participated."

"The moriscos have a difficult situation," explained Miguel. "They were forced to convert religions. Spain wants them to become assimilated, yet they are looked down upon and treated differently, sometimes harshly and unfairly. It is no wonder that it should take time."

"As usual, you are probably right, Miguel."

"I will ensure they attend church regularly as we do," Miguel assured him, "and we will rely on Father Giraldo as to their religious progress. I think the man might be a big help to Pedro. An outbuilding is available that can be converted for their habitation while we give him a try. I believe the idea merits a trial period. The man may prove to be valuable to our efforts with the plants from the Indies."

"Miguel, you seem convinced. I have reservations as I have stated, but if you think it best, you may proceed."

The next day, a man in his thirties came to see Miguel. The man named Joaquin was thin with a tanned complexion and a thick dark beard. He wore clothes and a straw hat that looked much like other workers. Miguel took him to meet Pedro who was happy to have added help in the gardens. If he could help with their potato seed problem, so much the better.

Miguel went with Pedro and Joaquin to see the garden where he would work. As Joaquin looked about with interest, Pedro told him that they were having trouble growing plants from some new seeds. He gave several seeds to Joaquin who examined them closely.

"I have not seen such seeds before, but they are not greatly different from other seeds. If we have difficulty getting seeds to grow, we soak them for a time, plant them in little pots and grow seedlings, putting them in a warm place where they are carefully watered and get sun. These seeds should be no different, I believe. What plant is this?"

"It is a new plant from the Indies called potato. The plant produces an edible bulb underground in its roots. I will show you."

They went to an outbuilding where a large table was covered with recently harvested potatoes.

"These are the bulbs, called potatoes, that the plant produces," Pedro told him.

Joaquin picked up several with great interest and closely examined them.

"I have not seen such a vegetable before. How do they taste? May I taste one?"

"No, they do not taste good raw. They must be cooked in some way, such as boiling or frying. They have a mild taste and go well with meats. We think of them as a bread-like vegetable."

"That is very interesting. I look forward to tasting one."

Looking at the potatoes on the table he asked, "Why are there so many different sizes, colors, and shapes?"

"We do not know."

"Did each plant produce a variety like this?"

"No, I believe the potatoes of each plant are similar in looks but vary a bit in size. But the potatoes of one plant can be different from those of another plant."

"That is interesting and important."

He examined a potato with sprouts already growing on it.

"This bulb, or potato as you say, has several sprouts. It appears to be starting new plants."

"Yes, new plants can be started either by planting a seed or one of these potatoes."

"Very interesting. Were these potatoes on the table produced from seed or planted potatoes?" he asked, pointing.

"These are from seed."

"Have you grown a plant from a potato such as this?"

"Yes."

"And were the potatoes produced by the plant the same as the potato that was planted?"

"Yes, I believe they were," said Pedro, after some thought.

"That is very important. If true, the potatoes of a plant grown from seed vary in their qualities from the potatoes of another plant grown from seed, as you see here on the table. But a planted potato produces the same kind of potato."

"Yes?" asked Pedro, not seeing his point.

"So, you use seeds to grow plants that produce potatoes that vary in their qualities. From those potatoes, you select the ones with qualities that you desire, things such as size, shape, color, taste, and yield. Then you plant those potatoes to grow more potatoes with the same desired qualities. With time, you will have many potatoes with the desired qualities."

Pedro blinked and looked a little startled at this.

"Joaquin, you have stated it very nicely," he said happily, "and have cleared up my muddled thoughts on what to do."

Miguel, who had been listening, said with equal surprise, "I agree. In a matter of minutes, Joaquin has clarified much for us. I am very surprised and pleased."

"Such things are not new. Only this plant is new."

"Let us go inside," said Pedro enthusiastically, picking up a good-sized potato from the table. "My wife Juana will cook one so you can taste this new vegetable and see why we are so interested in it and the other plants."

"I would like that very much, Señor. Thank you. Afterward, perhaps you will show me where my family will live."

11. With Child

JOAQUIN PROVED TO BE highly valuable to their gardening efforts. They were able to get their potato seeds to sprout reliably using his experience with other plants. Miguel asked Mateo to write down brief notes on his methods and insights on producing varieties of potatoes with desired qualities.

Meanwhile, from the variety of potatoes they already had, they began the process. They would begin with a white and a red variety. After sprouts started forming on candidate potatoes, they sampled them for taste, and if good, planted the sprouted potatoes to get more. Several rows of the two varieties were planted, and they now would keep better records of the results of the individual plants.

Joaquin's eye for growing things was also applied to the other new vegetables. For example, he was already experienced at growing chickpeas, which were a staple in morisco diet, and he readily applied that experience to growing the new beans.

Joaquin and his family were happy with the living arrangements in the outbuilding and with their life thus far on the estate. He had become a valued member of their estate and was treated so. He and his family went to church and interacted well with the other families. They still were able to keep in touch with their morisco culture and friends by periodic visits with the other nearby morisco families.

All was working out well with Joaquin. Lorenzo was pleased to find that he had been wrong. He told Miguel that they owed Don Alejandro and his overseer Hernán many thanks for letting Joaquin come to work there. They and their wives were invited over for a visit. On a tour of their garden, they were shown the potatoes as well as the other new plants. Joaquin was there and was praised for the valuable assistance he was providing to their gardening efforts.

Later at dinner, they sampled some cooked potatoes plus meat dishes seasoned with the dried peppers from last year's crop. Unfortunately, it was too early for the other new plants to be included and tasted. Even so, their guests were very impressed with the meal and especially the new peppers. Their sweet spiciness was so much better than the flavoring of the expensive peppercorns from Asia, which for centuries had been the only pepper spice available.

At the end of the meal, Lorenzo presented Alejandro with a small bag of potato seed and a small amount of the precious new pepper seeds. Smiling and greatly pleased, Alejandro thanked him enthusiastically.

Mateo and Luisa had thought beforehand of making an announcement at this dinner with the neighbors, but with all the excitement about new foods and the growing of them, they had decided to wait. The next day Mateo and Guillermo were talking.

"Guillermo, we are true friends still, are we not?"

In the past, they would tell each other a secret that they had told no one else to prove they were true friends.

"Yes, Mateo, of course," replied Guillermo, laughing and knowing what was coming. "But there is no need for you to tell me a secret to prove it again. Besides, I already know your secret."

"What?" exclaimed Mateo, laughing too.

"Yes, I already know it. Mencía told me the other day that she thinks Luisa is with child."

"Oh, I cannot believe it! How do these women know such things!"

"I do not know, Mateo, but it leaves you with no secret to tell."

"That appears to be the case," agreed Mateo.

"I am also without a secret. I am thinking of making a trip, but that does not qualify as a secret."

"Where are you thinking of traveling?"

"To visit your Uncle Diego, or should I say 'my father.' It is still awkward for me to call him 'my father' even if he is my natural father. I still consider Miguel to be my father since that is what I have always known until only recently."

"It is quite understandable, Guillermo. So you are planning a visit then? I wish that I could come with you. I have not seen Uncle Diego in such a long time and have never met your natural mother who is now there with him."

"Your company would be most welcome, Mateo. Then I could bring Mencía along, and you could be the duenna that your mother thinks so necessary," he said, chuckling.

"Mencía is quite different from the normal mold of traditional Spanish girl to which my mother is accustomed," said Mateo with a laugh. "You know, Guillermo, your trip might fit nicely with our baby news. Luisa's parents live along the way. She will, no doubt, want to visit them to tell them the good news and let them spend time with little Santiago."

After a pause in thought, he continued, "But Luisa's stay there must be longer and more relaxed this time. I wish no repeat of last year's visit when she was so busy and got terribly overtaxed."

"I remember how tired and weak she was when we arrived home. Your mother was not pleased."

"Neither was I. I should have been more careful with her. This time she should stay several months with her parents. If you and Mencía came with us, there will be plenty of time for the three of us to go on from there to visit Uncle Diego. It would only take two weeks, during which time, Luisa and little Santiago would be happily occupied there with her parents."

"Bravo, Mateo! I am for it! When do we leave?" declared Guillermo enthusiastically.

"I must talk first with Luisa. Three months will be a terribly long time away from her friend Ana. We may need to shorten it. Still, that will not affect our plans for seeing Uncle Diego. It may take several days to make arrangements for the trip with the baby and nanny. Tonight, we can announce at dinner that Luisa is with child and that we will be visiting her parents for several months."

"Oh, Mateo! This is one of those rare opportunities when you could say, 'Father, Mother, I have some good news and some bad news. Which would you prefer to hear first!'"

"How true! No matter which they pick, they will be happy in the end. You should get Mencía and be there to see it."

"It would be my great honor. We are still true friends, after all, even if we have no secrets today to share."

12. Visiting Family

AT THE DINNER TABLE that night, Lorenzo welcomed their dinner guests, saying, "Guillermo, Mencía, how nice of you to join us for dinner tonight. I wish to propose a toast." Raising his glass, he said, "To sons and daughters, God bless them."

They all happily toasted and afterward, Lorenzo continued, "Mencía, Guillermo, you are always welcome here, of course, but Mateo inviting you both tonight makes me suspect that something is afoot."

"Perhaps Guillermo and Mencía have an announcement to make," said Doña Antonia with a look.

This caused Guillermo to choke on his wine and cough uncontrolledly as Mateo pounded him on the back laughing. Mencía also was laughing but discreetly with her hand over her mouth.

"Antonia, my dear, it seems not to be the case," Lorenzo managed to say amid his laughter.

When things settled down, Guillermo told her, "Dear mother of my true friend, I am sorry to disappoint you, but we have no such announcement."

"A pity," she replied.

"Mateo, help me," said Guillermo with a strained face nodding toward the Don, urging him to get on with his announcement.

Amused by Guillermo's apparent desperation, Mateo struggled to assume a more serious tone.

"Father, Mother, since it is an announcement you wish, I have one. My announcement contains both good news and bad news. Which would you prefer to hear first?"

They were both taken aback by this.

"Mateo, what are you and Guillermo up to? What is this game?" asked his mother with annoyance.

"No game, Mother. As I say, I have some good news and bad news. Which would you prefer to hear first?"

With a sigh, his father said, "I suppose it is best to hear bad news first. What is this bad news, my son?"

"Only that Luisa, the baby, and I will be leaving soon to spend several months with her parents."

Deflating with disappointment, his father responded, "That *is* bad news. Must it be so long? Although, I suppose we have no right to keep you all to ourselves and must share you."

"Thank you, Father. That is most understanding of you," said Luisa.

"Well, what is the good news then, Mateo? I need it."

"One reason for the visit is to let them know Luisa is again with child."

At this news, his mother and father rose happily to hug Mateo and Luisa.

"Thank God for such good news," said his father.

"First Ana and now you, Luisa, how wonderful. You will be having babies at almost the same time," said Antonia.

"It must be something in the water, Antonia. Careful, you may be with child soon too! And you too, Rosa!" said Lorenzo, laughing and pointing first to his wife and then to the housekeeper.

This caused everyone to laugh, except for his wife who came over to whack him.

When the laughter died down, Antonia, said, "Enough of your rude jokes. Let us get back to the subject of this trip. I have concerns. Mateo, you must take better care of Luisa this time while there."

"But I will not be there, Mother. I am going on with Guillermo and Mencía to visit Uncle Diego."

"What?"

"Yes, though only for a short visit, and you may rest assured, Mother, that her parents will take good care of her while there."

"Mateo, why must you torment me so with your joking and drama. Luisa dear, you must promise me to take good care of yourself while there and somehow find a way to teach your husband more respect for his mother."

"I promise the former but cannot promise the latter. You need not worry though. Unlike last year, my stay will be quiet and relaxing, not busy," Luisa reassured her.

"Perhaps you should visit us there to check on me," she added.

"A fine idea, my child. Perhaps we shall," said Lorenzo brightly.

Hugging his mother, Mateo said, "I am sorry, Mother, I was just having a little fun. Are you not happy with our news?"

"Yes, Mateo. God has been good to us," she said less sternly.

Four days later, they were packed and ready to leave in the early morning. Ana and Bernardino were there with Mateo's parents and Guillermo's parents to wish them a good trip. After numerous hugs and kisses, Mateo, Luisa with little Santiago, and the nanny climbed into the carriage. Mateo had his horse tied to the back and all the baggage tightly secured onboard. Guillermo and Mencía were mounted on their horses.

With a wave, the little caravan headed away. Luisa was feeling good and experiencing only mild bouts of morning sickness. They planned to go slowly and avoid unnecessary stops or visits along the way. Still, they would stop briefly at Pascual's camp to say hello and show the women how big the baby was getting.

The next day in the late afternoon, they arrived at Luisa's parents, who were already hurrying out the door to greet them as they pulled to a stop, their approach having been noticed by excited house staff.

"Luisa, Mateo, what a wonderful surprise! Oh, look at the baby!" gushed her mother. "Here, let me have the little man while you climb out."

They were all smiles as they admired and fussed over the baby and hugged Mateo and Luisa as they emerged from the carriage.

"Guillermo, Mencía! It is wonderful to see you too. Welcome!" called Don Francisco, looking up and smiling.

After more hugs and greetings, Francisco said, "You all must be tired and hungry. Come inside and freshen up. We will get you something to eat. Leave your horses and things here. They will be taken care of. Let us all go inside."

As they started up the walk to the house, her father stopped and said, "Luisa, my child, I suppose you have something you wish to tell us."

They laughed at his statement because he had been so completely unaware the time before when she arrived to tell them she was expecting.

"Francisco, you are more observant this time. Yes, I think she is with child," said Luisa's mother.

Luisa nodded, smiling.

"Such wonderful news, dear girl," said her father, hugging her. "Actually, you look lovely as always. I see no difference and only suspected it might be the reason for your unexpected arrival."

"I saw it immediately," said Doña Isabel. "Men are so blind to such things."

"I freely admit it. Come, let us go inside."

As they started again for the front door, Luisa's younger brothers came bursting out.

"Guillermo! Mencía! Mateo! Did you bring your bows and arrows?" they called happily.

They then bounced excitedly around Guillermo and Mencía who smiled and laughed at their young admirers.

"Domingo! Gabriel!" scolded Francisco, "You *do* remember your big sister Luisa over here, do you not?"

"Oh, hi Luisa!" they said quickly waving, which made their father frown.

"Do not worry, Father. They are just being boys," she said laughing and waving back.

"Boys, stop your jumping around and ride over to tell Don Carlos and Doña Catalina that their cousins are here. They are invited to dinner tonight to celebrate."

"But Father, they just arrived!"

"Your father has spoken, now go!"

"Yes, Father," they said, running off to the stables to get horses.

"Mencía, shall we accompany them?" asked Guillermo.

"Why not," she said with a smile. "The horses are not tired."

They both quickly remounted, and Guillermo gave a little salute to the rest of the party, saying, "We will be back shortly."

Turning his horse toward the stables, he called ahead, "Domingo, Gabriel, we are coming with you!"

Luisa's parents were elated when they learned she and the baby would be staying with them for perhaps several months. They thought Mateo, Guillermo, and Mencía visiting Mateo's uncle was a fine idea. Naturally, the boys wanted to go along.

Before dinner, Francisco pulled Mateo aside and asked, "Mateo, would you and the others mind some company on the trip?"

"Certainly not, Father, we will be happy to take the boys off your hands for a week."

"Take the boys off my hands?" he said, grinning. "I wish to go too if you will have me. I have heard so much about the happenings there last year. Naturally, I want to see for myself. I met your uncle when he used to visit your cousins next door. But he has not done so in many years, so why should I not want to come along to say hello again."

At dinner, Francisco announced that he and the boys were going with the others to visit Don Diego. The boys immediately jumped up and howled with delight. Everyone laughed at their excitement as they bounded over to hug and thank their father, who grinned happily.

All laughed except their mother who declared, "Francisco, what kind of wild animals have we raised? Boys, sit down and calm yourselves."

When the commotion died down, Francisco said with enthusiasm, "Carlos, why do you not come with us?"

With a glance at his wife, Carlos replied somberly, "I would like it very much, Francisco, but the timing is unfortunate. Next Monday marks eight years since Cristóbal and Reynaldo left for the Indies. Catalina and I plan to spend the day in earnest prayer at church."

His wife grasped his hand and looked at him with emotion. After a moment looking sadly down at her hand on his, he perked up again, saying, "But please, I do not mean to dampen the celebration here. Catalina and I will write a letter to Diego for you to take."

"But Uncle, we can delay the trip and leave instead on Tuesday," offered Mateo. (Being the same age as Mateo's father, Mateo called Carlos his uncle instead of cousin.)

With a smile of gratitude, Carlos replied, "But that would delay the trip five days, Mateo. I thank you very much, dear boy, but you should go without me. I will stay this time, but greatly look forward to joining you on another trip."

"Come with us this time, Uncle. The boys can endure a delay of five days," said Mateo.

"Right, boys?" he said, turning toward them.

"Yes, I suppose," said Domingo with a deflated look.

"There, you see," said Carlos, laughing. "Such adventure must not be delayed. I will join you next time."

Looking around with his glass raised, Carlos announced, "You all must join Catalina and I for dinner tomorrow night so that we can see you off properly. We can toast your trip then, but I think we should toast it now as well. Here is to a safe and happy trip."

They all joined him in the toast and laughed at the suddenly jubilant boys, who bounded about happily again.

The next day was a day of preparation for the trip. Francisco and the boys had much to do in a short time while Mateo, Guillermo, and Mencía were already prepared.

Some of Mateo's seeds, brought back from the Indies, had been previously given to Dons Francisco and Carlos to attempt growing on their estates. Mateo had time during the day to visit with their overseers and gardeners and see their gardens. Their seeds had been planted two months earlier, and the growing plants looked healthy and well-cared-for. He talked with them about the plants and passed on the new insights about potato growing. Through the combined efforts of the various families, they hoped to succeed in learning to profitably grow the new plants.

Guillermo and Mencía also had time to visit with their friends in Francisco's stable. As they cleaned and groomed their horses, readying them for the trip, they reminisced quietly about their night of curate reform activity the year before. Thanks to the money recovered by their efforts, the parish church now had a new roof.

The boys were quick to finish their trip preparations so they could practice archery with Guillermo and Mencía.

After seeing them shoot, Mencía said with admiration, "No wonder you wanted to practice with us. You wanted to show us how good you have become."

"We've been practicing what you taught us several times a week," said Domingo.

"I am as good a shot as Domingo," Gabriel chimed in.

"We see that, Gabriel," said Guillermo. "Domingo has good power in his shot too. How old are you, Domingo?"

"Thirteen."

"Almost a man! We might be able to do some hunting on this trip, so take your bows," said Guillermo.

"We will!" shouted the boys happily.

"Perhaps we should fetch the arrows and shoot again, just to make sure those first bullseyes were not just lucky shots," said Mencía, teasing.

"Oh, Mencía!" they said with a look, before running to retrieve the arrows as she and Guillermo chuckled.

By the end of the afternoon, all preparations were done, and they were ready for leaving in the morning.

That night at Carlos' estate, they moved to a comfortable room after dinner for wine and dessert. Carlos was standing beside Mateo while Guillermo told the others more about their adventure with the merchant in Cordoba. With everyone's attention diverted, Carlos nudged Mateo and nodded toward the nearby doorway. Mateo followed as Carlos led him outside to the patio.

When outside, Mateo looked about and said, "Uncle, I have always admired your wonderful patio with its fountain and plants. This is the place where Luisa told me she would marry me."

"I did not know and am pleased to hear it." Then with a somber look, he said, "Mateo, I have something serious to ask of you."

"What is it I can do for you, Uncle? You have my full attention," said Mateo, now serious too.

"My dear wife and I find ourselves in a dilemma. As you know, we have heard nothing from our two sons, Cristóbal and Reynaldo, in the eight years since they left for the Indies. As we mentioned, we will soon be marking the day in church praying for them."

After a sigh, he continued, "Meanwhile, our daughter Angela is a nun and has sworn off such worldly things as possessions and a husband. In fact, we have not heard from her in many years either. It seems her order does not allow it. As a result, Catalina and I find that we have been spared the burden of letters with our children, as well as their hugs and kisses, much to our dismay."

"I surely regret that I could find no news of Cristóbal and Reynaldo while there in the Indies," said Mateo sadly. "I inquired about them at every opportunity."

"Yes, I am sure you did, Mateo. The Indies has many places, and your ship could only visit a few. Yet, the large size of it does not explain why we have not received a single letter from them. After so much time, I must face the sad reality that they are dead and not coming back. For reasons unknown to mortal man, it seems to be part of God's great plan that they should perish there. It must be so, otherwise we would have heard something from them after eight years. My dear wife, Catalina, still holds out some hope, but I have reconciled myself to the sad truth that they are dead. Drowning at sea, combat with natives, treacherous villains, or sickness. God only knows what happened to them."

He paused and added sadly, "Whatever it was that caused them to meet their fate, their mother and I must carry on here."

Mateo listened with great empathy as Carlos continued with emotion, "You, Mateo, are very fortunate. You have the start of your own wonderful little family. Your fine little boy provides an heir and continuation of the family line. Seeing little Santiago has given me pause to consider my own situation. Now you have another child on the way, which bodes well for even more in the future."

With tears welling, he said, "So now, Mateo, I finally arrive at the point of all this. I want to ask you, if in the future, you find you have sons to spare, would you possibly consider having one of them become my heir here to carry on my line."

With emotion, Mateo put his arm around his uncle's shoulder and said, "My dear uncle, I hope to God it shall not be necessary. We have much time before such things need to be decided. But, when the time comes, Luisa and I will help you and Aunt Catalina in whatever way we can."

"Thank you, Mateo. I knew you could be counted on. Please do not mention this conversation to my wife. It would break her heart to think I have given up hope of our sons returning."

"I will not mention it to anyone, Dear Uncle."

Looking back toward the house, he added, "Perhaps we should go back inside before we are missed."

"You go ahead, Mateo. I will just be a minute. I must compose myself."

"Yes, Uncle," Mateo said, patting him sympathetically on the shoulder and turning to leave.

The next morning, they set out early after many goodbyes, hugs, and kisses. It was early June and the beginning of the dry summer, so rain was unlikely. The sun would not be too hot and the nights not too cool. The trip would take one and a half days traveling along the north side of the Guadalquivir River on the well-traveled main road between Seville and Cordoba.

In this agricultural valley of the Guadalquivir River, wheat and other crops have been grown for over fifteen centuries since Roman times. It was not bandit country like the dry hilly expanses south of the river.

The trip would require only one night spent on the road, so they had brought bedrolls and would sleep around a campfire under an obliging cluster of trees. The added security of an overnight stay at a walled inn was not thought to be necessary. Bedrolls under the stars would be a good experience for the boys, and they hoped, not too taxing on their father. As a precaution, Mateo, Guillermo, and Mencía would stand watches during the night to ensure no thievery or other foul play was attempted.

13. Uncle Diego

AS THEY PULLED UP in front of the main house the next day and dismounted, Don Diego came out happily to greet them. He went immediately to Guillermo and Mencía.

"Hello, my son, you look well," he said, hugging Guillermo.

"And you too, Father," said Guillermo, smiling.

"Mencía, my dear, it is wonderful to see you again," he said grasping Mencía's hand and kissing it.

Mateo was now beside them, and Guillermo asked, "Father, you remember your nephew Mateo, do you not?"

"Hello, Uncle Diego."

"Mateo, dear boy. It has been such a long time. I have dearly missed you and your parents," he said, tearfully hugging him.

Pulling back and looking him over, he said, "You have turned into quite a man since we last saw each other. I deeply regret not being able to visit my dear brother, your father, all those years and not see you grow up. Though I suppose Guillermo has told you all about it."

"Yes, Uncle, and now that I see you and Guillermo together, I understand fully. You look very much alike. Anyone seeing you together would think Guillermo was your son, which would have been very disruptive and detrimental to his upbringing."

"Yes, I feared as much."

"Sadly, it kept you from visiting us all these years," continued Mateo. "My father, I know, has missed you very much. I am happy to say he and mother are in good health and send you warm regards. I have brought letters."

"Wonderful. I owe him so much. But I am neglecting your friends here, Mateo, please introduce me."

Francisco and his sons were formally introduced to Diego, who then came forward to happily embrace them.

"Welcome to my home. I am very happy to meet you. You all are my honored guests. Come now, let us go inside and get some refreshments for you after such a long ride."

Turning around and seeing others standing behind him, Diego said, "Ah, but first I must introduce you to the other honored guests residing at my home. First, my dearest friend, Floriana, her mother-in-law, Señora López, and this dear young girl, Beatriz, who is as precious to me as a daughter."

Guillermo and Mencía needed no introduction to them, but the others were introduced. Mateo, Francisco, and the boys came forward and exchanged greetings and pleasantries.

Looking about, Guillermo asked, "Father, where are those two intrepid brothers of mine, Andrés and Agustin?"

"In Seville as usual, I am afraid. They have been gone a week and should be back any day now."

"I hope so. I would not want to miss them."

With introductions made, they began to make their way inside. By then, the overseer Rodrigo had arrived with several stable hands to take care of the horses.

Guillermo had been instrumental in getting rid of the last overseer who had neglected the estate and in bringing Rodrigo here to take his place, so they had much good history. They greeted each other happily.

"Rodrigo, it is very good to see you."

"You too, Guillermo."

"I must say that the estate has been reborn under your guidance and looks much improved. Do you remember how it looked that day when I first brought you here?" asked Guillermo, laughing.

"Yes, it looked quite shabby. There has been much work accomplished since, but more is always needed."

Then turning to Mencía, he bowed and politely took her hand, saying, "Mencía, it is my great pleasure to see you again."

"It is good to see you again too, Rodrigo," she said, smiling.

"I must warn you, Mencía, that you are a legend here. You may see men pointing and whispering, 'Is it her, Mencía, the girl who threw the knives?' It is bound to happen."

This caused Guillermo to burst out laughing, but it subsided when Rodrigo told him, "Guillermo, you laugh, but you too are a legend here. One of the farm hands I kept on here hated the last overseer. He witnessed you thoroughly thrash him and run him off the estate and has told the story a hundred times."

Guillermo looked dumbly at him as Mencía now chuckled. Finally, Guillermo said, "Well, Rodrigo, you must tell them we are flesh and blood, not legends to be gaped at. There is no need for it."

"I will tell them."

Diego now emerged from the house and called, "Guillermo, Mencía, we have wine for you."

Guillermo waved and called back, "Thank you, Father. We will be right in."

Diego then called, "Rodrigo, you are invited to join us at dinner tonight. We are celebrating."

In reply, Rodrigo doffed his hat and called, "Thank you, Don Diego. You are most kind."

Mateo now joined them and said, "Rodrigo, I remember you from that morning when you left to come here. I want to tell you how impressed I am with your work here. The estate looks well managed. Guillermo has told me of its sorry state before."

"Thank you, Mateo."

"Rodrigo, I saw your large garden area and wanted to ask if you were able to raise potatoes over the winter."

"Yes, we did. We harvested a good number of seed pods and many bulbs, which we have been eating. The bulbs have become quite popular here, and I plan to plant many more of the potato seeds in the fall."

"Excellent, but do not eat all the bulbs. I will tell you what we have learned about potato growing. But we must go now and will see you at dinner."

"I look forward to it," Rodrigo said as they turned to leave.

Dinner that night was a happy affair with much talk about family, Diego's happy life, and the growing prosperity of his estate.

14. A Trip for Beatriz

THE NEXT MORNING, Guillermo and Mencía sat on the patio enjoying the morning sun and talking.

"Your father and Floriana seem very happy," mused Mencía.

"Yes, his fortunes are quite different from my first visit here a year ago when he was on his death bed. You can imagine my surprise at seeing him. Even weak and pale, I resembled him a great deal."

"I can imagine," said Mencía with a laugh. "You thought you were accompanying Don Lorenzo here so he could visit his dying brother only to find that you were the son of his brother who wished to see you before dying."

"Quite so, and now, he is in good health and has Floriana, her mother, and Beatriz living with him here, like a new family. I hope Andrés and Agustin come back soon. The celebration dinner last night was not complete without them."

"Your poet brothers, they are quite a pair," said Mencía with a laugh. "I talked with Beatriz last night. She has great affection for them, Don Diego, and Floriana. She also has great affection for you and me for rescuing her from that villain. It seems that you and I now have a new little sister."

"How she has blossomed after such an ordeal is most gratifying to see. She thanked me herself last night when I was talking with Rodrigo. I received a very pleasant sisterly kiss on the cheek and hug in the process. I think I shall enjoy having a little sister," he said with a smile.

"It is funny you should mention Rodrigo." Lowering her voice, she said, "You are not to tell anyone, but Beatriz confided to me that she and Rodrigo are in love and plan to marry. They have told no one."

"Wonderful! But I can say nothing or even congratulate them?"

"No, it is still their secret."

"A pity."

With a look of concern, Mencía added, "Despite such pending happiness, something seems to be bothering her. She would not say what, and I did not press her."

"She has been through much. It would not be surprising."

Just then, Mateo and the boys came out to join them.

"Here you are! We have been looking for you," said Gabriel.

"Good morning, boys, Mateo. We have just been enjoying the morning," replied Guillermo.

"Guillermo, when are we going hunting?" asked Gabriel.

"Patience, Gabriel. We just arrived," Mateo told him.

"As a matter of fact," said Guillermo, "I talked with Don Hernando and Martín last night. They said some deer are still in the high ground in the back of their estate and have not yet started moving to higher ground to avoid the summer heat."

"Did you hear that, Domingo!" exclaimed Gabriel excitedly.

"But before going hunting, you should practice more," Mencía told them.

"Aah, Mencía."

"Practice is always useful, boys," added Guillermo. "We can see Rodrigo after breakfast about setting up a place to practice."

Later that morning, Guillermo stood by Rodrigo as they watched Mencía, Mateo, and the boys practice their archery with the targets they had set up.

"They are good for their age," commented Rodrigo.

"They have a good instructor," replied Guillermo, smiling.

"Quite true. Mencía is quite remarkable."

With a grin, Guillermo told him, "Mencía talked a good bit with Beatriz last night. She said Beatriz is so grateful and devoted to Mencía and I that we have a new little sister."

"Yes, I believe that is true," said Rodrigo, smiling.

"Mencía said she is very happy here, and yet, she seems troubled by something. Have you noticed it?"

"Yes, I believe it has to do with her family back in Huelva. She misses or worries about them or something such as that, although I have never asked her directly about it."

"Perhaps, it is something she might unburden to a big sister."

"Perhaps. Did Beatriz tell Mencía anything else?" asked Rodrigo with a look.

"Yes," answered Guillermo with a smile, "and her big sister and brother promise to keep the secret."

Rodrigo laughed as Guillermo shook his hand and clapped him on the shoulder, saying in a loud whisper, "I believe congratulations are in order."

"Thank you."

"I am amazed you have been able to keep such a secret within this little estate community."

"It has not been easy."

"I will ask Mencía to talk to her little sister to see what might be bothering her. Perhaps we can help clear it up."

"I hope so."

"I suppose I should join the boys in their practice," said Guillermo with a yawn.

"Where is their father, Don Francisco?"

"It seems that he and my father have become fast friends. Since our arrival, they have been sipping wine and talking endlessly about family and other things. Many years ago, my father would visit with his cousin Carlos, the neighbor and friend of Don Francisco. They remember meeting at the time. I believe they feel like old friends as a result."

The next day, the boys were at it again, practicing their archery with Mateo. Guillermo and Mencía watched and stood talking privately with Rodrigo.

"Mencía, come join us!" called Gabriel, waving.

"I will in a few minutes. Move the targets back farther! You are getting too good at that distance!" she called back.

"All right, but hurry!"

"Mencía, they adore you so," said Guillermo, amused.

"I adore them too, but we must talk before I join them."

Turning, Mencía said in a low voice, "Rodrigo, I have talked with Beatriz, and she has told me what troubles her."

"What did she say?"

"You were right that it has to do with her parents," began Mencía. "As you probably know, she left home to learn flamenco dancing in Seville. Her parents were not in favor of such dancing, calling it sinful. Their parting was on bad terms. Unfortunately, she was abducted later while learning to dance in Seville."

"When we rescued her," said Guillermo, "we offered to take her back to her parents in Huelva, but she thought at the time that they would think her shameful and not accept her back. So instead, we brought her here."

Mencía continued, "But now, she believes she was wrong. She believes that her parents miss her, worry about her, and pray for her."

Mencía paused, sighed, and added, "Beatriz thinks she can actually hear their voices praying for her."

Rodrigo looked surprised but said nothing.

"Rodrigo, the obvious solution is to take Beatriz to visit her parents in Huelva as we originally offered to do. She can then show them she is fine and tell them of her happy life here," suggested Guillermo.

"I believe Huelva is a long journey from here," speculated Rodrigo.

"Mencía and I have looked on a map. It is about eighty miles from here and would take three or more days to travel at a pace not too difficult for Beatriz on horseback. Taking her there in a carriage would be slower and probably not any more comfortable. So it makes sense to ride horses. You are welcome to come with us."

Rodrigo thought for a minute and said, "The purpose of such a trip is for Beatriz to reconnect and spend time with her parents. My presence may distract too much from that. It might be better if I were not there."

"I do not know if you are right, but I understand what you mean," said Guillermo.

"However, I will go if security is needed on the trip."

"I do not know it to be bandit country on the way. Mencía, Mateo, and I will go. It is too bad Sebastian did not come."

"Martín from Don Hernando's estate will go. He would be greatly disappointed if we did not ask him," said Mencía.

"Another of Mencía's many devotees," said Guillermo, smiling. "And a good man to have along as well. I would think the four of us should be a sufficient escort for such a trip."

"Yes, I know Martín, and he is a good man. If it is not bandit country, that should be enough," said Rodrigo.

"We have no time to waste then," said Guillermo. "We must set the wheels in motion. After we finish our practice with the boys..."

Stopping abruptly and deep in thought, he added, "The boys. What about the boys?"

"They will surely want to go, Guillermo. We cannot leave them here for two weeks," said Mencía earnestly.

"I am not opposed to taking them. I do not believe the trip to be dangerous as I said, but we must first consult with Mateo and their father."

"First, I will talk with Beatriz, but I am certain that she will want to make the trip to see her parents," said Mencía.

Numerous discussions took place that afternoon. At dinner, it was announced that Mateo, Guillermo, Mencía, Martín, and the boys would be taking Beatriz to visit her parents in Huelva. The boys could barely contain their happiness and excitement. Francisco had decided to let the boys go, but he would stay and continue visiting with his old friend Diego. Martín was honored and gratified at being asked, and readily accepted. Martín would bring his cutlass and several pistols borrowed from Don Hernando. The others would bring their throwing knives and archery gear.

The next day was spent in preparation for the trip, and they left with great fanfare the morning after. They took bedrolls along but planned to stay in inns where decent ones could be found. With high surrounding walls and bolted gates, an inn would be safer at night since they didn't know the country along the route well.

Their route would take them southwest along the north side of the Guadalquivir River to the west of Seville where they would take a main road westward across the plains to Huelva.

On the first day, they rode steadily and in the early afternoon reached La Algaba, an ancient town along the river. There, they asked Beatriz how she was managing. They would stop at an inn in the town if she was tired or sore, but she told them she was fine, so they continued. In the early evening, they were passing through one of the ancient small towns west of Seville and found what looked to be a suitable inn, where they spent the night.

The next day they began their journey westward across the plains toward Huelva. They were traveling across an expanse of flat plains with an occasional small and large town, each with a surrounding area of wheat fields and orchards of olive and orange trees. They saw little traffic on the sparsely populated stretches of dry plains between the towns, mostly muleteers transporting supplies on the backs of their mules. Guillermo asked in the towns along the way if they should worry about bandits and was told, "No, not usually."

They were making good time that day when Guillermo looked up at the sun, high in the sky, and judged it to be an hour after midday. There should be enough hours left to make it to Niebla by nightfall. They were crossing one of the lonely stretches of plains between towns. He looked ahead and then behind, seeing no other traffic on the road. The trip thus far has been uneventful, he thought to himself.

15. Bandits

UP AHEAD, THEY SAW the road crossed a small tree-lined stream and knew they should be wary of possible bandits in such a place. They eyed it carefully without seeing anyone in hiding. Even so, when they reached it, six men armed with pistols and a seventh man with a machete suddenly jumped out in front of them from nearby bushes. Guillermo, Mateo, and Martín in front had no time to react to the six pistols suddenly leveled at them at close range.

"Gentlemen, if you would be so good as to raise your hands," ordered the leader.

Mateo, Guillermo, and Martín slowly complied without speaking.

"Very good," the bandit told them, "Now I must advise you not to move or we will be forced to kill you."

Eyeing the three men in the saddle, the leader said, "It seems you have been most unwise to carry no pistols in your belts. Have you no respect for men like us?"

"We were told no bandits were on these roads," responded Mateo.

"That was your misfortune, Señor."

As the bandits watched Mateo, Guillermo, and Martín very closely with their pistols leveled on them, the leader sent three men back to check out the women. Two of the men, sporting ugly grins, stared at Beatriz as they approached her, the first man armed with a pistol and the second with a machete.

"Ah, what have we here? Such a pretty señorita, eh, Sancho."

One of the bandits on the other side by Mencía's horse replied, "No, José, I have the pretty one here. And such a handsome riding outfit. She must have handsome jewelry to go with it. Is that not so, my pretty señorita?"

He stared greedily at Mencía for a moment as he stuffed his pistol into his belt in preparation to drag Mencía from her horse. Mencía looked at him but said nothing.

"Sancho, I think you must need some help, I am coming," said one of the four in front. He began walking back, keeping his eyes and pistol on Martín.

"I do not need your help, Ramon!" shouted the bandit Sancho, turning his head to him with a scowl.

Up front, the three remaining bandits had not taken their eyes off the eyes of Guillermo, Mateo, and Martín who remained motionless in their saddles with their hands raised. From their cover beforehand, the bandits had carefully inspected the group as they approached. Seeing the two travelers in the rear were just boys, the bandits paid no attention to Domingo and Gabriel.

"Ha, ha," said the bandit José beside Beatriz's horse as he stuffed his pistol into his belt. "Sancho and Ramon, they do not get along."

Mencía turned, exchanged a quick glance with Beatriz, and then returned her attention to the bandits beside her.

As the bandit Ramon came near, he glared angrily at the bandit Sancho.

"So you don't like my help, eh Sancho. Maybe, Sancho, I should use my pistol on *you*?" said the bandit Ramon.

"Maybe I should use mine on *you*, Ramon!" said the bandit Sancho, angrily pulling his pistol from his belt again.

The two bandits by Beatriz were now bent over, laughing and pointing at the two arguing bandits.

"Sancho! Ramon! Stop it before I shoot you both!" bellowed the leader still not taking his eyes off Mateo in front of him.

After scoffing at Ramon, Sancho shoved the pistol back in his belt and trudged forward, still scowling back at Ramon. When close to Mencía's horse, he was reaching up to drag her to the ground when Mencía kicked him hard in the face with the hard leather heel of her riding boot, sending him reeling backward. A split second later, she threw her knife at Ramon next to him. Wide-eyed and clutching at the knife in his throat, Ramon dropped his pistol, staggered, and fell to the ground.

Meanwhile, the bandit beside Beatriz jerked upright with a look of alarm, reaching for his pistol again. But Beatriz, in the meantime, had pulled from the folds of her billowy skirt a cocked pistol, with which she shot the bandit point blank in the face. The bandit behind him looked up in shock and then took an arrow in the side, staggering backward.

Hearing the commotion and a shot back where the women and boys were, the bandits up front probably thought at first that Sancho and Ramon were fighting. As they craned in surprise to see what was happening, they were distracted just enough for Mateo and Guillermo to throw their hidden knives with accuracy landing in the throat of one and in the chest of another.

The man with the knife in the throat, staggered backward, clutching at it in surprise. He started to slowly raise his pistol, but then received an arrow in the chest. He stared at it for a moment, dropped his pistol, and then collapsed to the ground. The man with the knife in his chest reeled, yelled out in defiance, and started to raise his pistol. But he was struck in the throat with a second knife and fell backward, firing his pistol up in the air.

The bandit in front of Martín had been craning to see in back when Martín slipped his pistol from hiding, cocked, and fired it in one rapid motion. He had to do it so quickly that he had succeeded in only grazing the bandit in the side.

Favoring his wounded side and peering through pistol smoke in front of him, the bandit was craning to take aim at Martín on the jittery horse in front of him when he received a knife in his arm holding the pistol. Clutching his painful arm in fear and surprise, he began to run off, still gripping the pistol.

Enraged by the attack, Martín pulled a cutlass from his pack and spurred his horse forward in pursuit of the man. As the bandit ran frantically, he grasped the pistol with his other hand and desperately turned and fired at Martín, missing him. Martín soon caught up to him and cut him down with a tremendous slash of his cutlass.

The bandit by Beatriz who had received the arrow had looked up to discover he had been shot by mere boys. He bellowed in fury and raised his machete, perhaps to attack the boys, but his efforts were cut short by another arrow in the side and a knife from Mencía in his throat.

Mencía then whirled around to see what had become of the bandit kicked in the face. She saw him on the ground writhing in pain from an arrow through his arm and a second arrow sticking from his leg. He started to rise, but a third arrow struck him in the hip, and he flopped back down in pain.

Seeing the pistol still in his belt, Mencía jumped from her horse and approached him with a throwing knife ready.

"Enough!" cried the man. "Tell them to stop!"

Having lost his enthusiasm for the robbery, he raised his uninjured arm in submission as Mencía plucked the pistol and several knives from his belt.

"Is anyone hurt?" called out Mateo with concern as he jumped from his horse and rushed back to Beatriz who still sat on her horse.

"I think I am fine, Mateo," Beatriz told him shakily.

As he helped her dismount, she avoided looking at the man she had shot. Looking back to see if the boys were unharmed, Mateo paused for a moment in surprise at seeing them standing by their horses with bows and arrows out and determined looks on their faces.

Looking down at the two dead bandits, one with two arrows in his side, he looked up at the boys in amazement.

"Domingo, Gabriel, it was you who shot the arrows?"

Guillermo, who was now with Mencía on the other side, called, "Mateo, come look at this one!"

Mateo went over and stood in amazement looking at the bandit with three arrows in him. Domingo and Gabriel walked over still carrying their bows with arrows in place.

"Domingo, Gabriel, I am very proud of you," declared Mateo.

"We all are," added Guillermo. "So brave and cool under fire, how remarkable for such young men."

"Are the others dead?" asked Mateo.

"Yes," replied Guillermo. "I checked the ones up front, and they were quite dead. I saw Martín finish off the one that ran. I believe Martín was unhappy with the man."

Martín was now back and jumped down from his horse. Looking around, he said, "Very impressive, Domingo, Gabriel. You did well."

Wiping the blood from his cutlass in nearby grass, he said, "That one will never point a pistol at me again."

Wiping a knife on the grass and handing it to Mateo, he said, "Your knife from his arm. I thank you for the assistance."

"You are most welcome, my friend," replied Mateo.

Guillermo put his arm around the shoulders of Mencía and Beatriz and said, "Mencía, Beatriz, we could not see what was happening back here, but whatever you did, you provided the diversion we needed. We are most grateful."

"Mencía kicked this one in the face with her boot and then Gabriel shot him with arrows," said Domingo.

"Bravo! Well done!" said Guillermo.

"Beatriz shot the one beside her in the face and then I shot the one behind him with arrows, as well as the one in front.

"Very impressive, to say the least," said Martín, looking at them with admiration. Then turning to the wounded bandit on the ground, he asked, "What should we do with him?"

Looking around at the scene of recent battle, Mateo said, "I suppose the thing to do now is pick up all the weapons and drag the bodies to the side of the road. We can pull the arrows out of this one and tie him up. At the next town, we will deposit him with the local officials and tell them where to find the others. We should not waste time, if we hope to make Niebla by nightfall."

A short time later in the next town, Mateo and Guillermo shoved their prisoner into the office of the constable. The constable sitting at a desk, looked up from his writing with annoyance at being disturbed.

Then with a look of surprise at the bloody, filthy man with his hands tied behind his back, he stood up and exclaimed, "Why, that is one of Black Tooth's men! Where did you find him?"

"He and his friends tried to rob us where the road crosses a creek about two miles east of here."

"I know the place, and what about the rest of them?"

"We left the other six dead by the side of the road."

The constable gasped and asked, "Did their leader have a black tooth?"

"Yes, I believe so. I noticed it when he talked."

The constable said with astonishment, "These men are ruthless criminals who come down from the mountains north of here to plague our roads from time to time. We have tried without success many times to capture them. You must have had a great many men to have defeated them."

"No, just three."

"What! How is it possible!"

He shot a questioning look at the unhappy, sullen prisoner standing in front of him.

"You! I recognize you. I believe your name is Sancho. How were three men able to overpower you all?"

The man only smirked. Unsatisfied with this response, Guillermo smacked him hard on his wounded leg and shouted, "Answer!"

The man doubled over in pain. Straightening up, he mumbled, "They just did! What does it matter how?"

The constable called to a man in the hallway outside and had the wounded bandit taken away to the warden of their jail. He handed paper and pen to Mateo and told him to write out a brief description of what happened. As Mateo was writing, Martín came in to see how Mateo and Guillermo were doing. He carried a sack which he plopped down on the constable's desk.

"What is the meaning of this?" asked the constable with indignation at such informality and disrespect.

"These are the valuables and money we found on the bandits," said Guillermo. "We did not have time to search for their camp or horses. You might want to do so."

The constable untied the sack without speaking, opened it, and looked inside. Reaching in, he brought out a handful of jewelry and coins, examining them.

"Incredible. These valuables would seem to confirm the truth of it," he said. "Finding the owners of this plunder may prove to be difficult, but you were perhaps wise not to leave these valuables along the road."

Letting the jewelry fall back into the sack, he tied it again, put the sack in a drawer of his desk, and locked it.

"By the way," he said, looking up, "I neglected to mention that a reward exists for Black Tooth and his gang. If Black Tooth is, in fact, lying there dead by the road, then the reward is yours."

Not wanting any more delays, Guillermo said, "We are traveling to Huelva and will pass through here again in about a week on our return trip. We can pick it up then."

"I will have it for you. The townspeople will be delighted to learn Black Tooth and his gang are dead. Most assuredly, they will want to thank you. You should perhaps set aside some time for it on your return trip."

"I do not know if we will have time. Our aim was not to rid you of them. We only defended ourselves. Still, we are glad to have been of help to your town."

The constable picked up and read Mateo's statement. He paused thoughtfully afterward before saying, "My assistants and I will leave soon to see the place and look for their camp. You are free to go, but before leaving, you must tell me how so few men were able to accomplish it. You did not provide such detail in your statement."

Just then, they heard a commotion in the hallway outside and someone rushed in excitedly, "Señor Constable! Black

Tooth and his gang! Someone has found them dead on the road!"

Turning to Mateo with a mystified look, the constable said, "You and your friends are to be commended, Señor. But again, how were you able to do it?"

"Well, our women and boys created a diversion by killing three of them and wounding one, enabling us men to kill the remaining three," Mateo told him matter-of-factly.

The constable looked at him with shock for a moment and said, "I must go out to see this group of yours and personally thank them. However, we must be quick about it."

They hurried outside to where the others were waiting by their horses. People in the street were rushing about, talking happily about the amazing news.

The constable shook hands with and earnestly thanked each in their party. He then announced to them, "And now I must be off to the creek and see this miracle you have performed. And you, my friends, must be on your way if you do not wish to be delayed by our grateful townspeople. If so, I thank you again, and God be with you. I will look for you again in a week."

They quickly mounted and with a wave were off, passing several excited people in the street hurrying to the town plaza after hearing the quickly spreading news. In a few minutes, they were out of town and riding past orchards and fields. Guillermo looked up with concern at the position of the sun and suggested they quicken their pace.

16. Reunion

THEY ARRIVED IN NIEBLA in the late evening and found an inn for the night. During the meal provided at the inn, Guillermo and Mencía asked Beatriz how she wanted to make herself known to her parents.

"If you want, Mencía or I could first visit their home to tell them you are well and here wishing to visit them," suggested Guillermo.

"No, I do not think it necessary. My mother attends midday mass every day at our parish church. If we can make it in time tomorrow, I will meet her there."

"Our innkeeper says Huelva is a four-hour ride at a quick pace, so we can make it," said Guillermo.

"I will wait outside the church and meet her as she leaves mass. I will know then whether I heard their prayers or not. Either she will cry out and rush to me, or she will look upon me with disgust and walk away without speaking."

"I can already see your mother crying out and rushing to you," said Guillermo optimistically. "Mencía and I will stay nearby. After your meeting, you can introduce us to reassure her you come with good company. Then you can go home with her. We can meet you again the next day, perhaps at midday mass, to see how you are doing."

"And where will you stay and what will you do?"

"We will find an inn and let you know where. While you spend time with family, we can see the sights of your ancient port city. See the fishing boats. Eat seafood, drink wine, and relax. I am sure that Huelva can occupy our interests for three days."

"When Columbus first discovered the Indies, he sailed from Palos, just across the river," offered Beatriz.

"Ah, I did not know. There, you see. So let us believe you will be happily welcomed back, and we will enjoy several days seeing the sights and relaxing in Huelva. We shall not consider any other result," reassured Guillermo.

Even so, Beatriz started shedding tears of worry, and Mencía gave her a hug.

The next morning, the innkeeper packed food for their ride, and they left early. They made good progress that morning and pulled up in front of the church at midday.

Mateo jumped down, walked to the front door of the church, and listened for a moment. Coming back, he told them, "They are about halfway through mass. It should not be long before they start coming out."

He helped Beatriz down from her horse and looked about quickly.

"While you, Mencía, and Guillermo wait here in front of the church," he said, pointing, "we will continue with the horses over to that side street where I see a bar. We will be there watching."

"That will be fine," replied Beatriz uneasily.

After Mateo and the others walked away with the horses, the three of them stretched and walked about after their long ride as Beatriz nervously eyed the closed front doors of the church. Mencía tried to reassure her. They stood for several minutes and then sat down on a nearby bench to wait.

In a few minutes, Mateo and the boys returned with glasses of wine for them, welcome refreshment after their ride as well as something to soothe Beatriz's nerves. They drank the wine down and thanked them. Domingo had also brought Beatriz's bag, which he gave to Mencía. After giving Beatriz a few added words of encouragement, Mateo returned with the boys and glasses to the bar.

After what seemed an eternity to Beatriz, actually about twenty minutes, the doors of the church opened, and the priest came out to greet the parishioners as they left. Guillermo and Mencía retreated a bit as Beatriz took several steps forward.

As the parishioners began to file out, Beatriz scanned them anxiously. She recognized her mother's friend Sancha as she emerged. After exchanging greetings with the priest, Sancha turned and saw Beatriz. She gasped with her hand over her mouth. Excitedly, she rushed back in, calling, "María! María! Come quickly!"

The priest and the others stopped and looked with puzzlement at her as she rushed back.

"Sancha, what is it?" Beatriz heard her mother say.

"Outside!" said Sancha, emerging from the door again and pointing.

Her mother appeared in the doorway and shielded her eyes from the sun as she peered out. The look of concern on her face turned into a happy tearful smile. Pulling a handkerchief from her pocket, she held it to her face as she scurried forward with one outstretched arm.

Seeing her happiness, Beatriz rushed forward, and they met in an emotional hug, which continued as the priest and others came down to welcome her back too.

Her friend Sancha blurted through her own tears, "María, you have prayed so often for this moment, and it is finally here! Thanks be to God!"

From a short distance away, Mencía and Guillermo watched happily. Guillermo looked over to the side street where Mateo and the others smiled as they watched. Domingo and Gabriel waved to them and Mencía waved back.

After a time, Beatriz was able to look up, acknowledge the well-wishers around them, thank them, and take her mother aside.

"Beatriz, you have come home. Thank God," her mother was able to say.

"Mother, I can only stay three days. I came to let you know I am well, so you will not worry about me. I live on an estate now. The people there are kind to me. I am going to marry their overseer. I wanted you to know."

"I am so happy for you, my child. We have worried so."

"Mother, you and Father were so unhappy with me when I left. For a long time, I thought you still were. I am sorry. Only recently did I begin to believe that you missed me, worried about me, and prayed for me."

"Your father, sisters, and I have all been praying for you."

"Mother, I heard your voices in prayer. I could actually *hear* them."

"I thank God for it," said her mother with emotion.

Her mother's friends were again close by, happily hugging them both. After a time, her mother thanked them and said they must leave to tell Beatriz's father and sisters that she was back.

Beatriz and her mother were able to break away from their friends and start home. As they walked arm and arm together away from the church, Beatriz stopped next to Mencía and Guillermo.

Pointing them out to her mother, she said, "Mother, these are my friends Mencía and Guillermo who are responsible for my present happiness. They and several others brought me here."

"Bless you. Bless you. Bless you," she said earnestly as she grasped and held a hand from both.

"We are very happy for Beatriz and for you, Señora Calleja," said Guillermo. "She is a lovely girl and much deserving of such happiness. We regret that she is only able to visit for several days, but at least, you can now rest easy knowing she does well."

"Yes, yes, thank you. Our Beatriz has been most fortunate to have found such good friends as you."

"Señora, we will let you and Beatriz make the most of your time together and will see you again tomorrow at midday mass," said Mencía.

"Oh, but you must come with us now so we can thank you for bringing back our Beatriz," she protested.

"We would be pleased to visit with you, Señora, but do not wish to take up your limited time with Beatriz," Mencía told her.

"Very well, but I look forward to seeing you again tomorrow. Thank you again so much," she said giving them both a hug and a kiss on the cheek. Then turning, she said, "Let us go, Beatriz, and give the blessed news to the others."

Mencía gave the bag to Beatriz, and they hurried away. Guillermo and Mencía watched them go, looked at each other, smiled, and turned to walk back to the bar.

They found Domingo and Gabriel just coming outside from the bar and sipping a glass of diluted wine. They waved excitedly at seeing Guillermo and Mencía.

As they neared, Guillermo asked, "Where are the horses?"

"Martín and I have already put them in a stable," said Domingo.

"And Mateo and I already found rooms nearby," added Gabriel.

"Very good. Let us go inside. I could use another glass of wine and something to eat," said Guillermo cheerfully.

Inside the bar, they found Mateo and Martín standing in the back at a tall table. When Mateo saw them coming, he waved to the host for more wine.

"So, it appears to have gone quite successfully," said Mateo happily.

"As you saw, her mother was very happy to see her. Beatriz's fears of being scorned were unfounded."

"Yes, they both looked very happy from where we stood," said Mateo.

The wine and accompanying small plates of snacks were brought to the table. Looking at the little plates of bread, sardines, and olives, Guillermo said, "I think I need more than just snacks. We should have a real dinner in a restaurant. The inn food on our journey did not suit me well. Did we not have some kind of stew every night?"

"Yes, I think so," said Mencía with a laugh.

Swelling with enthusiasm at a sudden thought, Guillermo asked, "Boys, how does a nice thick steak sound to you?"

"Yes! I am for it!" said Domingo eagerly.

"Me too!" chimed in Gabriel.

"I am buying steaks for everyone!" announced Guillermo. "We are celebrating! I brought plenty of money in case of emergency, so no arguments!"

"You twisted my arm, Guillermo! But I also have a good stock of coins with me, so I will buy the drinks!" said Mateo.

"Sounds good to me," said Martín.

"Bravo! Well done!" exclaimed Gabriel merrily.

At hearing this, they all turned in surprised amusement to look at Gabriel.

"Well, that is what Guillermo says," he told them innocently, which gave them a good laugh.

"You are right, Gabriel!" said Guillermo, grappling playfully with him.

"All right, little boys," said Mencía, "perhaps we should drink up, go to our rooms to freshen up, and then to eat. A steak sounds good to me too."

"It is unanimous," said Guillermo cheerfully. Then with a look at the boys, he added, "Bravo! Well done!"

With that, they downed their wine, left money on the table, and walked outside.

It was early afternoon, normally too early for a big meal, but they were hungry for one after their long ride. They were all in high spirits as they walked down the street.

As they talked about how good a nice juicy steak sounded, Guillermo noticed a pathetic, unkempt, ragged beggar up ahead. The beggar was sitting on the ground with his back against a wall and a basket in front of him. As people passed, he looked up at them with a slack-jawed, dazed, blank expression without saying anything.

"We happily go to eat a big meal of steaks, and that poor lost soul begs for coins to buy crumbs of bread," commented Guillermo, nodding in the beggar's direction.

As they passed him, he stopped, reached into his pocket, and pulled out a silver coin. The beggar watched him blankly as Guillermo stepped forward.

Looking down at the basket, Guillermo said, "Friend, this coin is worth much more than your normal copper ones. I had better put it in your pocket and not in your basket."

As Guillermo reached to put the coin in his pocket, the beggar grasped his arm weakly. The others had stopped to watch and were surprised to see something come over the man. He lost his dazed look and stared intently at Guillermo's face, examining it as he tried to speak.

Guillermo was unsure what to make of it but didn't pull away. The beggar weakly raised his other arm and felt Guillermo's face.

"What is it, friend? Are you well?" asked Guillermo.

The beggar continued to examine his face and then seemed to recognize him. He began to weep as he continued to try to mouth some words.

All the people in the street were now watching. They had never seen the beggar with anything but a dazed look.

With tears running down his cheeks, the beggar was finally able to weakly say, "I, I have been lost, but, but you found me." Letting the hand examining Guillermo's face weakly drop, he faintly said, "I do not know how, …but you found me."

"What do you mean, friend? I do not know you."

"Diego, do you not recognize me?" said the beggar weakly.

With a look of astonishment at hearing this, Mateo rushed forward and bent down beside Guillermo, examining the man closely.

"Thank you, Diego, thank you," the beggar mumbled and then passed out.

In shock, Mateo exclaimed, "Oh my God, Guillermo, this is Cousin Reynaldo! One of Uncle Carlos' two missing sons!"

17. Huelva

"WHAT! HOW IS IT POSSIBLE? They were in the Indies!" exclaimed Guillermo, bewildered.

"I do not know, but this must be Reynaldo! We must bring him back to our room," said Mateo as he bent forward and scooped up the unconscious man.

Rising easily with the light weight of the rumpled beggar in his arms, Mateo carried him hurriedly down the street.

Several minutes later, he laid him down on a bed in their room. Mateo checked his breathing and heartbeat.

"He seems to be alive. What should we do?"

"Send for a physician," suggested Mencía. "I will see the innkeeper about it."

A short time later, a doctor was beside the beggar, checking him over.

"He seems to be alive enough. I can bleed him if you wish?"

"No," said Guillermo.

"This beggar is a relative of yours?" asked the doctor incredulously. "He has haunted our streets for years, I believe. To my knowledge, he has never spoken a word but only wanders about in a stupor. Harmless enough and never a threat to anyone, our officials have not bothered with him. He has survived in this manner on the charity of others. The locals have given him a name, but I do not remember what it is."

"Where does he sleep?" asked Mateo.

"I am afraid that I do not know."

"Is he dying, or will he wake soon?" asked Guillermo.

"His heartbeat and breathing seem stable enough. He may awaken soon, but it is difficult to say. If he does, he will be thirsty, so give him water. After that, some wine and broth to build up his strength. Are you sure you do not wish me to bleed him?"

"I am sure. Thank you, doctor," said Guillermo.

"In that case, I can do no more and shall be on my way."

Mateo paid him and he left. Guillermo looked down at the beggar lying in the bed and then up at the others, watching.

"Mateo and I will bring the basin over and clean him up a bit while someone gets wine, water, broth, and perhaps some soft bread. After that, you should all get something to eat. Regrettably, we must postpone our steak dinner. Mateo and I will stay with him. If he remembers my father, he may also remember Mateo. Someone can bring food back for us."

A half hour later, the others were out getting food when the beggar began to stir, moving his head and moaning several times. Mateo and Guillermo rose from their chairs and stood beside the bed. They watched as he opened his eyes, slowly looked about, and saw them.

"Thank God, I was not dreaming. It *is* you, Diego," he said, reaching a hand to Guillermo.

"Is it truly you, Cousin Reynaldo?" Guillermo asked him sincerely, taking his hand.

"Yes, I am Reynaldo, your cousin. How did you find me? I seem to have been lost to the world for so long. It is only now at seeing your face that I have regained my senses. Oh, thank God, you found me."

"Cousin Reynaldo," said Mateo, which caused Reynaldo to turn and look at him. "Do you remember me? I am your cousin Mateo, Lorenzo's son."

"Yes, yes, I see it now. The younger brother of Santiago and Esteban, you were just a boy when I last saw you," he said reaching out and taking Mateo's hand.

"Yes, that is right," replied Mateo, not thinking it a good time to tell him that his brothers were now dead.

Mateo began again, explaining, "Cousin Reynaldo, we do most sincerely thank God for finding you, but must tell you that this is not Diego. This is Diego's son, Guillermo, who looks very much like him."

Reynaldo turned to look at Guillermo more closely and said, "He looks just like his father as I remember him when I was younger. Seeing his face and remembering Diego caused me to remember other things and somehow rise from my confusion and stupor."

He grasped Guillermo's arm tightly. "I do not even know you, my cousin Guillermo, and yet you came with Mateo to find me for my parents," he said with emotion. "I do not know how I can ever thank you both. Coming to the Indies to search for me is no small matter. How did you find me? I am so deeply indebted to you. What place is this? Mexico City?"

Guillermo and Mateo glanced at each other, and Guillermo said, "Reynaldo, you are not as indebted to us as you imagine. We are not in the Indies. We are in Huelva in Andalusia, Spain."

"Huelva! How did I get here? I have no recollection of it," he said, astounded.

"And we were not searching for you, but instead found you quite by chance."

"Found me by chance?"

"Yes, you were sitting on the ground along the street begging for money, and I stopped to give you a coin," said Guillermo.

"Dear God! I can only remember seeing your face in front of me, but nothing of begging or Huelva or coming to Huelva.

"You seemed to come out of your stupor when I bent to give you a coin."

"Yes, your face brought back memories of my childhood, family, and growing up. I remember going to the Indies with my brother Cristóbal…"

He stopped abruptly with a look of pain, shutting his eyes.

"Reynaldo, have some wine," said Mateo "It will make you feel better and give you strength."

Opening his eyes again, he sadly said, "Yes, thank you."

They put several pillows behind him to prop him up. Mateo then handed him the glass, from which he drank a swallow.

"Alas, my brave brother Cristóbal is dead. I loved him dearly. His death is the last thing I remember and precipitated my fall into what must have been an unconscious stupor," he said sadly to them.

"Do not think of it, Reynaldo. Get some food and rest for several days. If you desire, you can tell us about it when you are stronger. But now, you must get your strength back for your trip home. Your parents are well. You cannot imagine how very happy and relieved they will be to see you."

"My dear parents," he mused. "I am happy to hear they are well. We sent two long letters to them from the Indies but heard nothing in return."

"They did not receive them," Mateo quietly told him.

"Upon my conscience!" Reynaldo swore angrily. "We paid those scoundrels in gold to take the letters with them back to Spain and deliver them. And they did not!"

"So our parents have heard nothing of their sons for many years?" he asked, looking about in frustration.

"Eight," said Mateo.

Reynaldo gasped in surprise. "I have been senseless for a period of years, it seems. My dear parents must be distraught."

"It has been painful for them."

"I very much regret having caused it. Is there a way of sending them a message?"

"It will be faster to deliver you directly there ourselves. We are here in Huelva for three days and will start back on the fourth day. If you are unable to ride by that time, we can possibly buy a small carriage for the trip."

"I shall endeavor to get well enough to ride," he said taking another swallow of wine and handing back the empty glass. In doing so, he noticed his arm, which he examined in disbelief. He looked down at his torso and legs with equal amazement.

"My God, look at how thin and emaciated I am!"

"A doctor was here earlier. He said your breathing and heartbeat are stable. You are not sick, just undernourished. The doctor said you may want water. We have a pitcher of it here for you as well as some bread and a bowl of broth."

"I believe I will have some."

After taking a sip from the water glass handed to him, he laid back reflecting for a moment before accepting a piece of bread and another glass of wine.

"Friends of ours are out getting food. We can offer you more when they return."

"Thank you both, my cousins. I have returned to the world of the living and owe it to you."

After more nourishment and a restful night, Reynaldo felt strong enough in the morning to get up and walk about. He still seemed to be thinking clearly and remembering everything since recovering his senses the day before. With a fresh wash basin, Guillermo and Mateo helped him clean himself up, as best they could. Together, they ate bread and cheese for breakfast with some wine. Meanwhile, Mencía and the boys were able to find new clothes, shoes, and a hat for him. Now presentable enough to emerge from the room, Mateo and Guillermo took him to a barber. After coming back to the room and eating more food, he looked and felt much better.

Already stronger, they thought he should be able to travel in a few days, so Martín left to see about getting a horse for him.

Reynaldo had told them the night before that he wanted very much to find a church to pray for his brother's soul and thank God for bringing back his senses. That morning, they had worked hard to get him ready to go with them to the midday mass where they were to meet Beatriz.

With Reynaldo now ready, everyone set out with him for midday mass, where they joined Beatriz and her family. After mass, Reynaldo and the boys remained inside the church so he could light candles and pray at the altar. Meanwhile outside, Guillermo and the others were introduced to Beatriz's family.

Guillermo told them the incredible news that they had miraculously found their long-lost cousin. Beatriz was surprised to hear it, but her mother just nodded her head knowingly.

"It was providence. Clearly, God intended you to bring my Beatriz here to us so you would find your cousin."

Mateo told how they had discovered him begging, apparently he had been wandering the city in a daze for years.

"What? Our dazed beggar is your cousin! That was him inside?" exclaimed her father with surprise. "We did not recognize him. We have a good many beggars here, who come and go, but he is different. We see him regularly, and he gives us such a pitiful lost look that we sometimes give him a coin. People say a ship left him here several years ago. Some call him 'the barnacle' since he seems to have floated in and become attached to our city."

After more questions and amazement about Reynaldo, Beatriz told them how she was having a wonderful visit with her family. Her parents invited them to have food and wine at their home after midday mass the next day to thank them for bringing her daughter to them.

When Reynaldo emerged from the church with the boys walking alongside him for support, her family looked at him in wonder. After being introduced, he talked with them politely, saying nice things about their church. They were astounded that he had been the ragged beggar who, for years, had gaped blankly at them without uttering a word. Beatriz also recalled seeing the beggar before leaving Huelva two years earlier.

That afternoon, Mateo and Guillermo took him to a Moorish bathhouse to better clean off the dirt acquired from years on the streets. As he soaked and scrubbed, he proudly pointed out to them his many scars from battles with the natives of the Indies.

Meanwhile, Martín had been working to procure a horse and saddle for Reynaldo. To do so, he had first sought the advice of his local morisco kinsman. At the docks, he found and visited with several morisco dockworkers.

They traded stories, and he told them about their trip and their encounter with bandits. The dockworkers were greatly impressed to hear how they had fought off and killed the gang of ruthless bandits. Being great admirers of weapon skills and always seeking entertainment, his morisco friends greatly desired to see a demonstration of their knife-throwing and archery.

When Martín told them that he was looking for a place to buy a horse and saddle for their trip back, the enthused dock workers said they would talk to their friend who owned a stable. If Martín would bring his friends along to demonstrate their skills at the stable tomorrow morning, their friend would have a good horse and saddle there to sell him at a reasonable price. Martín agreed.

He returned to the others in the afternoon and told them of his success, but at the cost of a knife-throwing and archery demonstration. The three friends were amused at the request and readily agreed. Reynaldo was pleased at the prospect of getting a horse as well as seeing such an unusual demonstration.

They did not dine on steaks that night since money would be needed to pay for the horse and saddle. Without having planned it, several of them had fortunately brought along a few large gold doubloons for emergencies. Such high value coins would ordinarily not be carried, but the previous year, they had gotten an amount of them during their rescue of Beatriz.

After dinner, they went back to their rooms, and Reynaldo went to bed. Twelve hours later in the morning, he awoke refreshed and feeling stronger. He ate well at breakfast and was in good spirits as they walked to the stable.

When they arrived at the stable with their archery gear and knives, they found a large audience of Martín's kinsman eager to see their demonstration. Animals were cleared away from a section where wooden targets had been set up. As they were being introduced, Mateo, Guillermo, and Mencía surprised the crowd by suddenly turning and throwing their knives with deadly accuracy into the targets. Afterward, one would address the crowd as they went through various demonstrations as well as more unexpected throws.

Knowing the bandit attack was of interest, Guillermo told them how Mencía had surprised the ruffians by kicking one in the face and then immediately put a knife in the second one's throat. As he told of it, she performed the actions convincingly for them, and the crowd went wild with admiration.

It was such a big hit that Martín stepped forward and, handing her his cutlass, suggested that she should reenact her recent escape from and killing of kidnappers. He had heard all about it on the trip. As Guillermo described the action, the crowd watched in stunned awe as she banged on a door, threw her knives, and slashed and thrust with the cutlass. They were completely silent when she finished, before exploding into cheering and wild celebration. Amid the uproar, the threesome waved, bowed, and thanked the crowd.

When the noise died down enough, Mateo announced it was time to give the boys a chance to demonstrate their archery skills which had proved so useful against the bandits. The stablemen had pieced together sacks stuffed with hay to make a target outside in the shape of a man, topped with an old hat. On it were drawn eyes, an upside-down smile, and a heart. Everyone watched as Domingo and Gabriel shot four arrows in rapid succession from twenty paces. When done, their eight arrows stuck in or near the heart. Only seconds afterward, Mateo, Guillermo, and Mencía, who were standing to the side and ten paces farther back, fired a volley of arrows, all of which hit in the target's head. Then they rapidly fired two more each that left the target's torso filled with arrows. The crowd again cheered and rushed forward to inspect the target more closely.

Martín watched with admiration and enjoyed the attention his friends were getting. He had already told his morisco friends about his own more conventional use of pistol and cutlass against the bandits.

With the festivities over, Martín and the stable owner got together for business. Still excited and amazed after the demonstrations, the stable owner happily gave them a good price on the selected horse and saddle. Reynaldo was hoisted up onto the saddle and walked the horse around a bit, looking satisfied with his new mount. Their gold doubloons were able to cover the cost. They thanked the stable owner and the others who had come to watch, said their goodbyes, and led the horse away with Reynaldo riding atop it.

By the time they got back to their own stable, it was nearly time to go to the midday mass and then to Beatriz's home for food and drink afterward. The others left for the church while Martín stayed at the stable and took the new horse for a short ride to better check it out. Satisfied with the purchase, he put the horse away and walked to the church where he met the others as they came out of mass.

Martín was a morisco, a Muslim Moor who supposedly had converted to Christianity, but he practiced neither religion with any degree of enthusiasm. He could pose as a Christian, when need be, but was drawn to his Moorish roots and culture, although he drank wine and occasionally ate pork, things forbidden to Muslims.

After Martín was introduced outside the church, they all walked to Beatriz's parent's home, which was somewhat crowded when they went inside. Her parents made a great display of their gratitude to them. They could not thank them enough for bringing her to visit, one which had truthfully saved her parents from an early grave from worrying about her.

Reynaldo was still a source of amazement to them. Her mother's friend had beforehand scoured the town in search of their dazed beggar. Not finding him, she was convinced that God had miraculously changed their beggar into Reynaldo, just like water into wine. Yes, it was a miracle. At the party, she reverently approached Reynaldo and crossed herself. To his surprise, she then grasped and closely inspected his wrists.

"Sancha! What are you doing!" exclaimed Beatriz's mother.

"He is the object of a holy miracle. I wanted to see if he also bleeds from his wrists," she said with awe.

"I am sorry to disappoint you, my dear," Reynaldo politely told her. "But I am not holy essence, merely flesh and blood. Yet, I too thank God for bringing me back from the dead."

After a pleasant stay of two hours, Mateo and company thanked their hosts for their gracious hospitality and left to go back to their rooms at the inn. Upon arrival, Reynaldo said he was perhaps a little tired and would go to bed for a while. He fell asleep immediately and slept for fifteen hours.

The next morning, Reynaldo awoke feeling even more improved from the previous day. The many hours of sleep were a healing tonic for his once tortured mind. He was thinking clearly, although he could not remember any of his time in Huelva or how he got there.

Reynaldo was only in his late twenties but had felt like an old man when he awoke from his stupor. Now he was feeling much better, gaining weight and strength, and regaining a bit of his youth and vitality.

With several long days in the saddle facing him, Reynaldo wanted to get better acquainted with his horse beforehand. He and several others went for a leisurely ride through town and along the river. Reynaldo got along nicely with his horse and felt good to be up in a saddle again. Upon return, he declared himself fit for travel and able to depart in the morning, which pleased them greatly and caused a flurry of packing and preparations.

Mateo and company joined Beatriz and her family again at midday mass where they afterward told her all was ready for leaving the next morning. They said their goodbyes to her family who thanked them again with great emotion.

When they arrived outside her parents' home the next morning with her horse, only Guillermo got down to help Beatriz mount. After last minute emotional hugs, tears, and kisses with her family, Guillermo boosted her with cupped hands up onto her horse. With a wave, the travelers started down the street. Beatriz's sisters walked beside her for a time to spend a few last minutes with her before they stopped and waved a last time as the travelers rode on.

18. Homeward

THEY WERE SOON OUT of the city and heading northeast on the road through the grassy plain, scattered wheat fields, and farms along the Rio Tinto River. They planned to take the same route back, stopping overnight in the same towns, and staying at the same inns. They had kept the pistols which they had gathered up after their encounter with the bandits, and now the men and boys wore them visibly in their belts to discourage any further bandit attacks.

As they passed over a stone bridge across a creek, Mateo commented on what a fine bridge it was. Beatriz told him it was built by Romans, one of several in their area still in use over a thousand years later.

In the midafternoon, they arrived at the inn in Niebla. Although many hours of daylight remained, they would stay the night here. They had found the inn to be clean and comfortable on the trip to Huelva, and Mateo didn't want the first day of riding to be a long one for Reynaldo.

After getting settled in, they walked down to look again at the nearby Rio Tinto. They had noticed the river's strange orange and red color when crossing it before, and the horses had refused to drink its water. Since ancient times, the runoff from mineral mines upriver in the mountains has poisoned it.

Beatriz told them, "The locals say the river has been this way for a thousand years, that it is God's will."

Looking at orange lifeless rocks and water of the river, Guillermo commented, "Well, if this is God's will, then He is punishing the people here for something."

After dinner, they talked for a while, checked the horses, and went to bed. Mencía and Beatriz stayed in a four-bed room for women with a woman traveler from another party, while the men and boys fully occupied a six-bunk room for men.

During the night Mateo and the others were suddenly awakened by Reynaldo screaming and sobbing in his sleep. Mateo was nearest and shook him awake.

"Reynaldo! Wake up! You are dreaming!" he shouted as he shook the struggling Reynaldo.

Finally calmed down and awake, Reynaldo patted Mateo on the arm, saying, "Thank you, Mateo. I am sorry. A bad dream. I am still haunted by my brother's death."

"No apology is needed, Dear Cousin. We understand you have been through much," Mateo told him.

"Yes, thank you." Then looking around and seeing all the others awake and watching, Reynaldo told them, "I am sorry to have disturbed you all. I am fine now. Please go back to sleep."

The rest of the night was quiet, and in the morning, they were off again. Several hours later, they arrived at the town where the constable was holding their reward money. Mateo and the others had privately talked and decided the reward money would be Beatriz's wedding present.

As they entered the town, they were recognized by the townspeople. Soon a grateful crowd of people were beside their horses as they made their way to the constable's office at the courthouse. Already informed of their arrival, the constable was waiting for them as they pulled up outside his office, greeting them cordially as they dismounted.

While the others stayed outside with the horses, Mateo went in with the constable to sign for and collect the reward for the bandits. After accepting the small sack of coins from the constable, he reached out to shake the official's hand, but the constable said, "But wait. There is more."

He opened a drawer and pulled out another sack, explaining, "As you suggested, we searched for and located the camp and horses of Black Tooth's gang. We brought the horses and his gear back here, and they were sold. The money is rightfully yours too."

With raised eyebrows, Mateo took the second sack and looked up at the constable, who then continued, "As I predicted before, I have had little success in finding the owners of the jewelry and money you found on their bodies. I still have the sack that you left, and it is also rightfully yours."

"No," replied Mateo, not taking it. "It has only been a week. You keep it for a time to see if owners come forward. If not, sell it and use the money for the townspeople, as you best see fit."

With a smile of admiration, the constable said, "If that is your wish, Señor de Cordoba, I will do my best and thank you on behalf of our townspeople."

They shook hands. Mateo put the two sacks in his pockets and turned to walk back outside.

"Oh," said the constable, "before you go, let me show you something that you may find of interest."

Mateo stopped as the constable went into a back room and came back out holding a musket. It was not as bulky as the ones Mateo had seen before and its barrel was longer.

As he handed it to Mateo, the constable told him, "We found this at Black Tooth's camp. He apparently had no need for it in his ambush plans for that day. We test fired it and were quite impressed with it. It is accurate enough to actually hit its target at 50 to 60 yards."

Looking it over, Mateo commented, "I have seen muskets with flint firing mechanisms before, but not like this one. It seems that muskets are getting better, more accurate, and less cumbersome."

"I thought the same. I am commandeering this one. We cannot have highway bandits with better arms than constables."

Handing the musket back to the constable, Mateo said, "Several of us are skilled with bows and have enjoyed a range and accuracy advantage over these bandits with pistols and older style muskets. It appears our advantage is lessening."

"Yes, I saw that you carry bows. Being a man of arms, I thought you would be interested in this."

"I appreciate you showing it to me, Señor Constable. It seems my friends and I will need to be more cautious in the future as muskets such as this become more common."

Mateo waited as the constable returned the musket to the back room. Coming back out, the constable motioned graciously toward the door and said, "Well, my friend, shall we go outside and see what is happening. As I mentioned before when you were here, our townspeople are exceedingly grateful for what you have done. I believe we may find a great many people outside."

When Mateo and the constable emerged from the building, a large crowd of townspeople was there thanking their group. They brought flowers for the women as well as various foods and wine to share.

Surprised at the large crowd, Mateo made his way to Mencía and Guillermo. Mateo looked at them, uncertain what to do, and Mencía suggested that they satisfy the crowd to a degree by taking a break there and allowing them to show their gratitude. To leave abruptly, she told them, would be impolite.

Mateo reluctantly agreed and announced to the crowd that they were touched by their display of gratitude and would stay briefly to partake in their hospitality and celebration. The crowd cheered and quickly rounded up tables and chairs that were placed there in the town plaza for them.

When seated, various breads, meats, and fruits were placed before them. Oats and water were brought for the horses. Wine was poured and toasts made to their bravery. The constable and mayor gave speeches describing how Black Tooth's gang had victimized their town in the past and how the town greatly appreciated the remarkable event at the creek that had ended their crimes.

After an hour, Mateo thanked them for their wonderful hospitality and announced they regrettably must continue their trip. With difficulty, they were able to graciously break themselves away to remount their horses and start on their way as children trotted beside them to the edge of town and waved farewell.

At the creek crossing where the bandits had attacked them, they stopped briefly to point out to Reynaldo what took place. He marveled at and praised their skill and bravery.

"Thank God, you were successful," he told them. "If not, I would still be wandering the streets of Huelva."

After a last look around, the travelers were again on their way. They made their nightly stops as planned and encountered no bandits. Reynaldo had no more recurrences of bad dreams. The remainder of the trip was in all respects unremarkable.

In the late afternoon on the third day of travel, they neared the entrance of Diego's estate. Domingo and Gabriel wanted badly to ride ahead to announce their arrival. But thinking that the news about Reynaldo and the bandit attack would be a great shock to Dons Diego and Francisco, they were not allowed to, fearing that they might blurt it out.

As soon as the travelers pulled into the entrance drive, they saw a stir of activity, people running into the house and elsewhere. Turning in his saddle, Mateo said, "All right boys, we have been spotted. Remember, do not say anything yet about Cousin Reynaldo or the bandits. All right, you can go ahead."

At this, both boys let out a whoop and raced their horses forward. Beatriz also spurred her horse and raced forward. Soon people were coming from the house and the boys were hugging their father, and Beatriz was hugging Diego and Floriana. Diego's sons Andrés and Agustin rushed out, waving happily.

Elated at seeing his half-brothers again, Guillermo raced forward too. Jumping from his horse, he happily hugged and exchanged greetings with them and then with his father and the others. Mencía and Mateo soon arrived and joined in the happy reunion.

Meanwhile, Martín sat on his horse nearby, smiling and watching. Behind him, another man sat on his horse with his hat pulled down a bit.

Looking up from the crowd, Diego called, "Martín! Thank you so much for going along and for bringing them back safely. Come, climb down and join us in some wine. But who is that you have with you?"

Guillermo intervened, "Father, we have wonderful news, but you must prepare yourself for a shock."

"Guillermo, what is it?" pleaded Diego, already with a look of shock.

All who had come from the house now looked at him and amongst themselves in confusion.

Mateo came to Francisco and told him, "Father, you also should brace yourself. It is overwhelming, wonderful news."

Both dons looked at them with confusion, and Diego asked, "Guillermo, what is it? What is this news? Please tell us."

Holding Diego's arm, Guillermo said, "Father, we have found Reynaldo, the youngest son of Carlos and Catalina."

Diego and Francisco gasped and reeled in surprise. Andrés and Agustin also gasped at the news while the others looked about not knowing the significance of it.

"And we have brought him with us to take home," added Guillermo.

The two dons looked up in astonishment at the man behind Martín. Reynaldo raised his hat to reveal himself, dismounted, and came forward to them.

Staring at Reynaldo approaching him, Diego stammered, "Yes, yes, dear God, I believe I recognize you. How is it possible? Reynaldo, is it really you?"

"Yes, Uncle Diego, I am back and have my fond memories of you to thank for it," he said, coming forward with emotion.

As they hugged and wept, Francisco put his arms around them too and said, "Reynaldo, I am great friends with your parents. I cannot express in words what your return will mean to them."

Looking up, Reynaldo replied, "Yes, I believe I remember you, Don Francisco. I deeply regret that I have been away so long and have caused my dear parents so much pain."

Drawing back from their embrace, he added, "And now, sadly, I must also break their hearts with the news that my brother Cristóbal is dead, killed in an uprising of the natives there in New Spain."

"I am very sorry to hear it," said Diego in a daze. "Yet God has returned *you* to us, and we are most grateful for it."

Andrés and Agustin were now hugging their cousin Reynaldo and shedding tears of happiness.

"Oh, how absolutely wonderful! I am staggered and must sit down. Come, let us go inside," added Diego.

Still dazed and seeing Floriana and her mother, Diego stammered, "Floriana, my dear, help me inside. Reynaldo, these two ladies are my dear friend Floriana and her dear mother. I must introduce you to them properly, but first need a glass of wine to settle my nerves and overwrought mind."

Floriana took him by the arm, and they started inside.

"Mateo, how is it possible?" asked Francisco in amazement as everyone began to follow them in.

"It was most unexpected, I assure you, Father. We came upon him, quite by chance, begging in the street in Huelva. We will tell you all about it inside."

Rodrigo and his men from the stables were arriving to take care of the horses. Looking over and seeing Rodrigo discretely welcome Beatriz back with a polite handshake, Guillermo and Mencía smiled as they continued inside with the happy crowd.

A short time after going inside, Mateo took Francisco aside with the boys.

"Father, I regret to tell you that the trip was more dangerous than anticipated," said Mateo.

Francisco was taken aback but listened.

"A group of bandits tried to rob us, but we defended ourselves, killing six and capturing a wounded one."

"Dear God! And none of you were harmed?" he asked, excitedly looking his two sons over quickly.

"None of us were harmed, thank God. But I must tell you that your two sons bravely joined in the fight without our knowledge. Their arrows helped subdue them, and you have good reason to be proud. You will hear more of it, but I wanted to tell you first.

"You should have seen it, Father," said Gabriel excitedly. "Mencía kicked one in the face and then I shot him full of arrows!"

"And I got two of them after Beatriz shot one in the face!" added Domingo, equally excited.

"God in Heaven," said Francisco with a start.

"All right, boys, calm down. I am sorry, Father, there is much to tell, but Domingo and Gabriel did well and were calm and brave during the action. You can be proud of them. Even Martín was impressed."

"Well, Domingo, Gabriel, I am proud and want to hear more about it. Just please do not plan to become soldiers anytime soon. Remember, you are boys yet. Oh, what is your mother going to say?"

Their father gave them a hug and they rejoined the others.

The happy reunion lasted throughout the evening. They told of their encounter with bandits and the gratefulness of the town afterward. Beatriz told about the warm reception she received from her family. Guillermo and Mateo told of finding Reynaldo and his recovery of wits at the sight of Guillermo, who he thought was Diego. No one pressed Reynaldo for details of his time in the Indies or his brother's death. The plan was to rest and recuperate tomorrow and leave early the next day to take Reynaldo home.

When night fell, Mateo and Guillermo announced that Reynaldo was not entirely strong yet and needed rest after their long journey. With that, the party broke up, and they all filtered back to their rooms. Mateo, Guillermo, and Reynaldo were to occupy one guest room. The boys were with their father in another, and Mencía was staying with Beatriz in her room.

In the middle of the night, Mateo and Guillermo were again jolted from their sleep by the screams and sobbing of Reynaldo. They rushed to his bedside and quickly got him calmed and quieted down.

"I am sorry, my cousins. I am again haunted by terrible events."

He sat up and they gave him some wine.

"Reynaldo, you seem to carry a heavy burden. We wish to help if we possibly can. Would it help if you talked about it?" offered Mateo.

"They are events of the past that cannot be undone. I wish to God they could be," said Reynaldo, staring vacantly.

Then he pondered aloud, "Would it help me to burden you with these events? Perhaps. I do not know."

After a pause in thought, Reynaldo said with feeling, "Perhaps I should tell it so you can appreciate what a noble soul my brother Cristóbal was."

"If you wish to tell us, we will listen. Or perhaps you would prefer to unburden yourself to a priest."

"No, as I say, it is praise of a noble brother, not a confession of sin or wrongdoing."

"Let us all have a glass of wine, and I will tell it." They poured out glasses. Reynaldo took a sip and began his story.

19. The Brothers

"AS YOU KNOW," began Reynaldo, "my older brother Cristóbal and I were adventurous young men, much like Mateo's older brothers, Santiago and Esteban, who I look forward to seeing again."

Mateo nodded with a slight smile, without saying anything, and Reynaldo continued.

"Cristóbal and I were drawn to the idea of military service in the Indies, where the prospects of battle and riches seemed very good. We had heard such tales of gold, silver, and land grants that it was only natural for two adventurous souls to desire it.

"We were able to get passage to the Indies on a treasure fleet ship and after an uneventful voyage landed in Veracruz on the Spanish mainland. We immediately found service with one of the local military officials who was active in the continuing efforts to subdue the native tribes still refusing to become vassals of our holy king. They continued their resistance in the outlying areas of Spanish control, such as strongholds in remote mountain areas, high deserts, and in the jungles of Yucatan.

"Similar to the method of Cortes when he first set foot there, our captain sent messages to their chiefs offering peaceful, decent treatment of the tribes if they would become the subjects of our king. As in the past, the natives were unwilling to do so unless convinced of our strength of arms over theirs.

"Decades before, Cortes made such peaceful overtures to the local tribes near Veracruz where he established his initial colony. The tribes sneered at his paltry numbers and attacked him in great numbers with their spears, arrows, and swords. They were awed when his small number of Spanish soldiers defeated them in pitched bloody battles. Their priests consulted their demonic gods in their temple and were told by their gods that the tribe would be victorious in their next attack. When they were defeated again in bloody battle, the native chief believed our God must be more powerful than their gods, and they submitted. Cortez in victory treated them honorably and well. He forgave them for the losses he had suffered. They became his allies and supported him with native warriors and supplies. They revered him as long as he showed himself to be powerful and a help to them in defeating rival tribes. With his new native allies, the process was repeated on the next tribe, and the next. As his fame and the number of his native allies grew, Cortez was eventually able to conquer Moctezuma and the powerful Mexican (Aztec) empire, which had ruled and abused these tribes for so long.

"I am sidetracked but only mention it to describe our methods. We first tried to convince them to peacefully submit but usually had to convince them of it by defeating them in battle and capturing their villages and strongholds. Once they submitted, they were forgiven for their resistance and became vassals of our king, not massacred. The natives were valuable there as allies and labor assets, not enemies to be hunted down and killed. I wish I could say that, as valuable labor assets, they were always treated well, but that would not be true.

"In these battles with the unyielding native tribes, we soldiers showed our mettle and earned our rewards. In such pitched battles, we, with our native allies, fought desperately and tirelessly, knowing what would happen to us if captured. As our cavalry attacked them with lances, we foot soldiers poured cannon, musket, and crossbow fire into their masses. We stayed together, protected by our armor and shields, as they ferociously attacked us, and we, in turn, attacked them. After hewing them down by the dozens, their masses would finally break and run. Afterward, peace overtures were again sent to their chiefs.

"Our reward as a soldier for such fierce fighting was a share of the valuables taken and tribute paid plus a share of the native prisoners taken in battle, who were sold as slaves to landowners.

"Cristóbal and I fought in many battles and participated in bringing a number of tribes into submission as well as the suppression of native uprisings and revolts. We fought hard and suffered many hardships and many wounds. We saved each other's life numerous times and could not have been closer.

"We eventually accumulated enough capital to bribe one of the Spanish officials into awarding to us an encomienda, which is a trusteeship over land including the natives living on the land. This system of native trusteeship, which is perhaps just a more palatable word for ownership, had been officially banned for decades but was still in use in our area.

"Cristóbal and I had already picked out the location of our encomienda. For several months, we and several other soldiers had occupied the villages of a recently conquered tribe. During that time, we developed a mutual respect and trust with the native chief. We sought and were awarded ownership of his tribe's land.

"Our encomienda was not large or one with a valuable silver mine on it. Still, it would provide us with a comfortable income from tribute we would collect from the villages. The tribute represented an annual tax on the goods produced and maize grown by the villages.

"I am sorry to say that many newly arriving Spaniards received such grants and treated their natives badly. But Cristóbal and I had fought the natives and earned their respect. We respected them as well, and it was to our benefit to treat our natives well and be fair in our dealings with them. If not, with just two of us, they might rise up and kill us, or just flee, which would leave us with no labor and income.

"When we informed the native chief that we now had possession of the land and that his villages were to pay us an annual tribute on their products and provide us with labor, he accepted his new situation without complaint. It was much the same as their previous existence when they had been the subjects of another more powerful native tribe that had also demanded tribute and laborers from them. At least with us, the tribe would no longer have to regularly provide men, women, and children to be sacrificed and eaten.

"I must say briefly that Cortes may have had his flaws, but he was a religious man who tried to serve God well by demanding that the natives who came under his control should end their barbaric religious practices and embrace the Christian faith.

"In our soldiering, we saw much evidence of these barbaric practices. The native culture was an amazing one with large stone temples and palaces, large cities, and a capital city built on islands in the middle of a lake with causeways to the shore. Their civilization had domesticated various plants, such as maize, that they grew on large plantations for food.

"Nonetheless, their culture also included the regular sacrifice of people to appease or get guidance from their demonic gods. A common practice was for one native tribe to attack the village of another just to carry off men, women, and children to be sacrificed and eaten. They kept them in wooden cages beforehand to fatten them up. When Cortez was threatening the Mexican capital with a large army of his native allies, Moctezuma's priests sacrificed fifty of their own people in one day seeking guidance from the gods on how to advise him.

"The man, woman, or child to be sacrificed was placed on a large stone slab on the top of their stone temples where grotesque stone figures of their gods stood watching. They would cut out the victim's heart and present it to their gods still pulsating, then splatter blood on the walls, and cut off the head, sometimes fixing it to the walls. After cutting off the arms and legs, they threw everything down the steps of the temple to people below who would carry the body parts off to be devoured. Most appalling!

"We too demanded that our natives end such practices. We brought in a Catholic priest to visit and preach the gospel to them. A number were baptized, but not enough priests were available to visit regularly. Their teachings were too infrequent to have a great effect upon our tribe. Still, we outlawed such practices and tried ourselves in word and deed to show them the ways of our Christian faith. We had the stone gods destroyed on the top of their small temple in the main village and replaced them with a cross.

"Our natives provided us with labor to construct a house, stable, other necessary buildings, and their furnishings. They seemed satisfied with our treatment of them and with the amount of tribute we demanded. They viewed Cristóbal and I as conquerors who were interested in their well-being and protection. We enjoyed the respect of the chief, but such respect was fragile and depended on his perception of our continued strength and ability to protect the tribe.

"We made great progress on our encomienda for two years, but then disaster struck. One day, a large band of renegade Spanish soldiers passed through one of our villages killing, raping, and plundering. By the time we heard of it and got to the village, they were gone. The native chief was incensed by this unprovoked, senseless attack and was furious with us for not protecting his tribe. Without warning, they seized us and took us to their temple. They showed their scorn for us and our god by destroying the cross on it and throwing us in a wooden cage there at the top."

Here Reynaldo stopped his story as he sat shedding tears and staring down at the floor for a time.

"It was not long before they came for us. Reaching in the cage, they seized my leg and started to drag me out. Cristóbal and I fought with them and got my leg free. Then Cristóbal swore he would not let them take me first. He struck and dazed me long enough for them to get him out and close the cage door. I screamed and tried desperately to get out as he fought with them. He was able to get a knife away from one and kill several with it. But in the end, they subdued him.

"As they held him near the cage, he looked at me and said, 'Goodbye, my brother. I love you very much.' I was only able to cry like a baby and call his name as they took him to the stone slab.

"When I saw them hold up his pulsating heart to their gods, I started to scream and could not stop. I must have then collapsed into a half-conscious daze, for I cannot say for certain what happened afterward.

"I do not know who rescued me. I vaguely recall Spanish soldiers, possibly drawn by my screams and possibly from the same renegade group which caused our trouble. I do not know.

"I was in a state of shock afterward, dumb to the world. At some point later, I must have been put on a ship back to Spain. I cannot recall any of it. Apparently, the ship docked first in Huelva where they put me ashore with other cargo before continuing to Seville. Those times were all a haze of days turning to nights and nights turning to days. I was senseless and numb to the world.

"God, in his infinite wisdom, had struck down Cristóbal and I as we did our upmost to spread His word and enlarge His holy flock. He must not have been pleased with our methods.

"That day in Huelva when you, Guillermo, came near, I looked up and thought I saw a familiar face. It struck a chord within me, and my senses started to return. After a time struggling to see your face clearly, I then saw the uncle I knew when Cristóbal and I were boys. Your face brought back childhood memories deeply buried in my troubled mind. My sudden remembrance of family and upbringing somehow lifted me back to the conscious world.

"I tell you all this in hopes, as you say, of easing my burden. I ask you to keep these sordid details to yourselves and tell no others. I plan to tell my parents nothing of native sacrifices. I will only say that Cristóbal died coming to my aid during the native uprising, and I was pummeled by their clubs and left for dead. Knocked senseless by the attack, I never regained my senses until you found me in Huelva. It is not so far from the truth and will spare them details that would be too painful for them to hear."

Guillermo said solemnly, "Rest assured, my brave cousin, we will guard your secret. I ask that we may share it with Mencía only. She, Mateo, and I are true friends and can have no secrets."

"Yes, you may. I have great respect for her."

JOSEPH R. COSTA

Mateo had listened soberly to Reynaldo during his tale and
had shed tears with Reynaldo when telling the worst of it. He now
gazed sadly at the floor for a time and then looked up with tears.

"Reynaldo," he said, "your brother Cristóbal is truly a noble
soul, readily forfeiting his own life in hopes of saving his
brother's. It is unfortunate that it cannot be fully told. I believe
my two older brothers, Santiago and Esteban, were of the same
breed."

"You believe?" asked Reynaldo with surprise.

"I did not tell you before, but they both died in the king's
service fighting rebels in the Netherlands, about three years after
you and Cristóbal left."

Leaning back with eyes closed and a sigh of sadness,
Reynaldo said, "God in heaven, it grieves me greatly to hear it,
Mateo. They were good friends with Cristóbal and me. I had so
looked forward to seeing them again."

"Our family knows little of their time there in the
Netherlands, but we know they were brave and deserving of
honor. I have named my first son 'Santiago' to honor my oldest
brother and plan to someday name a second son after Esteban as
well. However after hearing your story, I desire first to name a
son after your heroic brother, if you will allow me."

With a sad but proud look, Reynaldo rose and embraced
Mateo without speaking.

"My wife is expecting a child. If a boy, I will name him
Cristóbal to honor your valiant brother."

"It would please me greatly, Mateo," he replied with emotion.

"Reynaldo, I am so thankful that we happened upon you,"
said Guillermo. "You may never have regained your senses, had
we not. Your parents will be very happy to see you."

"It was more of God's mysterious work," said Reynaldo.

Looking about, Mateo suggested, "Relating the story to us
must have been taxing for you. Perhaps we should get some
sleep."

"It has helped me greatly to tell it, but I am tired. Perhaps it
would be best."

142

20. A Day to Visit

THE NEXT DAY was spent in preparation for the trip on the following morning to take Reynaldo home. No big banquet was planned that night. The mood was sober. Thoughts were of getting Reynaldo speedily home to his parents again after being missing for eight years. Dons Diego and Francisco visited more with Reynaldo and heard again the details of finding him.

For their brave actions against the bandits, the boys were given two of the captured pistols, which they had worn proudly on the trip from Huelva. When getting ready, they asked their father for permission to wear their pistols for the remainder of the trip.

"What do you mean your pistols?" he asked uncertainly.

"They are ours, Father, our share of the pistols gathered up after the bandit attack. We earned them for our part in the fighting."

"Yes, I suppose you did," he said, proudly hugging them and nodding his consent.

Everyone leaving the next morning as well as Rodrigo and Beatriz went to Don Hernando's estate to thank Martín for accompanying Beatriz and the others to Huelva and to say goodbye. The boys wore their pistols in their belts to the delight of the stablemen, who were then told the story of their bandit encounter, which caused quite a stir. The travelers toasted to the great success of their trip. Respectfully holding Mencía's hand, Martín told her it had once again been his privilege and honor to be of assistance to her. He was ever in her debt and ready to serve whenever she should need him. The travelers said warm goodbyes and hardily embraced him in farewell.

The day was also an opportunity for Guillermo to spend time with his half-brothers, Andrés and Agustin. He had become quite attached to these two bookish poets. They had found and rescued his natural mother Floriana and had bravely assisted in the search for and punishment of the villain who had victimized her. He, like his father, had great affection and respect for them, even though they were quite different from him. Guillermo and Mencía were able to sit for a time with them drinking wine and chatting.

"Andrés, Agustin, I am so glad you were here when we returned. I was afraid we would not see you during our visit," Guillermo told them.

"When we returned from Seville to find that we had missed you, we were quite distraught," said Andrés.

"Yes, quite devastated," agreed Agustin.

"Of course, we stayed until you returned, wanting not to miss you and Mencía. You two are such sterling examples of gallantry and strength of arms. We want to write poems and plays based on your example, but we struggle to capture it."

"Thank you, Andrés, but you make too much of it," said Mencía with a laugh.

"It is you, Mencía, who is the cause of our difficulties. Composing flowery verse about valiant men slaying evil doers is normal and not so difficult. Depicting a brave young woman performing such deeds is much more difficult. Joan of Arc may have bravely led men into battle with her sword raised high, but she, herself, could not slay any men with it," said Agustin.

"Quite so, Agustin," agreed Andrés. "Such a thing is difficult to make believable without giving her a magic sword or some such thing."

Mencía and Guillermo could only chuckle at them, and Guillermo asked, "So that is what you do with your poet friends in Seville, wrestle with such questions?"

"Yes, I suppose we do. We also read our poems to one another. Agustin and I have written several plays and are working on another. Speaking of Seville, we must tell you about Matias."

"Ah, were you able to give Matias the gold coins we set aside for him? I still vividly remember my first glimpse of the villain Gómez at the club that night when Matias pointed him out as my mother's victimizer," said Guillermo.

"Yes, most assuredly, but only after waiting for the furor in Seville to subside."

"There was quite an uproar there when Guillermo and I passed through in the days after his body was discovered," said Mencía. "He was being described as a beloved, respected son of the city who had been egregiously murdered."

Guillermo snorted at hearing this exalted description of the villain.

"As you suggested, we waited before returning to permit the excitement there to subside," continued Agustin. "When we returned a month later, we heard nothing about Señor Gómez. He was forgotten. No one investigated his death or was ever accused of any crime. Apparently, everyone suspected his highly connected wife was behind it, so it might prove inconvenient to investigate. The truth probably also surfaced that he was, in fact, a despicable character who deserved the full measure of what he received. So they let the sleeping dog lie."

"But we should return to Matias," said Andrés. "We went to see him at the club where his flamenco company performed. When he saw us at the table during his performance, he became quite distracted."

"I regret to say that the quality of his dancing suffered due to our presence."

"Quite so, Agustin. I recall it too," said Andrés. "During the break in their performance, Matias hurried to our table and was elated to see us. He hugged us affectionately and sat down. With emotion, Matias said he had been looking for us for weeks, hoping we would show up again! When he heard Gómez and his bodyguard were dead, he knew who was responsible for finally bringing about such justice. He wanted to thank us for rescuing Floriana and avenging the honor of his friend Alvaro. He became quite overcome with emotion for several minutes thinking back on it. He saw his friend killed by the man in a duel, you remember."

"Shifting to a happier subject for the poor man," continued Agustin, "we told him that Alvaro's mother and Floriana were doing quite well and being treated with great respect and esteem. Floriana greatly appreciated his assistance and friendship during her times of trouble and hoped to personally thank him one day. He was very pleased to hear it."

Andres added, "We then told him that money was found at the place where Señor Gómez met his fate. We handed him the pouch, saying these coins had been set aside for him as a reward for his help in identifying the man. When he opened the pouch and looked inside, he gasped in surprise at the sight of the ten large gold doubloons. He was delighted and danced much better afterward."

"Yes, quite true, Andrés."

"It is truly amazing how well our adventure turned out and the good that resulted from it. I suppose you want to write a play about it," said Guillermo, smiling.

"Perhaps someday, but as I mentioned, we now are working on another interesting one," said Agustin.

"We are curious to hear about it," said Mencía.

"Surely. Andrés and I are quite excited about it. The play tells of a young man who consults a gypsy to find out who killed his noble father. The gypsy goes into a trance and tells him his uncle did it, because he coveted his brother's wife. The young man is startled by this revelation but thinks there might be some truth in it. He remembers his uncle being constantly at his mother's side since his father's death, affectionately consoling her. He hires a travelling theater company to present a play to his mother and uncle, in which the crime is reenacted. He then carefully watches to see the reaction of his uncle."

"A play within a play," inserted Andrés excitedly.

"The scene of the killing in the play causes the uncle to become upset and leave the room. So the son knows it to be true."

Agustin then paused, deep in thought.

"So what happens next?" asked Guillermo.

"That is an excellent question, one for which we have no answer as yet."

"Does the young man kill his uncle?" asked Mencía.

"Yes, but we have not decided how. We also have not decided if after killing his uncle, he then learns his uncle did not kill his father."

"Well, that would put a whole different shade on it," said Guillermo, sitting back.

"But it would add such moral tone to it," mused Agustin.

"Perhaps so, Agustin, but we do not want to make it too dark," said Andrés.

"It is another one of our dilemmas," said Agustin.

"Well, we look forward to seeing the play when finished," said Guillermo. "Now though, we must think of getting Reynaldo back to his parents."

"We *do* wish we could accompany you but, regrettably, have an unbreakable commitment in Seville this weekend," said Andrés with a sigh.

"That is a pity. We would have enjoyed your company," said Guillermo.

"If Mateo's wife, Luisa, will be there for a time," said Agustin with a desperate, yearning look, "Andrés and I *must* come to visit, perhaps in a month."

"Yes, truly," seconded Andrés. "We simply *must.*"

Excitedly, Agustin said, "Guillermo, you described her before as 'more divine than any distressed damsel in any castle tower.' Oh, if we could only behold such beauty. What inspiration she might provide to us and our poetry. Do you think she would mind greatly if we asked her to rise early one morning, so we could look upon her as she gazes into the warm glow of sunrise?"

21. Praise God!

THE TRAVELERS LEFT EARLY the next morning and made good progress, camping along the road that night. The next day, Reynaldo's spirits were high at the thought of seeing his parents again. When they passed the castle on the hill at Almodóvar del Rio, he was struck by his remembrance of it, and how it meant they were only an hour from home.

When they neared the entrance to Don Carlos' estate, Mateo nodded to his father, who then spurred his horse forward. They had decided beforehand that he should go ahead to break the news, in hopes of lessening their shock.

Francisco pulled up at their house, dismounted, and after a knock on the door, went inside. A surprised servant welcomed him back and went to inform the Don and Doña as he waited in their entry. The servant found him in his den and her outside on their patio, praying at a grotto.

They both hurried to happily greet him.

"Francisco, you are back!" said Carlos, smiling. "You were gone longer than planned. Did you have a good trip? Where are the others?"

"Francisco, you look so serious? Are you not happy to see us?" asked Catalina.

Now with a look of concern, Carlos asked, "Yes, Francisco, what is wrong? Did your trip not go well? Diego is not ill again, I pray?"

"Carlos, Catalina, my dear friends, I am indeed pleased to see you again. No, nothing is wrong. Our trip was far better than can possibly be imagined. I am about to share wonderful news with you."

The parents looked at him with dismay as he put a reassuring hand on Carlos's shoulder and grasped Catalina's hand.

148

"Carlos, Catalina, you must brace yourself for something extraordinary has happened. Your son Reynaldo has been found in Huelva."

They rocked backward in stunned disbelief.

"Yes, it is true," he assured them.

"Dear God! Is he, is he *well?*" stammered Carlos as Catalina tearfully put her hands to her face.

"Yes, Carlos, he has been in shock and senseless for several years but came out of it when he saw Guillermo and Mateo."

"In Huelva?"

Just then, the front door opened, and Reynaldo took a tentative step inside.

His mother and father seeing him, first gazed dumbstruck at him for a moment, and then rushed forward.

"Praise God!" his father exclaimed. The three of them hugged and sobbed for a good while. Finally, Reynaldo drew back enough to look at them and tell them as they listened in awe, "My dear mother and father, I am deeply grieved to have caused you so much pain for so long. I have wandered for several years without my senses or memory of who I was."

"But now, God has returned you to us. That is all that matters," his mother told him.

"Yet I also have tragic news for you. My dear brother Cristóbal is dead. During a native uprising in the Indies, he was killed while bravely coming to my aid," he said with a sob. "I witnessed it with my own eyes, and then was bludgeoned senseless by the devils."

At hearing this, they hugged and cried again.

Mateo, Guillermo, and Mencía came in and gave hugs of sympathy to Carlos and Catalina.

"Thank you all," Carlos told them with emotion. "God, with your assistance, has brought back our son. Today is San Juan (Saint John) day. We must go and pray to San Juan to thank him for bringing our son back."

The servants had been watching and also crying with happiness. Looking up, Carlos called to the housekeeper,

"Please Manuela, have someone from the stables bring a carriage around. We must thank God in our church where we have prayed so many, many times for this moment."

To the others, he said, "I do not know how to thank you or what to say. I only know we must thank God for returning our Reynaldo in answer to our prayers. Please, Francisco, my friend, you and the others should all go to your home, see your families again, and celebrate your return with them. We must devote ourselves to thanking God. Do not fret about us. We are now fine. Perhaps in a day or two, we can get together."

"As you wish, Carlos," said Francisco with feeling. "We will say prayers as well and will wait to hear from you."

After emotional hugs and goodbyes, the travelers returned to their horses out front, mounted, and rode away. The boys were already gone. Before coming inside, Mateo had told them to go ahead since they were eager to see their mother again, but he reminded them, "But remember, you are not to say anything yet about bandits!"

When they arrived at Francisco's home, the mood was less somber as they were happily greeted.

"Francisco, dear, welcome back," his wife Isabel said as they hugged and kissed. "Is it not wonderful that Reynaldo has been found? The boys told us."

"Yes, my dear. We were quite astounded when they arrived with him at Diego's. Carlos and Catalina are in shock and going immediately to church to thank God. It may take several days for them to recover."

"It is quite understandable." Then in a different tone, she said, "But Francisco! What has come over you? Why are Domingo and Gabriel carrying pistols in their belts?"

"Your little boys are not so little anymore, my dear. The pistols belong to them, the spoils of their brave action against bandits on the way to Huelva."

Their mother gasped.

"Yes, our brave sons earned them. Our trip was most remarkable, and we have much to tell. I had a wonderful stay with Diego. We have become fast friends. He and his two sons hope to visit soon. We will tell you and the others all about it, but first, I wish to see and hold my dear little grandson."

Meanwhile, Luisa had welcomed Mateo with hugs and kisses, and they had gone back right away to see little Santiago. Luisa had fared well during their absence and was in good health, suffering some from morning sickness, but getting much rest.

Everyone welcomed Guillermo and Mencía as they came inside to clean up. The staff bustled about preparing basins for washing and getting refreshments for the new arrivals. The boys were excited to be home and proudly walked about with their pistols in their belts.

Finally, their father told them, "Domingo, Gabriel, I believe we are safe enough inside the house. Your pistols are not necessary. Give them to me, and I will keep them for you in a drawer in my study."

Reluctantly, the two boys pulled the pistols from their belts and handed them over, much to the relief of their mother.

A few minutes later, everyone sat down for an afternoon meal. After the prayer was said, they began to pass plates of food and the questions about the trip started immediately.

"You say you found Reynaldo in Huelva?" asked Doña Isabel. "Why were you in Huelva?"

With that, the telling began.

That evening, Mateo, Guillermo, and Mencía were talking.

"Mencía and I will be leaving in the morning. Your parents will want to hear the news of Reynaldo's return."

"Frankly, I am surprised that they weren't here when we returned," said Mateo. "They talked before about coming."

"Yet, there is no need to ride hard to bring them the news," said Mencía. "Our horses have done well on the trip, put in so many miles. We have no need to push our good friends on the last leg of the journey. On the way, we thought we would visit our merchant friend, Señor Cruz, to see how he and Rachel are getting along."

"If you are leaving in the morning, I will let Luisa know. She will want to write one more letter to Ana. She already has several to take. I may give you a letter for my parents too."

"That will be fine. We have several already and I suppose a few more will not slow us down," replied Guillermo, casually.

"The boys will be upset that you are leaving so soon."

"We will miss them too. The trip was quite an adventure for them and us," said Mencía.

"Our stumbling onto Cousin Reynaldo still seems so amazing to me. And more so to his parents. I suspect they will recover soon from the shock of it," mused Mateo.

"I am sure of it. In no time at all, his mother will have young girls with duennas in trail coming to dinner to meet Reynaldo, like she did for you," said Guillermo, laughing.

"True enough. Taking Beatriz home, fighting bandits, finding Reynaldo. It has been a most extraordinary trip."

Chuckling and shaking his head, Mateo added, "And all because you wanted me to act as your duenna."

"What does *that* mean?" asked Mencía with a laugh.

"Nothing, nothing at all," said Guillermo sheepishly, "something about if he came along, then I could bring you too, and his mother would be happier."

"Happier that it would be more proper?" asked Mencía. "Does that mean you are courting me, Guillermo?"

"Of course not," said Guillermo with dismay. "I esteem you highly as my true friend, just like Mateo."

"Well, that will have to do for now, I suppose," she said with a smile and a look.

Turning with alarm to Mateo, Guillermo said, "Now see what you have done, Mateo. You have gotten me into trouble!"

"Guillermo, be calm. I believe Mencía is jesting," said Mateo, laughing.

"Yes, I am," said Mencía, grinning, "but I am pleased to hear you wanted to bring along your true friend."

22. Skills and Gardening

IN THE MORNING, Guillermo and Mencía were packed and ready to leave early. The boys were, needless to say, greatly disappointed when they heard Guillermo and Mencía were leaving so soon. To mollify the boys to some degree, they and Mateo would accompany Guillermo and Mencía to the merchant in Cordoba and then return.

"However! You are not to wear your pistols!" stipulated their mother.

Mateo and the boys were mounted and ready to go as Guillermo and Mencía said their farewells to the others who were all there outside to see them off. Guillermo and Mencía then quickly mounted, and they all started out.

They stopped only briefly at the merchant's place of business to say hello. Señor Cruz was happy and surprised to see them and greeted them warmly. Rachel brought in a tray with a bottle of sweet spirits and small glasses. They toasted to "life," which they said was prosperous and unthreatened after their recent kidnapping incident. Guillermo and the others were disappointed to find that Antonio was no longer there. He had decided to return to the streets after only working there a short time, which should have been no surprise.

After a brief pleasant visit, they all went outside where Guillermo and Mencía said their goodbyes and departed. Riding at a comfortable pace, they spent the night in an inn midway and arrived home before noon.

On the way, they had stopped briefly at Pascual's camp to visit Pascual and their friend Sebastian. Of course, they were questioned about their trip. When telling about their encounter with the bandits, Guillermo said, "Sebastian, we could have used you there."

"I wish I had been along," replied Sebastian longingly with a smile.

After hearing Guillermo's brief description of the bandit fight, Pascual stood, shaking his head and looking with admiration at Mencía.

Grasping her hand, Pascual told her affectionately, "Mencía, my dear, the world has underestimated you once more."

"Thank you, Pascual. I admit it is an advantage I have. Villains think I am a helpless woman while they tremble at the sight of that fearsome countenance of yours."

Laughing heartily at this, Pascual replied, "Quite true. Quite true. Mencía, you are a treasure. And I might add, a pleasant sight to the eyes of this fearsome countenance. You both must come back to tell us more of the trip."

"We will soon," Guillermo told him smiling as he and Mencía climbed onto their horses. Then with a wave, they reined their horses around and trotted away.

Upon arrival, Guillermo and Mencía stopped first at the main house to tell the Don and Doña the news of Reynaldo's miraculous return. As expected, they were astounded and wanted to hear all about it. News of their return soon reached Guillermo's parents, who arrived shortly. After several hours of refreshments and telling of their trip, Guillermo accompanied Mencía on her one-hour ride to her parents' house. It was something he ordinarily didn't do, but desired to do this time for some reason. After a brief visit with her family, he returned in the evening to his parents' house, to his room that looked strangely unfamiliar and empty to him.

The next morning, Guillermo was up early and joined his father as he directed the work of the estate. Guillermo had not been overly involved in growing the new plants from the Indies but was interested in their progress. Pedro, Joaquin, and Joaquin's family were in the garden working.

It was late June, and the tomatoes were ripening. The plants looked very healthy with a large number of reddening tomatoes on them. Joaquin was eager to taste one. He seemed to have an amazing knack for growing them, despite having never seen a tomato plant before. Through his careful examination of the leaves and blossoms of the plant, he experimented and found the right amount of water and mixture of soil nutrients to make them thrive.

That spring, Pedro and Joaquin had grown a great number of tomato seedlings for planting. All the families on the estate had been given seedlings for their gardens. They paid close attention to them as they grew, and now that the tomatoes were ripening, everyone was excited after tasting them with delight last year for the first time.

A good deal of potatoes from the winter crop were already available for eating. The last plantings in February would soon be ready for harvest as well. Pedro and Joaquin had made good progress with growing red and white potatoes from seed potatoes. Most of these potatoes were to be used for further planting and for selling to others.

They had also continued to plant potatoes from seed to see if a new even better variety might be found. The ones without the most promising traits from these efforts were of no use for further planting and given to the families for eating.

Much interest and ideas had been generated in how to best use them in Spanish cooking. A popular early dish was a potato tortilla made with diced potatoes, onions and eggs. Soon everyone was clamoring for potatoes to make the new dish.

When Mencía returned in a day, she and Guillermo went to visit Ana and Bernardino to see how their friend Ana was managing with her pregnancy as well as to tell them about the trip.

When they arrived, Felipe was there with Ana and Bernardino to greet them. They all sat down and chatted amiably. They listened with great interest as Guillermo told them about their added travel to Huelva and of finding their long-lost cousin.

Ana was doing well and experiencing no problems. She had greatly missed Luisa and was happy to get letters from her and to hear that Luisa was also doing well.

Bernardino told a little about his new life there on the estate. Under the guidance of the longtime overseer, the estate ran so smoothly that he had no need to get involved in its day-to-day affairs. He would ride about the estate periodically with Felipe to observe the farmhands at work, mainly to show interest in them. In his free time, he would occasionally practice with his pistols and still could shoot well.

Hearing this aroused Guillermo's interest, and he invited Bernardino to come to their estate to do weapons training with them. He could demonstrate his pistol shooting, and they could demonstrate their knife throwing and archery skills. Bernardino had heard of Mencía's skill with weapons and was eager to see it. Guillermo told him about their friend Don Tomás, a retired cavalier, who occasionally came out to the estate to instruct them with sabers and cutlasses. He suggested that Bernardino should join them in one of these training sessions, and he heartily accepted.

It was only two days later that they invited Tomás and Bernardino to their estate for one of these sessions. Bernardino still had his good right arm and was skilled with the saber. He also proved to be a crack shot with his pistol, a skill he had learned in the military, in case challenged to a duel.

Bernardino was greatly impressed with their knife throwing and archery skills. He couldn't compliment Mencía enough and told them a skilled archer was still of great value in land warfare. Yet such skills took so long to perfect that skilled archers were now a rarity. It was much quicker and easier to train a group of men to load and fire muskets, even though they were inaccurate and took much longer to reload.

Tomás showed Bernardino great respect and also saw his withered unusable arm as a badge of courage, something to be praised and proud of. They had great admiration for each other and talked happily together. When Tomás called Mencía a "warrior princess," Bernardino laughed and strongly agreed.

Dons Lorenzo and Felipe came and sipped wine as they watched and cheered on the participants. Ana watched proudly as Bernardino practiced with his saber. It was quite a day of training, wine, and tales of military service, followed by a festive dinner.

Two weeks later, the last planting of potatoes was ready to be harvested. The bean and pepper plants were doing well. Last year, they had only limited success in growing peppers. But based on what they had learned from Carlos' gardener, they had planted and fertilized them differently this year and had gotten many blossoms. It would be another month before the peppers and beans would be ready to harvest.

One day when Mencía was visiting, Miguel and Pedro were showing her and Guillermo the maize plants, which looked tall and healthy. Pedro peeled back the husk on one of the long hard seed pods for them to see.

"They are ripe by all appearances," Miguel told them. "The tassels on top of the seed pods are dried and shriveled. We will harvest some of them soon to eat fresh, but Mateo told us that in the Indies, they leave them on the plants much longer to dry out the seeds for making maize cakes, a staple food of the natives there."

"Unfortunately," added Pedro, "Mateo did not recall their method of making the maize cakes from the seeds. Last year, my Juana's attempts to make them were not very tasty."

"Perhaps a visit to Don Carlos is called for, so we can ask Reynaldo," suggested Guillermo. "He lived there several years with the natives and must have seen it done."

"The Don and Doña must be planning to go there soon. I am surprised they have not already gone," commented Mencía.

"I believe they want to give their cousins a little time to recover from the shock of Reynaldo's return," said Miguel.

Suddenly, they heard the pounding hooves of a horse and turned with concern to look. A stableman riding hard came into view and pulled his horse up sharply on the other side of the garden's high stone fence.

"Señor Miguel! Guillermo!" he shouted frantically. "Don Lorenzo wants you at the main house. There is some kind of emergency in town.

They looked at one another in wonder and started for the gate.

"Pedro, we must be off," called Miguel as he, Guillermo, and Mencía rushed away.

23. Emergency

WHEN THEY ENTERED the main house, they saw a frenzy of activity and excitement as they made their way through the house to find Lorenzo.

They found him in his study standing at his desk checking two pistols which he normally kept in a case in the drawer.

"Don Lorenzo, what is happening?" asked Miguel in alarm.

"Miguel, Guillermo, Mencía, we have troubles. The constable, who has just left, has informed me that a horde of bandits from the north is headed toward our area. They are discontented moriscos, who are attacking and looting small towns and estates in their path."

"A horde? Of how many?" asked Guillermo.

"Nothing certain is known, perhaps eighty or more. He is fortifying the town, blockading the streets, informing the estates, and recommending people come into town for safety. He asks for Pascual's assistance and wants us to ride to tell him."

"I will ride there right away," said Guillermo.

"Good, Guillermo. Thank you. Miguel, all our estate families must be informed. We must pack supplies and weapons and move everyone into town."

"How soon and for how long, Don Lorenzo?"

"As soon as possible, let us say within three hours. Plan to be gone for several days at least."

Miguel nodded and left.

"Are they also headed for the town where my family lives?" asked Mencía.

"I do not think that far west. We will learn more when we get to town."

"Mencía, I will ride to tell Pascual," said Guillermo. "You should ride to Don Felipe's to ensure they know. When you get back, perhaps you could gather up Mateo's weapons and all the arrows you can find."

With a frown, he added, "I wish we had not left our captured pistols with Mateo. They could be of use now."

"Maybe for the others, but I prefer my arrows," said Mencía as they both hurried out.

Mateo rode hard and arrived at Pascual's camp in twenty minutes. To his surprise, he found Mateo, Domingo, and Gabriel there. The boys had pestered their mother constantly for two weeks until she finally consented to let them go north to see Guillermo and Mencía. Mateo was along to accompany them. They had just stopped to visit Pascual on their way north when Guillermo arrived.

Pascual and the whole camp watched with concern as they saw Guillermo riding hard towards them. He pulled his horse to an abrupt stop and while still in the saddle, relayed his message.

"Pascual! The constable asks for the assistance of you and your men. A large horde of morisco bandits is pillaging estates and small towns. They come from the north and are headed our way. He is setting up barricades to keep them out of town and requests your help."

"Men!" shouted Pascual without hesitation, "Gather your weapons and some food! Guillermo, tell the constable we will be there soon. Juan, Jorge, you stay at the camp. If they head this way, we will return to either defend the camp or get everyone away to safety. We ride in twenty minutes!"

The camp became a frenzy of activity as Mateo and the boys jumped on their horses and rode away with Guillermo.

As they rode into the estate, they saw a similar uproar of activity as horse-drawn wagons were being loaded with supplies, weapons, and people.

They found Mencía inside putting a large number of arrows in a box. She looked up in surprise at seeing Mateo and the boys.

"Mateo, Domingo, Gabriel, you have come at a bad time, but we are happy you have."

"Fortunately, they pestered their mother so much that she let them come up," explained Mateo.

"Did you bring the pistols?" asked Mencía.

"Yes, all five and our archery gear too," said Domingo excitedly.

"They may be needed," said Mencía.

"Have we heard any more news," asked Guillermo.

"No, nothing more."

"And how about your family, Mencía?" asked Mateo.

"I am not so worried about them. Their town is larger, so the bandits will probably not attempt to attack it if they go in that direction."

"We should ride into town to see what preparations the constable has made," suggested Guillermo.

"Where did you get all the arrows?" asked Gabriel.

"While Guillermo was gone, I rode to several nearby estates, including Don Felipe's, to warn them and to gather arrows just to ensure they were brought into town."

They next went to see Mateo's father who they found in his study with Joaquin.

He was surprised to see Mateo and the boys but gave them a brief wave while continuing his conversation with Joaquin.

"Joaquin, are you sure you want to stay?"

"Yes, Don Lorenzo. If they come here, I do not think they will attack me and my family, since we are moriscos like them. I will tell them I work here, and you are good to us, that they should not loot your estate."

"Joaquin, I do appreciate that, but I believe it will not deter them. If they start looting, do not try to stop them. You need not put yourself and your family at risk. Are you sure you do not wish to come into town with us?"

"I think we would not be welcome there. I prefer to stay."

"You would be welcome with us, but I understand. If you stay, please do not endanger yourself or your family."

"I thank you, Señor, and hope they do not come here."

"I hope so too, Joaquin. It is all very unfortunate. May God protect you and your family."

"I thank you, Don Lorenzo," he said with a nod. Turning and seeing the others, he nodded to them and left.

After Joaquin was gone, Lorenzo sighed.

"Yes, very unfortunate indeed. Our past actions now return to haunt us. And I, myself, was part of it. After the morisco rebellion in Granada was subdued, we cleared out entire morisco areas and marched the people north into Castilian areas to be scattered amongst the population and be assimilated. I was one of the soldiers who marched them and saw how ill-treated they were. Many died on the march. Once there, instead of being assimilated, they were shunned. After a time, some of these moriscos resorted to banditry, and alas, we must now deal with the results of it. This bandit horde..."

"Don Lorenzo, we have no time to lament the past," interrupted Guillermo, "We must defend ourselves now."

"Yes, you are correct, Guillermo. I waste time."

"Mateo," said Guillermo, "you and the boys escort the Don and Doña into town when they are ready. Mencía and I will go ahead. Pascual should also be there soon. I will let the constable know and find out the latest on the situation."

"Good, Guillermo. We will see you there soon."

With that, Mencía and Guillermo rushed from the room, collected up their weapons, and raced outside to their horses.

24. Preparing Defenses

THE TOWN WAS A BEEHIVE of excited activity as people rushed about making frantic preparations for defense against the bandit attack. Mencía and Guillermo found their old friend Tomás in the town plaza collecting weapons and instructing men on their use. A number of weapons had been collected from the constable's stock, the townspeople, and surrounding estates. The collected cutlasses, machetes, pikes, pistols, bows, arrows, and crossbows were now being distributed.

Seeing Guillermo and Mencía, Tomás brightened and said, "Ah, my friends, your skills are sorely needed. The townspeople have spirit enough but lack such skills and training with weapons. We will have to teach them quickly though and defend our town with what we have."

"Don Tomás, how soon will they be here?" asked Guillermo.

"I do not know. I hope to have several hours to organize our defenses and get these men a modicum of training."

"Here are two more pistols for your men. Mencía and I will not need them," said Guillermo as they gave their pistols and ammo pouches to him.

"Very good. You should see the constable to find out the latest knowledge of the bandits."

"We will go to find him now. I also will inform him that I have been to see Pascual. He and his men will be here soon."

"That is good news indeed. Hurry back to help here if you can."

Then turning, Tomás hollered for two men who came forward and received the two pistols.

Mencía and Guillermo found the constable directing the townspeople in collecting wagons and furniture to barricade the numerous entrances to the town. Seeing them, the constable stopped momentarily to hear their news.

"Señor Constable, I have seen Pascual. He and his men will be here soon."

"Thank God. We will need them," said the constable with a look of relief.

"Señor Constable, what do we know of the bandits?" asked Guillermo.

"We are told they are a horde of eighty or more Morisco bandits from La Mancha, led by a villain named Comares. They swept down without warning from the hills to attack and plunder Tierracampo to the north. I believe they are still in that area and have smaller parties plundering the surrounding estates."

"That is only two hours ride from here if they decide to come this way," said Guillermo.

"I believe they are occupied with their plunder now and not on the move here. When Pascual and his men get here, perhaps they can find out more for us," speculated the constable.

"Guillermo and I will go with them. We will be helping Don Tomás until they arrive," said Mencía.

Not knowing Mencía well, the constable looked a little surprised at her statement, but soon his thoughts reverted to the defense of the town.

"So many streets into town," he agonized. "We must barricade them all and rush men to defend the ones that the bandits attack."

"Señor Constable," Guillermo told him, "a number of us are skilled in archery. You should place the street barricades in locations where we can shoot down on them from a flat rooftop as they attack the barricades."

Quickly looking around at the buildings along the street where they were overturning a wagon, he continued, "You see that flat roof with the facade rising on the front of it. It is an excellent place for us. Place the barricade fifty feet inside it, not where they are now overturning the wagon."

"I see what you mean, Guillermo. It is sound advice. We will place all the street barricades with that in mind."

Rushing off, he stopped the men overturning the wagon and pointed out to them where to put it instead.

Mencía and Guillermo quickly left and returned to help Tomás. Several other men had brought bows and arrows and had already stuffed blankets with straw from the stable to use as targets. They watched as Guillermo and Mencía shot several arrows and gave them instruction on aiming and shooting. Then the men began to shoot as Mencía and Guillermo repeated the instructions aloud for them.

Meanwhile Tomás was instructing several men on using cutlasses and sabers, demonstrating several basic slashing and stabbing moves. After a time, his trainees continued their practicing, while Tomás shifted to pistol training. With another group of men, he went over the steps for reloading, priming, aiming, and firing pistols. They repeated the steps over and over without actually firing them, so as not to alarm the excited townspeople.

A short time later, Guillermo looked up and saw the people of their estate arriving in a caravan of wagons. They jumped from the wagons and began unloading supplies and weapons. Soon the wagons were emptied, and the constable directed them to one of the town entrances where the horses were unhooked, and the wagons were overturned on their sides. Lorenzo, Miguel, and others from the estate then continued to help build the barricades.

Meanwhile, Mateo and the boys found Guillermo and Mencía.

"Good, you made it," said Guillermo. "You should turn your pistols over to Tomás for the men on the barricades."

"But *we* will need them on the barricades!" protested Domingo.

"No," said Mateo, "you will be more useful shooting the bandits with your arrows. Being on the barricade is too dangerous for you. My mother would never allow it. You can shoot your arrows from the barricade as they approach, but when they get close, you are to move back a distance, say a dozen paces, behind the barricades beyond the accurate range of their pistols. You can shoot them from there if they get up on top the barricade but be careful of hitting our men. Can you promise me that you will be good soldiers, follow orders, and will do that?"

"Where will you be?" asked Gabriel.

"We will be on a rooftop shooting arrows down on them, also too dangerous for you," said Guillermo.

Mateo and Mencía nodded their concurrence.

After looking at Gabriel and heaving a sigh, Domingo said, "We promise."

Gabriel dejectedly nodded in agreement.

"Very good. Now is a good time for practicing. Show these men how good you are with your bows," said Mencía.

Domingo and Gabriel reluctantly surrendered their pistols to Mateo who took them to Tomás.

The boys joined the men practicing their archery. Taking out their frustration on the targets, they shot their arrows with such determination, accuracy, and strength that the other archers were surprised and impressed.

From the crowd and clatter of arriving wagons, Bernardino now appeared with saber in belt and another man carrying pistols and gear.

"Bernardino, good to see you! Everyone made it?" asked Mateo.

"Yes, Ana and Don Felipe are unloading with the others." Then coming forward, he called, "Don Tomás, here are more pistols, ball, and powder."

"Ah, Bernardino," said Tomás, smiling as another man took them, "I have plans for you and your steady hand. We will feed you cocked and loaded pistols while you will shoot them down in droves."

"I will do my best," said Bernardino with resolve.

"But first, help instruct these men on some basic saber moves. And show them how to fend the attackers off with the pikes as well."

"It will be my honor." Then turning around, he hollered, "All you men with sabers and cutlasses! Follow me over here, and we will give you some instruction!"

With his saber raised in the air, he began to usher the men over to an open area.

Mateo and the others now heard excitement and the clip-clopping of many horses on the street behind them. Turning, they saw Pascual and twelve of his men arriving on horseback. Nearby townspeople were waving and thanking them for coming.

Mateo, Guillermo, and Mencía went to them. Lorenzo was also there greeting his friend.

"Pascual, how is it possible that we are so lucky to have such faithful friends as you and your men? You are at our side as always. Thank you for coming," he told Pascual as he dismounted.

"Don Lorenzo, it is us who are lucky and honored to have your friendship. Where is the good constable so we may render him our services?"

Guillermo was there now and said, "Come, Pascual, I will take you to him. He already has a job in mind for you."

They went to the constable who happily greeted Pascual and thanked him for coming so promptly. Guillermo, Mencía, and Mateo listened as he filled in Pascual on what was known. After hearing it, Pascual paused to consider it for a moment.

Guillermo suggested, "If they are sending small parties out to plunder estates, perhaps we can ambush some of them and cut their numbers down, not wait until they attack us here."

"I was thinking the same thing, Guillermo," said Pascual, looking up at the sky. "We have enough daylight left today for it. We should send out scouts now to make sure the way there is clear. Our larger party will follow them. Once there, we can see about attacking these estate raiders."

Turning around, he called, "Sebastian! José!"

The two came forward and he told them, "A large party of the bandits is in and about Tierracampo. They have smaller parties raiding estates, and we plan to attack those raiding parties if we can. We need you to scout out the way there. Ride out through the countryside on the west side of the road. Keep an eye out for them. We will leave in twenty minutes and follow you. We will meet you south of Tierracampo where the main road goes over the hill and the oaks stop. Do you know the place?"

"Yes, Pascual. We will be there," said Sebastian as he and José jumped on their horses.

"Be careful, my friends," Guillermo told them.

Sebastian smiled at this, waved, and then he and José were off.

25. Estate Raiders

AFTER AN ANXIOUS GOODBYE with their parents and
the boys, Mateo and Guillermo as well as Mencía left twenty
minutes later with Pascual and his men. They rode fast cross-
country through the oaks, avoiding the main road. With the
estates north of the town being less developed, they
encountered few high stone walls across their path. They slowed
as they approached the place where they were to meet Sebastian
and José and found them in the trees within sight of the road.

"What have you seen?" Pascual asked them.

"Nothing," said Sebastian. "We have seen no one along the
road. Not even people fleeing the town. They must be fleeing in
other directions or are hiding in the oaks."

Looking north, Pascual said, "We are about thirty minutes of
cautious riding from the town. What do you think, Guillermo?"

"Split up into two parties, one to the east side of the road
and one to the west side," suggested Guillermo as Mateo and
Mencía joined them.

"Yes, but we must be careful not to encounter a large party
of them," warned Pascual.

"What weapons do you think they have?" asked Mateo.

"Moors are great admirers of the sword, but these men
probably also have pistols," answered Pascual. "I would think
these bandits on horseback like to overwhelm their victims at
close quarters in surprise attacks, so I do not believe we will
encounter such things as muskets, crossbows, or arrows."

"That makes sense," said Guillermo, and the others nodded.

"Guillermo, Mateo, Mencía, how about if you three go to the
east," said Pascual. "Take Sebastian, José, and Manuel with you. I
will take the rest up the west side. We must strike fast and then
regroup here afterward."

"Agreed. Good luck to you, Pascual."

"You too, my friends, take care."

Guillermo and his group rode cross-country at a good pace in the concealment of trees, high weeds, and bushes as much as possible. They slowed when they got into an oak area and saw an estate house ahead in the distance. Continuing through the trees cautiously, they dismounted in some bushes several hundred yards from the house. They could hear a commotion there and continued to get closer, running from tree to tree.

Briefly stopping to watch, they saw several men coming and going from the house and throwing things into a horse drawn wagon next to where horses were tied. Several outbuildings were nearby on the right and a high stone wall was not too far away from the raiders, less than a hundred feet. Apparently, the family was either gone or dead, for they only saw bandits and looting activity. After watching for a minute, they estimated eight or nine men were involved, all busy and not being very watchful.

With a plan to approach the raiders from the concealment of the outbuildings, Guillermo motioned to the others to move to the right, which they did. Without being noticed, they succeeded in getting to the back of the buildings, where they listened and watched again for a moment. The bandits were now taking a break, sitting together, and having wine.

Guillermo said quietly to the others huddled close by, "There appears to be about eight of them, a small enough party to attack. Mateo, Mencía, and I will creep along behind the stone fence to get close. At my signal, we will attack them with our arrows. When they see our small number, they will charge us. Then you will attack them from this angle as well."

"I should be with you instead of Mateo. I have no wife and son," said Sebastian firmly.

"Sebastian, there is no need…," started Mateo.

But Sebastian cut him off, "I am sorry, Mateo, but I insist."

With a nod of his head and a pat on Sebastian's shoulder, Mateo said, "Very well, my friend, if you insist."

"Good, it is settled. I feel it necessary to mention that we cannot afford to take any prisoners," said Guillermo.

They all nodded with determined looks.

"Okay then, we are off."

Guillermo, Mencía, and Sebastian began to creep along the high stone wall. They had their bows out and arrows ready as they moved along unseen by the bandits. They were about three quarters of the way along it when a volley of pistol fire could be heard in the distance. They might lose the element of surprise if they waited. Guillermo looked at the others and they nodded.

They jumped up and saw the bandits now standing up and looking away in the direction of the shots. Three of them fell immediately as arrows struck them in the upper body. Looking around wildly, their leader saw the three of them at the fence.

With a shout and pointing, he rushed toward the fence with his pistol and his saber drawn. The others let out a yell and charged forward with him. Soon, another fell with an arrow to the chest and then another stumbled forward with an arrow in the hip. They began firing their pistols, but unwisely, from too far a distance to have accuracy. As the bullets whizzed by them, Guillermo, Mencía, and Sebastian let loose with more arrows.

The leader was hit in the gut and yet kept coming. Two others fell with arrows, picked themselves up, and stumbled forward. The others behind were taking arrows too. As the leader reached the fence with his saber raised high, he received a knife in the throat, then lurched forward with his body slumping onto the fence and his sword falling to the ground beside Mencía. The other two remaining attackers were still stumbling forward, several steps behind him. One received an arrow in the chest with such force that it knocked him over backward. The second halted, clutched at the knife he suddenly realized was in his throat, and finally collapsed to the ground.

Hearing the shouts and gunfire, three more bandits suddenly emerged from the house. They also rushed to attack, then halted when they saw the treatment the others were receiving. They then raced for their horses tied to the wagon.

All three tried to mount but struggled with the excited horses that were spooked by the gunfire and chaos. Two of them made it up as several arrows whizzed close by them. They started to escape to the right, and were surprised by Mateo, José, and Manuel, who had moved up closer from behind the outbuilding. The first one was shot by José who was now by the wagon. He slumped forward, managed to turn his horse around only to receive an arrow in the side, and fall from his horse.

The second bandit, seeing the ambush of the first, had reined around furiously to get away in the opposite direction. José shot at him with a second pistol but missed. The bandit, wheeling about on his excited horse, was about to fire his pistol at José when Manuel popped up from behind the wagon and shot him in the chest at close range. The man went limp and tumbled backward from the horse to the ground.

Off to the left, the third bandit was trying to escape by running beside his horse, using it to shield him. After making it past the end of the house, he was about to mount, but Mateo had raced to stand beside the house where he had a clear shot at the man. His arrow struck him in the hip, and the bandit stumbled and lost the reins of the horse, which ran off leaving him exposed. He desperately fired his pistol at the archers who approached from the stone wall, without hitting them. Seconds later, two arrows struck him in the chest, and he went down.

With all the bandits down, the attackers all hastily converged on the wagon near the door of the house.

"Quickly, Mencía and I will check the house," directed Guillermo. "You others make sure they are all dead, and collect the weapons and our arrows to take with us!"

With pistols and knives out, he and Mencía hurried inside and quickly came back out.

"No other bandits inside. We found two dead people who did not make it away," reported Mencía.

"We must hurry back to the horses," shouted Mateo, and they started running. Soon they were remounted and riding full speed through the countryside back to the meeting point.

Looking back, they saw a group of men on horseback in chase. They swerved about in the countryside with the bandits not far behind them. They made for their meeting place where the main road crossed a hill and the oaks ended.

When they reached the road and galloped up the rise to the top of the hill, they saw Pascual discretely wave from his concealment behind a high stone fence along the road. As they rode past, Pascual discreetly motioned and pointed to the road in front of him. Guillermo understood his meaning. The six of them rode a bit farther and pulled their horses to a stop in the road and dismounted.

The leader of the bandit group slowed when he saw this. He looked about quickly, seeing no others. The group ahead of them, only six he thought in amazement, were walking toward them with their bows and other weapons out. He had to admire them for their courage even if he had to kill them. They were thirty yards ahead when he saw them start to shoot their arrows. One arrow barely missed him, and two of his men were hit.

It is time to put an end to their sport, he thought as he raised his saber. When turning to command his men to charge, he spotted horses back in the trees.

With sudden alarm, he shouted, "Horses! There must be others here! Quickly! Back to…,"

His shout was interrupted when Pascual and his men popped up from behind the nearby stone wall and discharged ten pistols at close range into them.

Although wounded by a bullet, the leader was reaching for his own pistol when he was hit by two arrows. He crumpled and toppled from his horse with a boot still caught in a stirrup.

Behind him, the horses nervously dashed about in confusion. After this surprise attack, the two bandits, still on their horses, fired their pistols, wounding one of Pascual's men. Two other bandits had also fired shots without aim or success before collapsing from their horses.

One of the two bandits remaining on horseback then charged the fence with his saber raised. Pascual's men prepared to receive him with their cutlasses. However, an arrow whizzed close by the bandit and then a second arrow struck him in the side. He crumpled forward but managed to rein his horse around and stay in the saddle as it galloped off.

The second bandit still on his horse, reined around and followed the other's example. The rest of the horses chased after them at a run, including the horse dragging the dead body of the leader whose boot was still stuck in the stirrup.

Pascual looked about and saw no other bandits moving. Only two had gotten away.

With the action over, Pascual shouted, "Collect all the weapons and make sure they are all dead!"

One of Pascual's men was bleeding from a bullet wound in the upper arm, while a second man had a saber cut on his shoulder from their previous encounter. The wounds were quickly bound, and both men said they were able to ride.

"It is a good thing that we were here waiting and able to ambush them," said Pascual, scanning about cautiously.

"Yes, all worked out well," agreed Mateo, soberly.

"We have done enough damage for now and should get back to town," recommended Pascual.

"Agreed," said Guillermo, retrieving an arrow nearby from the body of a bandit on the ground.

In a minute, they had finished gathering weapons and Pascual's men raced back to the horses in the trees. Meanwhile, Guillermo and the others had remounted their horses on the road and joined them. Glancing back in the direction of the town, Pascual saw no one coming. As Guillermo came up to him on horseback, Pascual asked, "Guillermo, did you have any success before being chased?"

"Yes, we killed eleven of them," he replied.

"My God, we had more men and thought we did well in killing seven!" said Pascual, impressed.

"I counted nine on the road here, and the one being dragged makes ten," said Mateo.

"Their leader, this glorified thief and murderer, Comares, will not be pleased. Let us be off," said Pascual as he reined his horse around, and they started back.

26. Comares Attacks

"SOMEONE WILL PAY FOR THIS," snarled Comares with venom. Less than an hour after the attack, the bandit leader sat on his horse with a terrible scowl on his face as he surveyed the scene of his dead men lying on the road.

Only one of the riders fleeing the scene had made it back to town to report to Comares that their party had been ambushed. The second wounded man with an arrow through his liver had finally passed out from loss of blood and fallen dead from his horse on the way. Comares was enraged at hearing the news of their loss.

"The fools! They rode right into a trap!" he swore as he gathered up his nearby men and rode out to the place. They found the mangled remains of the group's leader halfway there. Being dragged through heavy brush had finally torn the dead man's boot free of the stirrup.

Seeing his body as they passed, Comares paused for only a moment, saying, "The fool! Lucky for him, he is already dead, or he would suffer my fury!"

Riding on, they cautiously approached the place of ambush, coming in from different directions to ensure they would not be surprised again.

When first arriving, Comares looked about and could see the trail of trampled grass leading back into the trees.

"Rashid!" he shouted to one of his men. "Take some men and follow those tracks. Find out where they rode."

The order was acknowledged, and soon a number of men were trotting their horses along the path of trampled grass back to the trees. After eyeing the ground there, they rode off through the trees to the south.

When they returned a half hour later, they found Comares in a black mood, sitting on a stone waiting. Rashid reported that a group of fourteen or more had ridden south through the countryside in the same direction of the road. They had seen no town and could not tell the distance to one in that direction.

"Fourteen or more townsmen! Not even soldiers, but mere townsmen! I cannot believe it. Kareem said they showed great bravery and skill with their weapons. Well, these townsmen will pay, skilled or not. We will collect up all the men and move farther south during the night. We will then find this town and, at first light, attack it. No one will be left alive when we are done with it. Mount up! We go back now to collect the men and our wagons."

When Comares got back to Tierracampo and was told that two of his raiding parties had also been wiped out, he stormed about in a fury and swore vengeance. He had lost twenty-nine men and had less than sixty men left. Nevertheless, he would level this town. He would rush upon its defenders at dawn and show no mercy.

With a half dozen wagons loaded with plunder and supplies, they set out that night from Tierracampo along the road south. A party of scouts rode ahead to clear away any would-be attackers, but none were encountered. After several hours of advancing cautiously, the scouts came over a low hill and saw a small town in the distance. The cover of the oaks ended shortly beyond this hill leaving over a mile of open fields to the town.

In the dark, they could not make out any defenses. The town was dark and quiet. Stone walls separated the fields outside the edge of the town. They watched for several minutes, saw little or no activity, and rode back to report to Comares.

"A small town, you say," asked Comares, "and you saw no people or activity?"

"No, Comares. The town was dark and quiet. The moonlight did not permit us to venture out into the open to get closer."

"Perhaps they abandoned it and sought the protection of a larger town," Comares pondered, stroking his beard. "If so, we are too late to kill the men who attacked us but still can have our vengeance upon their town. We will burn it to the ground. We make camp for the night here in the trees away from the road and make ready to attack at dawn."

Early the next morning, Comares and three of his deputies stood beside an oak tree and strained to see the town in the grey dawn. He had left four men back at the camp to protect the wagons. The rest of his men were nearby in the cover of the oaks awaiting his orders.

Their vantage point was as close as they could get to the town without being seen. From there, they could still see no activity in it.

"I see two main roads into the place on this side, and it looks like they have barricades in the streets where they enter the town," pointed out one of his deputies.

"Yet, we still see no activity. What does it mean?" pondered another.

"That they built defenses and then decided to abandon the town, or they are still asleep, or possibly they lie quietly in wait," speculated Comares.

"Perhaps they have barricaded only the streets on this side from where we would come. I can take some men and circle around the town to see," said one.

"No! My blood is up! I do not want to wait!" said Comares with a vicious look. "Rashid, you will take half the men to storm the barricade on the left, and I will take the other half to storm the one on the right. I will meet you in the center of the town. Anyone we find will be put to the sword."

Ten minutes later, Comares was mounted on his horse back in the oaks with his men. As his men on their horses looked at him expectantly for his signal, their horses stepped and turned about nervously.

With a fierce look toward the town and his sword raised, Comares shouted with fury, "Let vengeance be ours! Let none remain alive!"

Then pointing his sword in the direction of the town, he screamed, "We ride!"

The bandit leader spurred and whipped his horse viciously as it burst forward, and the men cheered and followed. With a thunder of hooves, they emerged from the trees. It would take them three- or four-minutes riding hard to cross the open area to the barricades. Soon, they split into two hordes racing at full speed along the two roads toward the town.

As soon as the bandits emerged from the trees, they heard church bells begin to ring and saw a scramble of activity in the streets. After they split into two groups, they began to see more activity behind the barricades and on the roofs nearby.

"They have not fled! Now they will pay!" shouted Comares above the thunder of the charging horses.

The street ahead had the typical look of these towns, a narrow street lined by a continuous block of two-story stucco houses and shops. The barricade, a short distance inside the start of the buildings, looked to be a jumbled mass of wagons and furniture too large and high to jump. His men would have to overwhelm the defenders and pull it apart to get by. Most of the buildings along the block had sloped tile roofs, while some had flat roofs with a raised facade on the front, from which someone could shoot down upon them. He dared them to do it. He would shoot them down like dogs.

He could only see several men poised behind the roof facades above the barricade and a small number of men behind the tangled barrier.

"They expect to repulse us with so few? These non-believers are either fools or up to some devilish trickery. They will learn more respect!" thought Comares. Such disrespect only enraged him more, and he spurred his horse furiously.

When he was two hundred feet from the barricade, the place came to life. Armed defenders came running and took positions behind the barricade where protruding pikes suddenly appeared. From behind the roof facades, archers rose and began a steady fire of arrows at the onrushing horsemen, long before they could respond with their pistols and swords.

Ignoring the arrow that whizzed by, narrowly missing him, Comares turned to shout encouragement to the men behind him and noticed one was already down. A steady stream of arrows soon greeted them and began taking a toll on his men. When he entered the narrow street and neared the barricade, an arrow caught him in the shoulder of his rein hand, and he struggled with it to control his horse. Yet, he was able to stay on his horse and continue waving the sword in his other hand to urge his men forward to the barricade.

The archers on the roof were shooting down on them and then ducking down behind the façade as they quickly readied the next arrow. Then they would pop up suddenly and fire down with deadly accuracy.

"Shoot the archers on the roof!" screamed Comares to his men. But their pistols were ineffective as they rode forward toward the barricade and shot from excited horses at the archers.

Some attackers were now close to the barricade, shooting pistols, dismounting, and rushing to it, where they faced a barrage of pistol fire that took a further toll on their numbers. The gunfire and smoke were spooking the horses and creating chaos in front of the barricade. One bandit who did make it to the top of the barricade, was shot. As he staggered momentarily, he received an arrow in the throat and fell forward inside the barricade. He then was immediately beset upon by several men who thrust him though several times with cutlasses and dragged his body out of the way.

From the smoke of the pistol fire, more bandits emerged, rushed the barricade, and scrambled up the tangle of furniture. Men behind the barricade jabbed at them with their pikes. As the attackers fended off the pikes and tried to get at the defenders with their swords, they received pistol fire, killing several attackers who crumpled and fell backward from the barricade. Others, even though wounded, continued to struggle up the barricade to get at the defenders.

The street in front of the barricade now became a maelstrom of screaming, frantic, riderless horses as pistol fire was exchanged and arrows continued to rain down upon the attackers. One of the archers on a rooftop was shot and fell forward over the facade onto the street below. The leader Comares received a bullet in the arm and another arrow in the leg before finally signaling to the others to retreat.

He and his nine remaining men, all of whom were wounded, rode back out of range of the arrows. Sixteen of his men didn't make it out. Comares stared in furious amazement at the sight of the few remaining men gathered around him. Violently reining his horse around to look at the recent scene of action, he could see horses still nervously racing about in front of the barricade in the street littered with the bodies of his men.

He gritted his teeth and screamed at the top of his lungs. In a rage, he pulled the arrow from his leg, broke it in two, and threw it to the ground.

He looked over and saw the remnants of his other attacking party also ingloriously retreating. He only counted nine remaining from the twenty-six attackers sent there. His deputy Rashid was not among them.

Nothing more could be done now, but to ride back to their camp and get away from this devilish town. They would retreat north back into the remote hills of La Mancha, where they could rest and recover. The wagons would have to be left, so they could travel fast. He swore he would return and punish this town or else his name was not Comares!

He gathered up the remnants of his men and rode back through the oaks to his camp. In twenty minutes, they arrived at the camp. The four men guarding the wagons looked at them with surprise and alarm when they saw them coming. They had expected only a few riders to help them drive the wagons to the vanquished town.

Seeing the returning wounded men and anticipating the probable need to flee, one guard called, "Comares, the wagons are loaded and ready to go. What are your orders?"

"We leave the wagons! We must travel fast to get away. Take the most valuable things and put them in sacks for the pack horses. And supplies too. And be quick about it!"

He shouted to the others, "Dress your wounds, quickly! And reload your pistols! We must ride soon from here without the wagons!"

He dismounted and said to the man beside him, "Ameer, break off this arrow in my shoulder and pull it through."

Ameer did as he was told, and Comares winced in painful fury as he jerked the broken shaft of the arrow through his shoulder.

"Wrap some cloth on the wound on my arm. Then ride a distance back toward the town. Stay there while we get ready to leave in one half hour. Ride back to warn us if you see anyone coming out to pursue us."

"Yes, Comares," he said as he grabbed a satin scarf from the loot on a wagon. After quickly tying it around Comares' bloody arm, he rode off in the direction of town.

Comares then shouted commands and directed the men as a wild scene of preparations to flee commenced. Sacks of rice, bread, and cheese were tied to pack horses. Men frantically threw the piles and boxes of loot from the wagons looking for jewelry, gold and money. When they found any, they hurriedly gathered it up and threw it into sacks that they then tied to the packhorses. They worked frantically and filled sack after sack of loot. It was a scene of bedlam until a shout was heard, and everyone turned to see a riderless horse coming their way.

"Curses!" shouted Comares, "It is Ameer's horse! I sent him out to be a sentinel. Quickly, we have little time. Get the last of the things, and then we ride!"

As the men rushed to pick up final things to take and get to their horses, several arrows came streaking in among them. One narrowly missed Comares, who looked about in disbelief. Sixty yards away standing in front of a stone wall and walking toward them were four archers, who were shooting arrow after arrow at them. More arrows landed barely missing several men.

When an arrow struck a wagon close by, a horse spooked and threw its wounded rider to the ground. He got up painfully holding his shoulder with a bullet wound from earlier. Two others grabbed him, hoisted him back up on the horse, and handed him the reins.

One man had been standing in a wagon searching through their plunder when he stood up to look. An arrow struck him in the chest, and he toppled backward with a cry over the side of the wagon and onto the ground. Several seconds later, another man was hit in the hip.

"There are only four of them!" shouted one of the men. "Let us charge them and cut them down!"

"No! It must be another trap! Mount up and follow me!" shouted Comares as he raced to his horse and painfully hauled himself up into the saddle.

A man, previously wounded in the attack, was being helped from the ground when he went limp and died. The two men, helping him, then let him fall to the ground and ran for their horses. Another man had just tied a sack onto a pack horse when an arrow struck him in the back of the leg. He then hobbled painfully to his own horse and managed to climb on despite the arrow sticking from his leg. One man was in his saddle and awaiting Comares' command to ride when an arrow struck him in the side. With a cry of pain, he slid from the saddle and collapsed to the ground with a thud.

Comares, waving for the others to follow him, raced off through the oaks away from the attackers with his greatly diminished band of men following closely.

Soon, they were across the road and headed northeast cross-country through the oaks at the fastest pace they could make, given their heavily laden packhorses. Comares looked behind several times without seeing any pursuers, yet he knew these demons with their arrows would pursue them.

After riding ten minutes, Comares was unsatisfied with their speed, so he called them to a stop to shed some load from the packhorses. The heavy sacks of jewelry and coins were quickly removed from them and carried to a nearby rock outcropping. They laid the sacks behind the rocks out of sight as the dismayed and unhappy men watched.

"Have no fear. We will retrieve these valuables when we come back to destroy that town!" he shouted to them as he hurried back to his horse. Before leaving, he quickly scanned about trying to remember the place. In less than a minute, they were off again at a more rapid pace.

Some wounded men could not keep up the pace for a long period and started to fall behind. One of the wounded riders passed out, fell from the saddle, and landed hard on the ground, where he lay in a motionless heap.

Comares kept up the fast pace for about six miles and then stopped by a small creek for a brief rest and to water the horses. He was anxious to keep moving. The La Mancha border was only an hour or more away. They should be there by midmorning.

As the horses stood in the creek and bent to drink, the men beside them scooped water with their hands to drink. One more of his men came straggling in and Comares quickly counted. He cursed at finding he had only sixteen men. Two more had been lost during the ride.

"Comares, what is the plan now?" asked one of his few remaining deputies.

"We must continue to ride hard in this northeast direction. As soon as we cross the Rio Guadalmez, we are back into La Mancha, away from the arrows of these Andalusian demons."

"You do not think they will follow us into La Mancha?"

"No, I think not. We will then be La Mancha's problem for the Castilians there to deal with. They will not want to trouble themselves and risk their lives to chase us once we leave Andalusia. They will congratulate themselves and return to their town. So we must keep up the pace. Once across the river, we can slow the pace and, after a time, find a place to recover from our wounds."

"I hope you are correct. Our men are wounded and exhausted. They can still fight, but we could not withstand another such attack from these fiends with their cursed arrows."

"By what witchcraft has this happened!" shouted Comares furiously in a fit of rage with clenched fists. "We roamed freely throughout remote La Mancha for months without difficulty, always able to evade soldiers and to plunder at will!"

"We were nearly ninety in number when we entered Andalusia!" he shouted angrily.

"Now look at us," he said pointing. "Those devils with their arrows will pay for this! No amount of witchcraft or magic will stop me! We will return from La Mancha with an army of our kinsmen to level that town!" he declared with anger and determination.

Staring down fiercely with gritted teeth, he said, "Gather up the men. We have rested long enough and must go."

In half an hour, they crossed another main road and a small creek on the other side of it without stopping. They saw no one on the road as they crossed. Looking behind, Comares still could see no pursuers.

North of the road, they had to slow their pace as the terrain of rolling oak-covered hills became rockier and rougher. They should be back within La Mancha in less than an hour, thought Comares. The dry, hilly countryside was sparsely populated with very few estates in the area. They didn't encounter anyone as they made their way over and around hills toward the northeast. They kept up a steady pace with no stragglers falling behind.

When Comares saw the river ahead, he felt relieved to have made it without being attacked. The river was shallow, not very wide, and totally dry in some places. When they arrived, he stopped briefly to give their horses a drink. He dismounted and splashed some water on his face. It did not help. He was still furious. Looking up at the sun, he noted it was still well before midday. Much of the day remained for them to continue. Now at the border of La Mancha, Comares thought only two more hours of travel would get them sufficiently into the safety of La Mancha and away from the treacherous Andalusians.

After several minutes of rest at the river, he gave the order to move out. The hilly terrain continued to be sparsely populated, dry, and rocky, with a covering of mostly scrub brush. They could slow their pace a bit now.

In two hours, they would begin to look for a place where they could finally stop to get some food and rest and attend to their wounds. They would need a creek with water in it, where they could camp in nearby trees for several days to recover before continuing.

27. Nearby Estate

GUILLERMO PULLED UP his horse in front of the Rio Guadalmez. Looking it over, it did not impress him as being much of a river. Mencía and Mateo stopped their horses beside him. Sebastian and José were already dismounted and in front of them examining the tracks in the mud.

"They stopped to water the horses here. About an hour ago," said José. He walked across the ankle-deep water to the other side and inspected the tracks there.

"I count twenty horses," he called back as he continued to inspect their trail.

"We saw them leave with three pack horses, so that means seventeen bandits," said Mencía.

José and Sebastian were now examining their trail beyond the river.

"They slowed their pace and do not hurry anymore," called José,

Pascual and the rest of his men were now there too. Mateo, Mencía, and Guillermo walked their horses into the water to let them drink. Pascual joined them with his horse.

"Pascual, did you hear José? The bandits, probably seventeen in number, crossed an hour ago. I am for continuing. What are your thoughts?" asked Guillermo.

"Well, if I were this Comares fellow," said Pascual stroking his beard thoughtfully, "I would want revenge for what happened to me. It would be far better to finish him off now than to wait for his return in the future to have it."

"I also believe that to be the case," said Guillermo.

"Destroy them as they flee in defeat. Those were Don Tomás' words to us," said Mencía with resolve.

"Sage advice from a veteran campaigner, I believe," said Mateo. "They are not many and probably tired and wounded. We should continue the pursuit." All nodded in agreement.

"Thus far, they have kept up a fast pace to escape us, yet José says they slowed their pace there on the other side," said Guillermo, thinking.

"It leads me to believe they think themselves now safe in La Mancha," he concluded. "They will camp for the night ahead, and we should attack them there."

"The moon is only a sliver now at night, so it will be dark," said Mateo. "We can get into position during the night and attack them in the morning."

"A good plan," agreed Pascual.

"More men to help surround the camp would be nice. The estate we passed a mile back is the only one in the area. Despite the high walls of the enclosure around the house, they are still vulnerable to attack from bandits. They will want to help when they learn that a vengeful Comares and his men will soon return this way unless we finish them off now," said Guillermo.

"All true, I suppose," said Pascual.

"Perhaps you should wait here and send Sebastian and José to scout ahead. Mencía, Mateo, and I will go back to the estate. We will be back soon," offered Guillermo.

"That will be fine," said Pascual, nodding in agreement.

Ten minutes later, the three of them approached the closed gate of the enclosure at the estate. Several armed men appeared above the top of the masonry wall on each side of the gate.

"Stop there! What business have you here?" challenged one.

"You probably saw our group pass by a short time ago. We are chasing a group of bandits who passed by an hour earlier."

"We saw both you and the first group. If they were bandits, then they are gone into La Mancha and no longer a threat here."

"There you are wrong," responded Guillermo. "They may not be a danger to you at this moment, but they will be back. Their leader is a bandit named Comares and…"

"What did you say? That was Comares!" interrupted a second man in surprise. "We have heard that he commands a horde of cutthroats and have feared that he would come our way and attack us."

"He did until yesterday, but that ragtag group of seventeen wounded bandits is all that is left of him and his horde. We have slain a great many of his men and pursue the rest. We plan to attack their camp in the morning to put an end to them. We ask if you can spare some men to help?" called Guillermo.

After a moment in thought, the man said, "Tie your horses to the post outside and leave your pistols with them. We will then open the gate so you can come inside and tell us more."

Once inside, introductions were made. The man in charge was Señor Lopez, who was the overseer for the Don and Doña who owned the estate but spent most of their time at their villa in Cordoba. He was astounded to hear Comares had been defeated and was now on the run. Señor Lopez applauded their efforts and wanted to help. He expressed his regret at not being able to go himself to help. Being responsible for the estate, he could not. Instead, he would send his deputy Simón and four good men. In an hour, his men would be at the river crossing to join them. Mateo thanked him, and cordial goodbyes were said.

As they started to leave out the gate, Señor Lopez could not help but express his curiosity and surprise at seeing a young pretty woman taking part in such a dangerous mission. They had all been eager to make her acquaintance during the introductions and had complimented her on her attractive riding outfit.

"Pardon me, but why do you risk this lovely young lady on this dangerous pursuit? She can stay here with us if you like until you return," offered Señor Lopez.

With a laugh, Guillermo turned to Mencía and asked, "Mencía, my friend, perhaps these gentlemen are curious to know how many of these bandits you have already killed with your arrows."

As she paused before replying, they all listened with great amazement for her answer.

"I am sorry," she replied nonchalantly with a shrug, "but I have lost count."

In an hour, the five men arrived on horseback and were welcomed by the others. They dismounted and the overseer's deputy Simón introduced himself and his men. In turn, Guillermo and Pascual introduced their group. The newcomers were still intrigued by Mencía, and one asked if she really was good with her bow. The men laughed at the question.

"I assure you that she is," Pascual told them. "If you wish a demonstration, go to the other side of the river and stand. She will shoot the hat from your head."

This caused a great deal of laughter. With a wink at Mencía, Pascual then added, "Perhaps, you would prefer to see a demonstration of her knife throwing?"

As the men were digesting this unexpected new offer, she turned and rapidly threw two knives that stuck close together in the trunk of a tree twenty feet away. The new men looked in amazement as the others laughed at their reaction.

Pascual declared, "Gentlemen, you may rest assured that our lioness Mencía is quite skilled with weapons. Now back to the serious business at hand, I see you have brought your own weapons, but what is that you have wrapped in the canvas?"

"Torches. Señor Lopez suggested it. They can be easily lit with a flint and may be useful at night as well as for starting fires to smoke out prey or spook horses."

Pascual looked at Guillermo with raised eyebrows and said, "Quite true. I never thought of it. They may indeed prove useful, not while we creep up on their camp at night, of course, but it will not hurt to bring them."

"I agree. It was good of Señor Lopez to think of it," said Mateo.

"Yes, a good notion," said Guillermo, "and now we should be off. They are two hours ahead of us and leave a trail a blind man could follow. They seem to be relaxed in a belief that no one will pursue them further. We shall give them a rude awakening in the morning."

28. Into La Mancha

AFTER CROSSING THE RIVER, they followed the trail of the bandits across the dry rocky terrain covered with scrub brush, dry grasses, and a scattering of scrub oaks. The trail led them over a low range of hills, along a dry creek in the valley beyond, through a gap in another range of hills, and along a dry creek in another valley.

"I can understand them not stopping along here," Mateo commented to Guillermo. "What dry, inhospitable terrain this is. I have not seen a good place to camp either. Perhaps we will need to travel farther into La Mancha than expected."

"It seems longer in this rocky desolation, but we have only gone perhaps eight miles. These hills probably look much better in the springtime. At least, we make very little dust," replied Guillermo.

"I cannot stop thinking of Don Tomás," said Mencía sadly. "He was badly wounded on the barricade. I pray not too badly."

"I know. I have thought of him much too," said Mateo. "We can only pray that his great spirit will help pull him through. He was so adamant for us to pursue the fleeing enemy though. We had no chance to see how bad his wounds were."

"We are doing exactly what he trained us for and what he wanted us to do, to chase down and destroy these bandits as they flee in defeat. That must content us until we get back to see how he does," said Guillermo.

Mencía and Mateo nodded in agreement.

Their party continued to carefully follow the trail for miles along the narrow valleys of scrub brush and dry creeks.

Up ahead, they suddenly spotted Sebastian riding toward them. At first, they feared bad news, that he and José had been attacked and José killed. However, Sebastian didn't appear distressed as he neared. They slowed and stopped as he pulled to a stop in front of them and reported.

"Comares has made camp in a cluster of oaks along a creek with water about an hour ahead. José is on a nearby hill and keeps watch on them."

"How many are there?" asked Guillermo.

"We counted twenty horses, just as José said before. Seventeen riders and three pack horses."

Pascual looked up at the midafternoon sun and said, "Very good then, we have plenty of daylight left to get there and look over this camp."

"Bravo, Sebastian, to you and José," said Guillermo. Seeing Sebastian notice their added men, Guillermo explained, "Yes, Sebastian, my friend, we have reinforcements. Simón and his men from the nearby estate have come with us to help. Perhaps we should dismount and stretch our legs for a minute, and they can tell you about Mencía's knife throwing."

They dismounted with a laugh, and quick introductions were made.

"Well, we have work to do and should be at it without further delay," suggested Pascual a few minutes later.

They were soon remounted and rode off at a faster pace. Sebastian started in the lead and was quickly joined by Mateo, Mencía, and Guillermo.

As they rode, Sebastian told them, "We were traveling along the base of a hill and saw clearly in some dirt how fresh the trail was. We could see a gap in the hills ahead and suspected they would go through it, so we climbed up the hill for a better view and spotted them as they reached a creek running along the other side. We watched as they followed the creek back toward us along the other side of the hill. After about a mile, they stopped and made camp along it."

"You and José were quite clever," said Guillermo.

A half hour later, Sebastian pointed to the hill on their left and said, "The bandits are camped along a creek on the opposite side of this hill. José is up there on top. You can see his horse there below, tied to the bush."

As they looked up and spotted the horse, the rest of the group came up behind them. It was decided that Sebastian, Mateo, Mencía, Guillermo, Pascual and Simón would ride up the hill to join José. They would observe the bandit camp from there and be back shortly. The others were to stay quietly below in the shade of a small cluster of oaks.

After tying their horses to bushes near José's horse, they cautiously walked from there to the top of the hill where they found José sitting amid the scrub brush. He looked happy to see them as they crept up next to him.

"There, along the creek," he said in a low voice, pointing and handing something to Pascual next to him. Pascual was about to ask, "What is this?" But then he saw it was the brass spyglass wrapped in a shirt to prevent any reflections. "Good thinking," he said instead, then peering through it down at the camp.

"In this desolate country, they managed to find the only creek with some water in it," quietly observed Mencía.

"Perhaps enough daylight remains to get into position and attack them this evening," pondered Guillermo, looking up at the sun.

"It may be difficult to do so without being spotted," said Mateo.

"They have good concealment in the trees at the base of the hill along the creek. I believe I see their horses in the trees on the right side of the camp," said Pascual as he handed the spyglass to Guillermo.

"Yes, the horses are on the right," said José.

"It would be nice to shoot down on them from our hill, but the trees at the camp are too dense," said Guillermo.

"It seems we must approach them along the creek from upstream, downstream, or both," suggested Mateo.

"Two separate groups might risk one of them being attacked and overwhelmed," said Pascual with concern.

"Keeping them from escaping on the horses is of primary interest so it makes sense to approach the camp from the right where the horses are tied," suggested Pascual and the others agreed.

"Two groups attacking may still be a good idea if they are not far apart and can support each other," said Mateo.

"One attacks from the trees by the horses and the other from the creek. If we can keep them from the horses, any bandits trying to escape on foot will head upstream along the creek and we can chase them down afterward."

"The ground between their camp and the creek is somewhat clear of trees, a good place for shooting our arrows. We should kill as many from a distance with arrows as we can, minimize the fighting at close quarters," suggested Mateo.

"I suppose there is no use in asking them to surrender, is there?" asked Mencía.

"No, these men know they will be killed should any authorities get their hands on them, and most likely by being publicly burned at a stake. They will fight to the end or try to escape, but they would never surrender."

"We can approach them in the dark and attack at first light. We should be prepared, however, to fight at night, should we be discovered," suggested Guillermo.

"They seem to be fixed in position there, and I see no need for further watching from here," said Pascual. "Thank you, José. You and Sebastian have done well. Let us all get back down."

As they descended the hill on their horses, Guillermo looked several times at the sun and finally said, "Pascual, I have been thinking. It is only late afternoon, and we have many hours of daylight remaining. It would not take long to ride around this hill and get close enough to the camp to set out on foot to attack them before sunset. We will see their camp and the lay of the land better during the daylight and better finalize our plan before attacking."

"And if they see us approaching?" asked Pascual.

"We attack them anyway from a distance with our arrows. Whittle away more of their numbers and continue to pursue them if they escape on horseback."

"Hmm," said Pascual as he thought about it. The others had now stopped and were listening.

"If we can surprise them, attacking from the trees along the hill, we may get close enough with the torches to create havoc with the horses and keep them from escaping on them. I noticed from my brief glimpse through the spyglass that the area around their camp looked to be dry grass," said Guillermo.

"An interesting thought," mused Mateo. "If concealment exists along the creek, perhaps a group of us with bows can get into position ahead of an attack. We can help cover the attackers along the hills."

"Better yet, we should surprise them with our arrows from the creek. The attack from the trees should be a feint to draw them out, not an actual more dangerous assault," suggested Mencía.

"I concur," said Guillermo. "From my brief glimpse, I believe the distances are good for accurate shooting."

"Well," said Pascual, "what do you all think?"

They all nodded in agreement.

"Then we should waste no time in getting to the other side of this hill where we can then proceed on foot."

As they approached the bottom of the hill, Pascual was already waving to the others to get mounted and follow them. The men all quickly mounted and joined them as they rode by.

Peering through the trees along the bottom of the hill, José crept forward to the next tree. The camp was less than a half mile ahead. He moved forward from tree to tree several times and then could see the men in the camp up ahead. He turned and waved to the men behind him. They in turn waved to the others further back, who dismounted and tied their horses in the bushes out of sight.

Pascual and Guillermo came up behind him and peered at the camp and the terrain along the trees. Guillermo pointed along the bottom slope of the hill.

"Look how it is already dark and shadowy in the trees along the bottom of the hill. That is a good route for attacking," said Guillermo.

Pascual nodded in agreement. Guillermo then craned to look at the terrain along the creek. The creek bed looked to be sunken and edged with dry grass and periodic bushes, which should allow them to crouch down and sneak along it without being seen. He looked up ahead at the camp, about twenty yards from the creek.

"Pascual, we do not want to get too close. We will stop at a spot by that single tree and bushes." He looked again at the terrain and added, "It looks to have a clear shot from there at defenders coming out. We will get into a position there where we have the best shot at them."

"What signal shall we use to start things?" asked Pascual.

"Have someone positioned to see us in the creek bed. I will signal when we are ready with a wave forward, and he can relay it to you. Remember that we hope to avoid an actual assault and are just trying to draw them out. Rush forward through the trees as if you are attacking but stay out of their pistol range. If you can get close enough, throw torches in among the horses, otherwise hang back. When they come out and start shooting, tell your men to fall back a bit to draw them out more."

"He probably respects your arrows and may not come out."

"If he does not suspect we are part of this attack, he may. We must hold our fire until more come out. It may become dangerous for your men. Reassure them that falling back is part of the trap we set and no reflection on their manhood."

Looking around quickly, Guillermo said, "We only have an hour of daylight. We must get into position in the creek. I will take four of your men with us. Good luck, my friend."

"Good luck, my friend," said Pascual.

29. Camp Attack

BENT LOW, THEY CREPT along the creek carefully and noiselessly across the rocks and through the shallow water. Guillermo was in the lead with Mencía, Sebastian, and Mateo close behind. They carried a bow in one hand and a full quiver of arrows in the other. Along with them were four of Pascual's heavily armed men who also carried several unlit torches.

In fifteen minutes, Guillermo was peering at the camp from the location he had pointed out to Pascual. They were about forty yards from the edge of the camp and could hear the men talking. With only a half hour left of daylight, it was already starting to get dark in the shadow of the hill. From behind the bushes, the others took turns quickly surveying the scene, looking along the trees where they would be shooting. If they could draw them out far enough, it would be less than thirty yards to the targets.

Looking up at the sky, Guillermo said, "We have no time to lose, everyone get ready. Do not show yourselves until I say so. Is everyone ready?"

They were now in a line along the ditch with their bows and arrows poised. They nodded to him, and he made the signal to the man down the ditch.

Immediately, a roar of voices could be heard as Pascual's men rushed forward through the trees toward the camp. They stopped outside pistol range but fired their pistols at the camp. The bandits in the camp were up immediately and a volley of pistol fire erupted from the camp, but without hitting anyone. When several of the bandits showed from the cover of the trees and moved tentatively forward at them, Pascual's men fired and retreated to another tree. Seeing the quick retreat of the attackers, the bandits rushed forward boldly with their sabers out, but they received a volley of close-range pistol fire from others hidden behind trees that killed one and wounded another. The third bandit and the wounded man then rushed back to their camp.

Now a new set of attackers with fresh pistols moved forward again from tree to tree as the bandits watched from their camp. One of them carried a burning torch that he flung a good twenty yards and landed amid the horses. It immediately caught the dry grass there on fire causing chaos as the horses screamed in fear and tore at their tethers. Three of the horses got free and raced across the field toward the creek and away. The remainder of horses jerked desperately at their tethers to get away, with two more succeeding. Several of the bandits were in amongst them trying to put out the fire and get them under control.

Comares had been cautiously watching, not wanting to fall into any more traps, but when he saw another man run forward with another burning torch, he had no choice but to order his men to charge the attackers. A dozen crazed bandits shouted and rushed out. Seeing the charging men, the man threw the burning torch in their path and ran back among the trees. Pascual's men fired their pistols at the onrushing bandits as they retreated, without hitting any. The bandits now had their blood up. They raced forward with their swords out and held their pistol fire until they got closer to the fleeing attackers.

Suddenly, two of the bandits fell with arrows in their sides. Another was hit in the hip and knocked to the ground. He got to his feet and began limping back to the camp. In their fury, the others didn't notice. Soon two more fell and one was hit in the leg and struggled to continue forward. The others suddenly noticed the arrows. One stopped and turned to look around only to see an arrow streaking at him, but too late to avoid it as it struck him in the chest.

The leader of the charge called and waved for them to turn back. As the bandits ran frantically back, three more were hit, one collapsing immediately to the ground and the other two struggling to continue. As three of the bandits were about to reach the camp, one of them was struck in the chest and collapsed forward, falling at the feet of Comares.

By now Pascual's men in the trees were rushing forward again firing their pistols and swinging their cutlasses to finish off any stragglers. The dry grass was now burning in front of the camp.

With the number of bandits greatly reduced, Guillermo and the others moved down the creek closer to the camp and began to shoot at anything they could see through the smoke of the fires. Several more horses now had frantically broken their tethers and ran from the camp.

One of Pascual's men again raced forward with a lighted torch and heaved it over the horses catching the dry grass behind the camp on fire. Others moved closer to the camp and fired into it with their pistols from behind trees.

Darkness had now set in. Guillermo had one of the men in the creek light a torch, run forward a bit from the creek, and heave it into the camp. A shot was fired at him as he did so, but it missed, being well out of its range.

The camp illuminated by the fires appeared to be in chaos as arrows came streaking in and bullets pinged nearby. The bandits there hid behind trees and on the ground behind piles of their saddles. Occasionally, one of them fired a futile shot at their attackers.

As they continued to shoot arrows into the camp at the dark figures moving about, one of them stood up and shouted, "You fight like women from the distance and darkness! Come out and fight like men!"

"I am Comares! Who is man enough to come out and fight me!" he screamed as he took several steps out away from the trees and into the area of burned grass.

"No, Guillermo! Do not do it! He cannot be trusted!" said Mencía desperately, beside Guillermo.

"Such a challenge deserves to be answered," he told her as he jumped up.

"I will fight you, Señor Comares!" he shouted with determination as he walked forward with his cutlass drawn.

All shooting stopped as the attackers and bandits watched in silence. They both stepped farther forward until they were separated by about ten paces. From the dim light of the nearby fire in the grass, Guillermo perceived from the limp, the tilt of his body, and slackness of his arm, that Comares was wounded.

"Ha! So you, a dusty townsman, not even a soldier, accept my challenge and come out for the honor to fight Comares, eh? And who are you?" asked Comares boldly.

"Honor, you say?" replied Guillermo. "What honor is that? I shall feel no honor when I strike you down, only that I have finished off a wounded murderer and thief."

Outraged at such disrespect, Comares' face contorted with teeth-bared fury as he snarled, "Then there will be no honor!"

The arm that had appeared slack suddenly had a pistol that he quickly fired at Guillermo, who fell to the ground.

With an evil, triumphant laugh, Comares took a step forward to finish him off with his sword when he suddenly felt a sharp pain in his side. Looking down, he saw a knife imbedded deeply in it. Then looking up, he saw a dark figure racing at him at full speed from a nearby bush with cutlass poised to strike.

He barely had time to brace himself as the racing figure with a scream of rage made a vicious slash with its cutlass at his neck. He got his sword up just in time to stop it, but the impact of the cutlass on his sword drove him savagely backward to the ground. He looked up quickly to fend off the next attack, but the attacker was now kneeling beside the man he had shot.

He suddenly realized with astonishment that he had been viciously attacked by a woman with amazing, almost superhuman strength. In shocked disbelief, his distraught mind began to suspect some kind of magic, that these attackers were supernatural fiends, not ordinary mortals. With growing superstitious fear, he picked himself up painfully and suddenly gasped in surprise and pain when another knife magically appeared in his gut. Terror-stricken, he scrambled painfully back to the cover of the trees.

Meanwhile, Mencía was at Guillermo's side and asked, "Guillermo, are you hurt badly?"

Looking up at her worried face, he said, "The bullet hit me on the side of my chest. Nothing vital was hit, I think. Help me up, Mencía."

Mateo was now there too, and they hurriedly helped him to his feet and back to the cover of the creek, where they laid him down in a dry area of the creek bed.

She opened his jacket to see blood oozing from his shirt on the side of his chest. Mateo, beside her, stuffed a cloth under his shirt onto the wound and held it to stop the bleeding.

Mencía, in a fury, jumped up and shouted into the darkness to Pascual and the men, "Guillermo was hit but not badly." Then she savagely shouted, "Throw more torches into the camp, and let us finish it!"

In less than a minute, several men raced forward with burning torches and the camp became illuminated by the burning grass in the camp. Mencía, Sebastian, and Mateo moved from the creek bed closer to the camp, and the men racing about inside it were easy targets. Soon they were falling.

With more fire about, the horses were again excited and screaming as they jerked on their tethers and nervously pranced about. One wounded bandit managed to mount one but was immediately stuck by an arrow and fell lifeless to the ground.

With a roar, Pascual and his men charged the camp from the trees. Hearing this, Mencía and the men along the creek let out their own roar and charged as well. They burst upon the camp, shooting their pistols and slashing with their cutlasses. The bandits in the camp who were unable to flee were quickly dispatched. One of Pascual's men suffered a bullet wound in the leg during the assault.

The remaining bandits fled on foot into the dark among the trees as the attackers looked about victoriously in the camp.

Pascual, Mateo, and Sebastian happily celebrated their triumph. Glancing about, Mateo saw Guillermo gingerly walking toward them with one of Pascual's men supporting him. With concern, he asked, "Guillermo, should you be up so soon?"

"Yes, I came to see the body of that detestable villain."

He looked around at the bodies without seeing him. With sudden realization, he asked frantically, "Mencía! Where is Mencía?"

Suddenly aware that she was not celebrating the victory with them, they hurriedly looked about and called her name without answer.

"She must have gone into the dark after Comares! She was in such a rage," said Mateo.

Pascual shouted, "Quickly! Four men stay here, but everyone else! After them! Mencía is out there with them!"

This caused a great uproar of shouts as the men rushed from the camp in the direction where the few remaining bandits had fled. Once in the dark among the trees, they spread out as they cautiously hurried forward.

After a time advancing through the trees and bushes, they saw up ahead a figure on the ground beside a bush with another figure kneeling nearby.

Mateo and Sebastian cautiously approached and saw the kneeling figure was Mencía.

She pointed and said quietly, "Two more are up ahead on the left in those bushes."

Sebastian stole over to the left where he found Pascual and several other men. He told them what Mencía had said, and they crept off into the darkness. A minute later, Mencía and Mateo heard shouts, the slashing of swords, cries, and then silence.

"I think that is the end of the last of them," said Mateo, crouching beside Mencía. Bending down to see the body beside him better, he could make out the man had a vicious bloody gash in his neck down through his collar bone.

"Is this Comares?"

"Yes," said Mencía standing up. "He was collapsed there when I found him. He was still alive enough, however, to look up at me in horror and shriek 'You!' before I dispatched him."

"You gave him quite a stroke, Mencía. You were probably a little upset with him," said Mateo drolly.

"He paid for his dirty trick. I thought I had lost Guillermo when I saw him fall."

"We should hurry back and tell Guillermo you are well. He was worried about you when he did not see you in the camp afterward," said Mateo.

"Sebastian!" called Mateo into the darkness, "Mencía and I are going back to the camp to see how Guillermo fares."

They heard Sebastian reply, "Very good, Mateo."

"Mateo," they heard Pascual call, "Simón is here and tells me that he counted fourteen dead in and around the camp. These two are dead. Both had arrows in them. Your dead one makes a total of seventeen. That is the lot of them."

"This one here is Comares. Mencía killed him," Mateo called back.

"Well done, Mencía. We will drag him back to the camp and will see you there."

"Very good."

Back at the camp, Guillermo looked up with relief when he saw Mencía and Mateo come in from the darkness.

"Mencía," he said happily, "I do not know why I should worry about you, but I did. It is indeed good to see you are unharmed."

Mencía gave him a careful hug on his uninjured side. When she drew back, Guillermo noticed tears in her eyes.

"Mencía, there is no need for tears. I think my wound is not serious. A glancing blow along my ribs I believe."

"I thought you were dead when I saw you fall. It was quite a scare for me," she said, giving him another tearful hug.

Drawing back and wiping her eyes with embarrassment, she smiled and said, "I thought I had lost my true friend."

30. Wounded

THE TORCHES HAD PROVEN to be quite valuable in the battle with the bandit gang. The fires started by them still burned slowly up the hill and in places away from the camp. The remaining fires in and around the camp were small and quickly put out. Other torches were lit to provide light for the immediate cleanup after the battle. The men collected the bodies and laid them in a row near the camp. Before attacking, they had tied their own horses to trees and bushes a distance away, and men were sent to retrieve them. Once these two tasks were done, the men returned to the camp. Gathering up weapons and rounding up escaped horses could wait for daylight.

As they collected afterward in the camp, they happily congratulated one another for the success of their efforts. One of the men led them in a prayer of thanks. They rearranged the camp quickly to move gear and saddles to unburnt areas and were then able to settle down around a campfire for some food and wine they had brought.

Meanwhile, an estate man named Hector had been tending to the wounds of Guillermo and Ruiz, Pascual's man was shot in the leg as they assaulted the camp. Hector had been the barber-surgeon for some time at Señor Lopez's estate and had brought along his medical bag.

First, Hector worked on Guillermo's more serious chest wound. As Mateo held a torch for light, Mencía and Hector cut away one side of Guillermo's jacket and shirt to get them off and inspect his bullet wound. When they removed the cloth stuffed under his shirt, blood oozed from two separate wounds. The bullet had entered the side of his chest at an angle, bounced along the outside of his ribs, and exited his back. Luckily, no large blood vessels had been hit.

He cleaned the bloody wounds, made up a poultice from herbs in his bag, and applied it to them. A small amount of blood was oozing from the wounds, which he said was good so any infection could also escape. After putting a clean cloth on the wound, he wrapped Guillermo's chest and made a sling for his arm, using the cleanest cloths that could be found.

Next, they attended to the leg wound of Ruiz, who had patiently waited nearby with a bloody cloth wrapped around his pants. Not wanting to embarrass Ruiz, Mencía took a break while they cut the pant leg to expose his wound. Fortunately, the bullet had passed through the flesh of his thigh without hitting the bone. Hector would treat this wound similarly to Guillermo's.

When Hector finished with Ruiz and rose to collect his things, Guillermo reached up to grasp Hector's arm.

"Thank you, Hector, for patching us up. Again, we have Señor Lopez to thank for thinking of sending you."

"You are most welcome, Guillermo. You should rest tonight, and I believe you both will be able to travel tomorrow." With a smile, he added, "And, I must add that it was our great honor to have accompanied you and the others. To have participated in the destruction of Comares and his gang is something I will remember and talk about to the end of my days."

"I am glad. Still, we were fortunate to have your company," replied Guillermo.

"Yes, we were indeed!" chimed in Pascual who had just joined them.

Turning around with a big smile and a wave to Simón, he called, "Simón! Gather your men together. We want to salute and thank you with a toast!"

Simón waved back happily.

"Whatever cups we have, fill them with wine. We can share cups if needed," Pascual shouted gleefully.

With Simón and his four men together and the rest of the men surrounding them, Pascual said with raised glass, "To Simón and his men, a salute to your bravery and friendship!"

Simón quickly reciprocated with his raised glass, announcing, "And we salute you, compadres. It has truly been our honor to accompany such brave men…" He stopped, realizing his error, and corrected himself, saying, "and you, of course, brave Mencía, on such a worthy and daring exploit!"

"Here! here!" said Mateo, and they all lustily drained their glasses. Then began a great free-for-all of cheering, hugs, and back slaps. The high spirits continued for some time as they ate, drank wine, and talked.

Pascual, Mateo, Mencía, Sebastian, and Simón gathered around Guillermo as he lay on a soft cushion of several blankets.

"We should talk about tomorrow," suggested Pascual.

"Hector said Ruiz and I should be able to travel, so we can start back," said Guillermo.

"It may take some time before we are ready to leave," said Pascual. "We can send out men first thing in the morning to bring back the escaped horses. As far as Señor Comares lying over there, we must take his body back as proof of his death. But what is to be done with the remaining sixteen bodies?"

"I suppose we should not leave them for the buzzards. Do we bury them here before we leave?" asked Sebastian.

"We do not have tools with us for so much digging in this dry hard ground. It may make more sense to carry them back to our estate and bury them there," offered Simón.

"These morisco bandits are Andalusians," Mateo thought aloud, "whose families were gathered up from Granada and scattered about in Castile after an unsuccessful rebellion. Their banditry is not a surprising outcome of it. Perhaps it is fitting for them to be buried in their native soil on the estate."

They were considering this a moment, when Mencía asked, "Simón, if we take them back, would Señor Lopez object to burying them there?"

"No, I believe he would not."

Looking around at their faces, Pascual said, "Well, I do not know if they deserve to be buried in their native soil or not. I do know it would be difficult to do otherwise. So it is settled. We will tie them to their horses and take them with us. We should get them on their way as early as possible. It will not be long before they become unpleasant. We will make an early start in the morning. As for tonight, I think a single sentry during the night is a good precaution. My men can do it. Very good then."

Getting up, he added, "I will now get some sleep and see you in the morning. I should also mention that you all are to be commended for your bravery and fine performance today."

With a wave and a smile, he turned and went to find a patch of unburnt grass to spread out a blanket and lie down. Next, Simón excused himself and left, leaving Sebastian, Mateo, and Mencía there with Guillermo.

"How are you feeling, Guillermo?" asked Mencía.

"As well as can be expected, I suppose."

"I will get you more wine to help you sleep," she said, getting up.

"Bring more for the rest of us too, Mencía, if you would," requested Mateo.

Mencía returned with a wine bag and a cup. As Mateo gently propped up Guillermo and supported him from behind, she handed him the cup of wine. He drank it down and handed it back, saying, "Well, drink up, my friends, we have earned it today."

The cup was passed and refilled, and they each drank a glass down. Afterward, Guillermo drank two more glasses of wine and said, "That should fortify me for the night. Mateo, please lie me back down."

He did, and then Guillermo added, "Thank you, my friends. You are all cordially invited to stretch out with me here if you like. Mencía, please remember to keep a proper distance, and Mateo, you are to act as duenna if you would?"

They all chuckled at this as they laid down. In a short while, they were fast asleep.

31. The Dead

AT EARLY LIGHT the next morning, the camp was astir with activity. The eleven bandit horses that did not escape were saddled and loaded with eleven of the dead bodies. Strips of cloth, cut from clothes of the dead bandits, were used to secure them on.

Simón, his estate men, and part of Pascual's men busily readied their own horses for taking this first installment of dead bandits back. Simón's man Hector would go later with the wounded. With a wave to Pascual and the others, Simón and his group set out at a brisk pace leading the eleven horses.

Meanwhile, several men rode out to retrieve the escaped horses, while others rapidly searched the camp area and woods to recover weapons and valuables. As riders brought in escaped horses, each horse was quickly saddled and loaded with a dead body. Within an hour, they had another group of horses ready to go back, six of them loaded with the remaining bodies. They tied a special red bandana on Comares' body to mark it. With a wave, Pascual and his men set out with the horses for the estate back in Andalusia.

In preparation for the ride back, Hector inspected the wounds of Guillermo and Ruiz, seemed satisfied with the look of them, and replaced the bloody dressings with fresh ones.

As Mateo helped Hector ready the wounded for the ride back, Mencía and Sebastian left to retrieve the two remaining escaped horses, which had been spotted during the earlier searches. They returned with them shortly. Soon, the horses were saddled and loaded with the remaining gear and supplies to be brought out. Their party was now ready to leave.

Guillermo and Ruiz were carefully lifted into their saddles and shifted themselves around to get more comfortable. They both looked well enough, not pale, and they nodded that they were ready. The others mounted, and they started out at a walk. Their planned steady slow pace would get them back to the estate by late morning. The others who had left before were well ahead and would arrive at the estate long before them. They probably would start burying the dead soon after arrival.

As they rode along, they saw no one in the desolate landscape. Guillermo and Ruiz must have felt some pain and discomfort during the ride, although they tolerated their pain without complaint. Hector checked the wraps on the wounds during a rest stop on the way and saw no excessive blood loss. As they began the climb to cross over the final chain of hills, they were buoyed at the thought that soon they would reach the shallow river and not far beyond was the estate.

As they approached the enclosure around the main house at the estate, Señor Lopez and Pascual came out of the open gate to greet them.

"Guillermo, Ruiz, you made it. You look tired but not in bad shape," called Pascual.

"Hector, how are they?" called Señor Lopez.

"They seem to hold up, Señor Lopez, with no great loss of blood from the ride."

"Very good, bring them inside to the front of the house. We have two comfortable chairs awaiting them there. Everyone, come inside our walls. Refreshments are being brought out."

As they rode through the gate, Señor Lopez happily reached up and shook hands with them in greeting.

"Welcome, welcome," he said excitedly. "What you have done is magnificent! Who could believe your success would be so complete!"

Pascual was cheerfully welcoming each of them in his happiness at their safe arrival. They pulled up their horses in front of the main house and dismounted. Guillermo and Ruiz were helped down and directed to nearby cushioned chairs.

After they sat down, they were able to clean up a bit with a wet cloth and have a glass of wine. Looking over at a horse tied to a post a distance away, they saw the red bandana around the neck of the body draped over its back.

"Where is everyone?" asked Mateo.

"They are burying the dead off in that direction," said Pascual, pointing.

"It is a place where they will not be disturbed. Burying them in their native Andalusian soil is perhaps a fitting end to their unfortunate lives," said Señor Lopez in a thoughtful tone.

"I am interested to see it," said Mateo.

"I will come with you," said Sebastian.

They looked at Mencía, who said, "I will stay. You go ahead."

Mateo and Sebastian remounted and headed out in the indicated direction.

It was only a short distance before they came upon the men at work with their shovels. They were filling in the last of four mass graves. Piles of boots, coats, cloaks, and hats were nearby on the ground, along with a small bulging sack. Not being a great distance from the enclosure, the men had walked the horses with the dead bodies out there and tied up the horses nearby.

The men greeted Mateo and Sebastian as they rode up and were happy to hear that Guillermo and Ruiz had done well on the ride back.

Only a few minutes later, the burial work was done, and they paused for a few moments looking at the graves. One of them asked if something should be said over the graves.

Mateo spoke up and said, "They were Muslims and would not wish a Christian prayer said over them, so perhaps it is best just to ask that God have mercy on their souls."

With that they collected their tools and walked to the horses. Simón walked over to Mateo and Sebastian and handed Mateo the bulging small sack.

"These are the valuables found in the saddle bags and on the bodies before we buried them. They are for you to take with you."

Mateo looked inside and saw various pieces of jewelry and money.

"Thank you, Simón. I will turn them over to our constable back home."

"We also removed those other articles from their bodies, since they looked to be in good condition. The dead men have no further need for them," he said, pointing.

"Quite so, Simón. You and your four men should have a share in them."

"A wagon will be out soon to take them back so the men can look through them."

The men now began to walk the horses back to the main house. With the smell and blood of the dead bodies still on the saddles, no one was willing to sit in them.

Mateo and Sebastian rode ahead. When they got back to the others relaxing in the pleasant shade in front of the main house, they got a glass of wine and some bread. The others were cheerfully talking when Mateo took Pascual aside.

"Pascual, the men are bringing back the horses that the bandits have so graciously left for us. I propose that each of the men who participated in our adventure should get a saddled horse as a reward for their part in it."

"Mateo, I had the same thing in mind. I propose we leave six horses here as thanks to Señor Lopez and his five men. We will leave it to him to allocate them to the individuals. I will quickly pick out six to leave. They all look to be good horses."

"That leaves fourteen for you and your men," said Mateo.

"Thank you, Mateo, but we are only thirteen in number. We will only take thirteen. You, Mencía and Guillermo can fight over the remaining one."

"Agreed," said Mateo with a laugh.

"Before burying the bodies, they also took what boots, clothes, and hats from the bandits that looked still usable. The men can sort through those to see if they want any."

"Good, the dead bandits certainly have no further need for them," said Pascual.

"Simón gave me a small sack of the valuables taken from the saddle bags and dead men before burying them. I will…"

"What was that?" Pascual interrupted.

"I said that Simón gave me a small sack of the valuables taken from the saddle bags and dead men before burying them. I put it into my saddlebag and will take it back to the constable."

"Hmm," said Pascual, scratching his beard thoughtfully.

"Does Hector think Guillermo and Ruiz are well enough to travel the remaining three hours back?" asked Mateo.

"Huh, oh yes," said Pascual, coming out of his deep thoughts, "they seem to have no complaints about the ride here. Hector did an excellent piece of work bandaging them up last night and has just refreshed their poultices. My other men Alfonso and Sancho had their shoulder and arm wounds dressed earlier in town, but Hector will refresh them as well. I told Hector he was so good at his craft that I wanted to steal him away from the estate. He laughed and said he will give us some of his medicinal herbs to take with us."

"That is good to hear. Hector was indeed a fortunate addition to our enterprise. If they are well enough to travel, then as soon as your men can get some wine and food, we can thank our gracious host and be on our way."

"Agreed," said Pascual, happily slapping Mateo on the back.

As they rejoined the others, the men started to walk into the gate with the horses. Pascual went out, eyed them as they came in, and had six of the horses tied up apart from the others.

The men saw the food and wine set out, and Pascual announced to them, "After a bit of these fine refreshments, which our host Señor Lopez has so graciously provided, we will be departing. So eat and drink up!"

They must have been either hungry or eager to get home because they hurried forward to the food. Pascual and Mateo rejoined Guillermo and Mencía who were thanking Señor Lopez for thinking of the torches and telling him how useful his torches had proven to be.

"The first burning torch caused great chaos among the horses. The sight of the second one coming convinced Comares to come out to attack us. That enabled us to shoot them down with our arrows and not have to overwhelm them in more dangerous close combat."

"I am so gratified to hear it. Still, it was your bravery and skill that subdued them. But I am pleased to hear the torches were of value."

When all the men seemed fed and rested, Pascual loudly announced, "Men, before we go, we have a bit of news!"

After a look toward Mateo, he announced, "Mateo and I think the participants in our recent pursuit performed with such exceptional bravery that a reward is in order."

There was silence as he paused, and the men eagerly waited to hear more. He then continued, "Therefore, as a reward for your gallant service, each participant will receive one of the captured horses and its saddle!"

A great cheer went up from the men as they waved and shouted. Señor Lopez clapped and came to Pascual and Mateo to warmly shake their hands.

When the cheering died down, Mateo added, pointing, "We have set aside six horses for Señor Lopez and his five men for their greatly appreciated assistance. We will let Señor Lopez decide how they are assigned."

Pascual then announced, "As for my men, each of you will get one too. We will decide which ones when we get back, so do not lose any! Mount up and grab a horse to take with us."

This caused a great commotion of farewells, gratitude, and promises to visit one another. After a round of cheers, the men rushed to their horses. The saddles of the bandit horses were given a rapid cleaning with wet rags as each man gathered up a horse to lead.

Several of the saddles had gotten singed and blackened by the fires in the attack on the camp. Mateo laughed when he overheard Pascual's man Sancho pointing out the burned marks to another man.

"Marcos, look at the burn marks on this saddle. I pray to God that I get one like it. People will see these marks and ask about them. Then I will tell them how it happened and that I was one of the party that chased down Comares, stormed his camp, and finished off him and his gang of thieves! God, I hope I get one of these saddles!"

In a few minutes, Pascual's men were mounted and ready to leave. Guillermo and Ruiz thanked Hector again and were helped back up into their saddles. Pascual and Mateo said heartfelt thanks and farewells to Señor Lopez and Simón. Sebastian took the horse still carrying the body of Comares. Mencía and Mateo took the two remaining captured horses. With a wave and a cheer, they all rode out the gate.

Once outside and away, Pascual shouted for everyone to stop and then addressed them.

"Men, we will be returning on the same route we took yesterday. José will be in the lead. We will stay together and travel at an easy pace for our wounded."

Pascual gave a nod to José, who then reined his horse around and headed off toward the trail that the bandits had taken past the estate. Everyone followed behind him. José soon found the trail and turned to follow it back toward their town. The trail was not hard to follow. After all, it was the day-old trail of both the bandits and their party pursuing the bandits. Yet, José carefully looked at the ground as he rode.

Mateo, Guillermo, Mencía, and Sebastian were riding near the back but could see the close attention that José was paying to the tracks.

"Sebastian, what is it with José? What is he looking for?" asked Mateo.

"I do not know. He seems to be looking for something."

When Pascual came back to ride with them, Mateo asked, "Pascual, why is José inspecting the tracks so closely, and why are we even following them?"

"I confess that it is my doing, Mateo."

"What are you up to, Pascual?"

"Where is that sack full of valuables taken from the saddlebags and bodies of the bandits?"

"Here in my saddlebag," said Mateo, patting one behind him.

"Does something not strike you as odd about it?"

"No, I plan to turn it over to the constable and have paid little attention to it."

"How about you, Mencía? Does anything strike you as odd about it?"

"Now that you mention it, there is not very much of it," she replied with sudden realization.

"Exactly, my dear. These bandits have been on a rampage, plundering towns and estates. And we found only one small sack of valuables on them or in their camp. Where are the jewelry and money that they must have accumulated?"

"So you think that they hid it along the trail?"

"Perhaps they carried heavy sacks of valuables that were slowing them down. So, they stashed them quickly somewhere, intending to return some day to retrieve them."

"They were ransacking their wagons when our arrows interrupted them," said Mencía, "probably pulling out the most valuable things to take."

"I agree. It looked like that to me too," said Sebastian.

"I remember getting one man in the leg as he was tying a heavy sack on their packhorses before they fled," said Mateo.

"There, you see. So where are the heavy sacks of loot that were on the packhorses. We want a slow pace on our trip back anyway, so I told José of my suspicions and directed him to follow the trail back and look for any tracks leading away from the main trail," said Pascual with a grin.

"Very clever, Pascual," said Guillermo.

"Perhaps I should go up to help José," said Sebastian.

"Yes, Sebastian, but just you and José. Too many cooks might spoil the soup."

"Sebastian, let me have Señor Comares. I doubt that he will tell you where he hid the loot," said Mateo.

With a smile, Sebastian passed the horse carrying the dead bandit leader to Mateo and then rode forward to join José.

With the chase of the bandits over, Mateo, Mencía, and Guillermo began to think and talk about their friend Tomás, who had been seriously wounded during the fighting in town. The retired cavalier had taken great pride and pleasure in their saber and cutlass training and in their archery skills. Now on their way home, they began to think and worry about their great friend and mentor.

After an hour of travel, their party crossed a creek and road as they continued cross-country along the trail toward the place where the bandits had fled from their wagons. The two trackers found no sign of men dismounting to hide loot.

After another hour of travel, they stopped to rest at the same creek where the bandits had rested briefly during their flight. Pascual thought that it was a likely place for Comares to have hidden the loot. As the group rested, Sebastian and José continued to search about carefully without finding anything. Pascual sighed with disappointment at the news and called for everyone to mount up and continue.

As they rode, they passed the bodies of two bandits who had died of their wounds during their flight. They had seen the bodies during their pursuit and had already been checked for weapons and valuables. Pascual had no interest in spending time now to bury them. The constable could send someone later to do it.

Another hour passed and not much trail remained before reaching the place where the bandits had left their wagons. Pascual was becoming concerned, and Mateo tried to console his friend.

"I am sorry, Pascual. You must be right that they hid their plunder somewhere along the trail, but it appears that we will not find it. You really should not think of it as hidden treasure anyway. It should be returned to the constable and the people who were robbed of it."

Pascual sighed and said, "If we do not find it, news of "the lost treasure of Comares" will spread like wildfire, and every scoundrel in Spain will be combing the area, looking for it. If they were to find it, I doubt that the constable would see a single copper coin of it."

"Regrettably true," replied Mateo.

"Wait!" said Pascual, sitting upright and staring forward.

Mateo followed his gaze forward and saw that José, up front, had pulled his horse to a stop and was sitting upright in his saddle, intently examining a grassy area along the trail. He waved for everyone to stop. Sebastian stopped his horse nearby and also stood in the saddle, intently eyeing the grass. He pointed and José nodded to him.

Pascual rode to the front of their group to better see. Everyone watched as José and Sebastian dismounted and carefully walked through the dry grass, stopping frequently to examine ahead. The trail of crushed grass led to a low outcropping of rocks. José and Sebastian carefully approached the rocks and took a long time examining the crushed grass and weeds in front. Pascual held his breath as he watched.

After examining the front of the rocks, José looked on the other side and suddenly stiffened. Sebastian now looked, turned with an elated smile, and waved Pascual over.

Soon, everyone was dismounted and walking over to see what was there. José and Sebastian brought out six hefty sacks from behind the rocks. Pascual untied one of the sacks and his eyes lit up when he looked inside and saw the coins and jewelry. He lifted a handful out and everyone gasped.

Mateo was now there and heard Pascual tell them, "Señor Comares knew we would be after him. He stopped to quickly hide these heavy bags here so he could travel faster. I suspected as much and told José to look for tracks of them doing it."

"Hooray for José!" shouted one of them, and several slapped him enthusiastically on the back.

Guillermo, Mencía, and Ruiz were now there too, still on their horses and watching.

"Is it ours to keep then?" asked another.

"Well, I am not sure. What do you think, Mateo?" asked Pascual, causing his men to shift their excited gazes to Mateo and listen for his answer with bated breath.

"Well," said Mateo, "much of it may be from Tierracampo and the owners will want it back. The jewelry might be family treasures and keepsakes passed down from generation to generation. If you were to keep such things, you would be little better than the bandits themselves."

The excitement of the listeners dimmed noticeably.

"On the other hand," continued Mateo, and the men perked up again, "the coins are a different matter. To sort out and verify claims of stolen money will be a difficult task. So the coins are a messy business anyway. I do not think it would be wrong to set aside one sack with just coins in it as a reward for recovering the valuables, as well as a reward for your bravery in bringing in that gentleman with the red bandana over there tied on the horse."

The men burst into wild cheering and excitement as Pascual came over and hugged Mateo to thank him. As the men watched excitedly, Pascual and Sebastian dumped the contents of several sacks onto blankets and sifted through the valuables, putting back jewelry and filling one of the bags with gold and silver coins. In a matter of minutes, they were done, and Pascual hoisted the heavy money bag up for them to see. The men cheered again.

Carrying the sacks back to the horses, Pascual told Mateo, "I will keep the bag of coins for us, but perhaps you should carry the other sacks. I do not trust myself to do it."

"You are a good man, Pascual," Mateo said with a laugh as he attached the sacks to the saddles of his and Mencía's extra horses.

32. Success At Great Cost

A SHORT TIME LATER, they reached the spot in the oaks where the bandits had fled from the wagons. The place was now only a trampled dry grassy area with several fresh graves nearby. The wagons and the things that the bandits had hurriedly flung from them were gone.

"The people from Tierracampo probably came to gather up their things and take them back," speculated Mateo.

Looking about, Guillermo said, "There is nothing for us to do here, so we can be on our way to town."

"I believe a triumphal procession is appropriate as we enter town!" declared Pascual with enthusiasm.

He turned and shouted, "Men, straighten yourselves up! Look your best! We are going to parade in triumph into town!"

This announcement was received with a lusty cheer from his men and started a bustle of activity as they straightened up clothes, wiped off boots, put cutlasses and pistols in belts, ran fingers through hair and beards, and gave hats a dashing tilt.

"I give the honor of leading the procession to Mateo, Mencía, and Guillermo!" announced Pascual, and the men heartily cheered their agreement.

"Sebastian, José, and I will be next, but I want the honor of leading the horse carrying Comares!" More cheers. "Everyone three abreast behind us. Look proud, my fine fellows! You have a right to be!"

They howled their agreement and then excitedly formed up into a column three abreast, each with a riderless horse in trail.

"God, I wish we had some flags to carry as we ride in," said Pascual as they sat in readiness to go.

"You are perhaps getting a little carried away, Pascual," said Guillermo with a laugh.

"Perhaps, but one must savor such moments. They come too infrequently. Ah well, let us get started, flags or not," he replied cheerfully.

As the column made its way through the oaks and then onto the roads toward town, it seemed incredible to Mateo that so much had happened since just yesterday. At dawn the previous morning, the town had repelled the attack of the bandits, and shortly thereafter, they began their pursuit of Comares. Mateo smiled at Guillermo and Mencía and they smiled back. Guillermo was riding in the middle of their threesome to protect his wounds from happy, congratulating townspeople. He had taken off the sling on his arm, thinking that it detracted from a look of triumph.

As they approached the outskirts of town, several people saw them and stopped to look. Then waving happily, they ran into town to announce their arrival.

As they reached the edge of town, they noticed that the barricades had been pushed aside and most of the material removed. The street was still a mess of debris from the battle the morning before.

As they rode along slowly, the happy townspeople came hurrying out, and a crowd was forming beside their horses. The people were welcoming and praising them when they noticed with concern the dead body on the horse. Several came forward to tell Pascual how sorry they were that one of his men was killed. He was to be honored by the whole town, they said.

Pascual listened to them with a serious face and then proudly announced, "Comfort yourselves, my friends, my men have no need for your grief. None of them were killed."

The people looked at him with surprise, then at the dead man, and then back at Pascual with a questioning look. Meanwhile, Mateo, Guillermo, and Mencía had turned around to witness with amusement the dramatic performance of their friend Pascual.

"You see all these riderless horses!" he declared, sweeping his arm along the line of riders. The people turned to look at the many horses they were leading.

"There is a great number of them. Do you not think? Only yesterday, a swarm of murderous rabble were riding them. Now their riders are all dead and buried. This body you see here is Comares! We destroyed him and his entire gang!"

The crowd looked up at him with stunned, open-mouthed shock for a moment and then erupted into jubilant celebration that grew as the news spread. They continued to ride slowly to the center of town as the growing crowd of people celebrated around them. The mayor and constable worked their way through the crowd to them. They shook hands happily with Mateo, Mencía, Guillermo, Pascual, and the others as they heaped praise and congratulations upon them. The constable lifted the head of the dead man to look at him.

"So this is Comares. The nearby towns will be happy to hear he is dead. You have done well and are to be congratulated. I will send out a rider right away to announce the good news."

He turned and was looking for one of his men when Mateo called to him over the noise of the crowd, "Señor Constable, how is our friend Don Tomás doing?"

The happy smile left his face as he told them, "I am sorry to tell you that he died this morning. He tried hard to last until you got back, to hear your news, but alas, he was too badly wounded."

Mateo, Mencía, and Guillermo were struck by the news. Closing their eyes sadly, they slumped forward deep in thought, remembering their friend.

Pascual lost his jubilance too, telling them, "A terrible pity, my friends. I know he was a great friend of yours and a gigantic fighting spirit. I am very sorry to hear it."

The constable eyed them sadly and said, "He and two other men were killed in the battle and are being honored. Their coffins lie in state in the church. I will go with you to let you see him. But first, I must send a rider to the other towns. It will only take a moment."

"Señor Constable," called a subdued Mateo, "we also have something to take care of first. We have sacks of valuables stolen by the bandits to turn over to you."

"Very well, please continue to my office, and I will take possession of them. I will be there in a moment."

They were waiting for the constable at his office when he arrived and let them inside.

"Several locked cabinets are in the back," he said as he led them into a back room of his office. He unlocked a cabinet there and watched as Mateo, Sebastian, and Pascual carried in the bags of valuables and put them in the cabinets.

He locked them back up and told them, "After you left, I found the wagons in the oaks and went to Tierracampo to let them know. Their constable was killed in the raid, but the mayor luckily escaped. He sent some people to collect the things there and take them back to their town."

With a sigh, he continued, "They probably are still too overwhelmed to know what valuables are missing. I am guessing that many of these things are from Tierracampo. It will take time to sort such things out, and I will have to help them since their constable is dead. But now, let us go visit our brave fallen friend, Don Tomás."

As he started to usher them out the door, Pascual stopped him and said, "By the way, Señor Constable, you need not concern yourself about a reward for my men for returning the valuables. I have already kept a bag of coins to save you the trouble."

The constable looked at him with a smile, put his hand on Pascual's shoulder, and said, "I greatly appreciate how you and your men came to our assistance so quickly and fought bravely in our interests. You and your men deserve and are welcome to every one of the coins."

"I knew you would think so," said Pascual with a smile.

"You may be in line for even more coins. I will inquire if a reward exists for this villain Comares."

Several minutes later, they all filed solemnly into the church and were met by their priest Father Giraldo. He sadly greeted them and led them to the closed coffin of their friend.

As they gazed upon it, Mateo commented, "It is the simple wooden coffin of a soldier, just as he would have wanted."

They all nodded in agreement. The three of them knelt before it to pray for their friend as the constable, Pascual, and Sebastian stood back respectfully and watched. After a time, the constable asked if they wanted to look inside.

They said yes, and the top of the casket was lifted off. With teary eyes, they gazed upon him. He was dressed plainly but wore the red sash, medals, and saber that he liked to wear on special occasions. He looked contented with almost a smile on his face.

"The old soldier wears the things of which he was so proud," said Mateo with emotion.

"It was your father who suggested it," said the constable.

"And he was right. They suit him well," said Guillermo.

"He looks happy," noted Mencía. "I think he died happy, the way he would have wanted, in glorious battle as he used to say."

"I believe you are right, Mencía. I am happy for him. It is only for us that I am unhappy."

"We will miss him. We were great favorites of his and he of us," said Mateo.

"He was a good man who died an honorable death. There can be no better epitaph for any man," said Pascual.

"Goodbye, old friend," they said as they patted his arm before closing the lid again.

On the way out, Father Giraldo told them, "Praise God for bringing you back safely. Your parents were here earlier praying for Don Tomás. They will be very happy to see you."

As they exited the church, they immediately saw Domingo and Gabriel racing up on their horses. They pulled to a stop, jumped off, and ran excitedly toward them, shouting, "Guillermo! Mencía! Mateo!"

Mencía stepped forward with arms outstretched to intercept them, saying, "Boys, we are happy to see you too, but you must be careful of Guillermo. He is wounded and cannot be hugged."

"Guillermo, are you badly hurt?" they asked with concern.

"No, only a scratch," he said, turning and opening his shirt so they could see the bandage, now showing two patches of blood.

"There, so you see," said Mencía. "We are on our way back to the estate now. You can ride with us."

Then with some concern, she said, "Guillermo, you are bleeding again. We should put your sling back on and get you home to change your dressings and let you rest."

"I agree," said Mateo.

"Well, I guess we should be on our way then," said Guillermo.

"Let me collect up my men," said Pascual, "and we will ride with you. It is time for us to be on our way home too."

They left the body of Comares with the constable. After putting the sling back on Guillermo and helping him gingerly get up on his horse, they said farewell to the constable as he thanked them one more time.

Meanwhile, Pascual had gathered up his men and horses. They all rode through the crowd of townspeople who were still celebrating and waving to them. They, in turn, looked down happily from their horses and waved.

33. Spreading News

AT THE ENTRANCE to the estate, Mateo, Guillermo, Mencía, and the boys stopped and waved as Pascual and his men passed by and continued.

As they rode up the drive, the estate workers came out to welcome them. The boys rode ahead to the main house to announce their arrival. The Don and Doña were outside in front waiting with the boys when they arrived. Mateo dismounted and hugged his parents, while Mencía and Guillermo stayed mounted, so they could continue to his home where he would convalesce. The Don and Doña offered to care for him there in the main house, but Guillermo thought being home with his parents would be better.

"Then we will come and see you shortly, when you are settled," said Lorenzo.

Mencía and Guillermo rode on to the overseer's house where Guillermo's mother and father hurried out to see them. They helped him down from his horse and walked with him inside. Soon, they had his dressings changed, and he was resting comfortably in bed. His wounds had bled some but looked clean and not infected.

Mencía knew Guillermo's mother would pay close attention to his needs, and yet she wanted to stay a day or two to see that he was recovering and out of danger. She would spend the night in the main house, which she had done so often that they had a bedroom set aside for her.

That evening, Mateo, his parents, and the boys came to visit. Guillermo moved out to a comfortable chair on the patio where they sat, drank wine, and talked.

"A mass to honor the town's fallen dead is to be held tomorrow morning," Lorenzo told him.

"I will attend to honor them, especially Don Tomás," said Guillermo.

"I have not heard any details of how he received his mortal wound," said Guillermo. "Mencía and I were at the other barricade and know little about it."

"Sebastian and I were there nearby on the roof," said Mateo, "but did not see it in all the turmoil."

"Maria, perhaps we should go inside and prepare some snacks," said his mother, thinking they probably wanted to talk in private about the fighting.

After watching them leave, Lorenzo began, "I was there beside him. Three of the bandits were climbing over where we were on the left end of the barricade. Two of us shot the first one down. He and the one behind him had already discharged their pistols, so the second one was atop the barricade and Tomás was fighting him with his saber when the third one shot Tomás in the side. He stumbled back a step for a moment and then was at it again slashing at both with his saber.

"Some of Pascual's men were there, and I think it was José who shot the second bandit in the face. One of the others got at the third one with a pike and then someone shot him down. I saw Tomás was wounded and helped him back to a bench. Others took our place on the barricade as the bandits continued to come. Thankfully, we had many pistols captured from your raid. The people behind were reloading them continuously for us, and we seldom wanted for a loaded pistol."

"Domingo and Gabriel were behind on the right end of the barricade harassing them with their arrows," said Lorenzo, proudly looking at them.

"We wounded two as they approached. After we moved back from the barricade, we had to shoot high over our men, so we did not hit very many, only one in the arm and one in the throat," said Domingo.

"Still, I am sure your misses were a distraction and concern to them," said Mateo. "In the wildness of the fighting and the horses racing about, I also had many misses. Yet, Sebastian and I were able to reduce their numbers that made it to the barricade."

"After the bandits gave up and retreated," Mateo continued, "I looked down and saw Father with Don Tomás and that he was wounded. Sebastian and I went to see him right away. They had a bandage on his side and were getting ready to take him to be treated.

"He lit up when he saw us and said with great enthusiasm and pride, 'What a glorious fight! We showed them, did we not! I am proud of you all.' Then he paused in pain for a moment and added, 'Do not mind me. You and the others must follow up our victory and pursue the enemy. Cut them down while they are disorganized and in flight. That is the proper thing to do, follow up the victory. Destroy them as they flee in defeat. So you must go now. Do not mind me. I will be here when you get back. God be with you.' I assured him we would be off after them very shortly, to which he smiled and squeezed my hand before several men carried him away."

"When you told us he was wounded, Mencía and I went to see him quickly, and it was much the same with us," said Guillermo.

"He said he was very proud of his pupils and called me 'his warrior princess' before telling us that we must be going," said Mencía with tears.

After a pause of emotional silence, Lorenzo said, "I was with Tomás early this morning when he died. He thought so very highly of you all. He lived a long active life, seen many things, fought in many battles. Despite that, he told me again that his participation in your training was the highest honor of his life. I believe his last thoughts were of you."

Mateo, Guillermo, and Mencía wept silently for a time at hearing this.

"And we shall always hold him in the greatest esteem and honor him," said Guillermo.

Later, Mateo, Mencía, and the boys rode to Don Felipe's estate. Bernardino had been on the same barricade as Mencía and Guillermo during the attack. Their arrows and Bernardino's bullets had taken a heavy toll on the bandits. As others handed him one loaded and cocked pistol after another, he had stood erect at the barricade, firing calmly at the bandits trying to scramble onto and over it. Somehow, he had come through it unscathed.

When they arrived at the estate, Felipe, Ana, and Bernardino all came out to meet them. Ana rushed to hug Mateo and Mencía, saying, "Dear God, I am so happy to see you back. We have been praying constantly for your safe return."

"Domingo and Gabriel rode over earlier to tell us that you were back," said Bernardino, coming forward to welcome them. "They also told us that Guillermo was wounded. How is he?"

"It is a serious wound, but we do not believe he is in danger. He is recovering at home," replied Mencía.

"That is very good to hear," said Bernardino.

With a somber note, he added, "I am so sorry that your great friend Don Tomás was killed. I can only praise him. I went to see him after the fighting, and even though in pain and knowing that he was dying, he was buoyant and proud. He was a valiant soldier, content to be dying from wounds received honorably on the field of battle."

"The town's defense came at great cost, and we will greatly miss him," replied Mateo.

They paused a moment deep in thought.

"I will miss him as well," said Felipe. "He was a close friend of Mateo's father and me."

"He would have been proud of us," offered Mencía with a weak smile. "We chased down and destroyed the enemy fleeing in defeat as he so adamantly urged us to do."

"Your success was a fine tribute to him," said Bernardino.

"I wish you could have been there, Bernardino. Our destruction of Comares and his bandits was complete," said Mateo.

A truly amazing accomplishment. You and the others deserve such accolades!" said Bernardino, shaking his head with admiration. "I wish I could have been there as well, but with

Don Tomás seriously wounded, the constable asked me to stay to direct the continued defense of the town. Not knowing if we might be attacked again, we kept vigil on the barricades until the afternoon. With the imminent danger judged to be over, we only then began to take down the barricades so that people could return home.

"But not before visiting our church to thank God for sparing our town," added Ana.

Thinking again of Guillermo, Bernardino said, "I am so glad to hear that Guillermo is not in danger and is recovering. We will visit him after he has a chance to rest. Were any others wounded or killed?"

"Three of Pascual's men were wounded, none seriously."

"That is good to hear. Pascual and his men are to be highly commended. They were in the thick of the fighting on the barricades as well," said Bernardino with respect.

Turning to Felipe, he said, "Father, we should send them a token of our appreciation from our animals or supply room."

"I agree, Bernardino. They certainly deserve it."

"I must also say," said Bernardino to Mencía with admiration, "that you and Guillermo were fantastic. I wish we had archers like you at the bridge we stormed in the Netherlands."

"Thank you, Bernardino. I only got a glimpse but saw you shooting them down 'in droves' as Don Tomás had hoped," replied Mencía with a sad smile.

"I did my best, but everyone there was fighting with spirit."

Turning to Ana, Mateo asked, "Ana, you look in good health. No ill effects from all the excitement?"

"No, I am well, thank you, Mateo."

"Perhaps we should go inside," suggested Felipe. "We will say a prayer of thanks to God. Then we can have some wine, and you can tell us more about your chase."

"A fine idea," agreed Bernardino as they turned to walk inside.

The next morning, they all went to the mass for the fallen men and prayed for the soul of Tomás as well as the other two men who had been killed in the fighting.

The family was in a solemn mood that afternoon when unexpected visitors called. A prosperous-looking man and woman pulled up in a carriage and asked to see Don Lorenzo. Upon being cordially received by the Don and Doña, the visitors introduced themselves as Barros and Elvira de la Rocha, the Don and Doña of an estate near Tierracampo.

Apologizing for their intrusion and thanking Lorenzo for receiving them, Barros explained that the constable in town had suggested the visit. They were seeking information to explain the sad and puzzling scene they found when they returned to their estate after the bandit attack on their town.

Barros told them that on that terrible day, they had left their estate in great haste when they heard bandits were attacking their nearby town. When they returned the next day, they found the bodies of their two friends from town inside their house and the bodies of many bandits outside.

They were astounded to see someone had killed the bandits before they could get away. They wished to express their deep gratitude to whoever had done it. Having heard the rapidly spreading word that the local townspeople here had fought and killed Comares, they came to ask the town's constable if he knew who had been to their estate. Not knowing who deserved the credit for the dead bandits, the constable had recommended they see Don Lorenzo and had given them directions. Lorenzo listened kindly to them and then responded.

"First, let me say that we here were all heartsick at the news of your town's misfortune. You have our greatest sympathy and are in our prayers."

"Thank you, Señor."

"I do not know who was at your estate," continued Lorenzo. "However, my son and his two friends were part of the attack on the raiding parties and perhaps will know. They are nearby, and I will have someone fetch them. In the meantime, please sit down and have some wine with us."

As they waited, Barros talked about how they had fled with their estate people to his brother's estate in a town to the east.

When Mateo, Guillermo, and Mencía were told of the visitors, all three of them came at once. Guillermo had his arm in a sling but looked well. Domingo and Gabriel came with them and stayed in the back watching. After introductions, Lorenzo told the threesome what their visitors had said.

"You say two people were dead inside and eleven bandits dead outside?" asked Mateo.

"Yes," replied the visitors.

The threesome looked at one another, and Guillermo said, "There were six of us that attacked the bandits there as they were looting the house and throwing things into a wagon, us three and three others. We surprised them with our arrows from behind the stone wall and the nearby outbuilding. Afterward, we found the two people already dead inside the house."

After their initial surprise, the couple came forward with emotion to thank them with teary hugs, handshakes, and kisses on cheeks. Meanwhile, Lorenzo and Antonia watched with pride. Finally, everyone sat down, and Barros told them more.

"In the rush to leave, we could only bring away our most valued family heirlooms. Upon return, we found our other valuables still there, to our surprise, in the wagons and on the dead bodies of the bandits."

Mateo explained, "Our objective was to surprise a small party of them, kill as many as we could, and get away quickly, nothing more. With the large number of bandits in the area, we only had time to ensure they were dead and collect up weapons before leaving."

"And why would you take this young woman on such a dangerous mission?" asked Barros.

"Looks can be deceiving, Don Barros. She is quite as skilled with weapons as we are. Mencía, maybe you should continue the telling of it?" said Guillermo.

The visitors stared in disbelief at Mencía as she said, "It was fortunate that we got away on our horses so quickly from your estate, because we soon found we were being chased by another group of bandits. We were able to lead them into a trap along the road where we and others killed ten more of them. Only two got away from there and fled back toward your town."

The visitors were still staring in surprise as she finished.

"You must excuse our surprise at hearing that a young woman, such as yourself, was part of the fighting at our estate. How very brave of you," said Elvira.

"I only wish we could have saved your friends. After killing the raiders outside your house, we hurriedly searched inside and found them dead, apparently killed before our arrival," said Mencía.

Barros replied sadly, "Our purpose in coming today is to express our deepest gratitude to those responsible for killing the devils who murdered our friends. And we do so now, most sincerely. They lived in town, and we feel great remorse that we could not bring them with us to safety. One of our neighbors sent someone to tell us the town was overrun by a great mob of bandits, and we should flee. We listened and could hear the gunfire and noise in the distance. We could see the smoke of fires."

"The town was already overrun," said Elvira, sobbing into a handkerchief. "What chance had we of getting our friends out?"

"There was probably very little you could have done," said Lorenzo sympathetically.

"We heard from others afterward that our friends were among the people who sought sanctuary in our church. When the heathen bandits burst in, our priest confronted them. Holding up his cross, he declared firmly, 'This is a house of God and a sanctuary for those inside! You cannot enter!'

"The devils slapped away the cross from his hand and began to beat him. Others inside rushed to help the priest, but they were beaten as well. But greed soon overcame the bandits, and they curtailed the beatings in favor of looting. The heathen beasts began running about the church stealing anything golden and smashing everything else. They smashed the cross and altar, broke stained-glass windows, and started a fire with vestments they found. In the melee of greed and destruction, the people inside fled with our priest.

"We know nothing more about our dear friends after that. They must have gotten separated from the others in the confusion in the streets, fled the town, and made their way through the oaks to our estate. But we were already gone. They must have been trapped in the house when the bandits suddenly arrived. I shudder to think of it."

Poor Elvira began to sob again.

"If it is any solace to you," said Guillermo with conviction, "none of the bandits at your house escaped. Whichever of them killed your friends was killed by us."

With a weak smile, Barros said, "It *is* a comfort. Truly so. It is our only comfort, and I am glad to hear it. I confess that I came hoping to hear it. I do not view it as revenge, but rather as justice for our dear friends."

"We also lost a dear friend in the fighting," said Lorenzo. "A retired cavalier, a brave man full of life, he was mortally wounded in fighting when the bandits attacked our town."

"I am very sorry to hear it," said Barros. Then looking at Guillermo's arm in a sling, he asked, "And you, Guillermo, you were wounded in the fighting as well?"

"Not in the fighting here in town, but during the fighting when we killed Comares."

"So you all were there as well?" he asked.

"Yes," said Lorenzo proudly, "these three and our friend Pascual and his men were the ones who pursued and killed them."

"Actually, we also had five men from an estate near the border who came along into La Mancha and fought with us," added Mateo.

"Did you say Pascual? The one who charges for passage along the road?" asked Barros with surprise.

"Yes, the very one. He is a great friend of mine and of our town. Not only did he and his men help defend our town when the bandits attacked it, but afterward, they helped chase Comares down," said Lorenzo.

"I had no idea. So that is why he is allowed to charge money for passage. The constable can rely upon him in such emergencies. I have new respect for him and his men."

"His benefit to our area is well worth the paltry money he charges to pass," said Lorenzo.

"I see that now," said Barros.

"Mateo," inquired Lorenzo, "you mentioned the five men from the estate near La Mancha. I am greatly interested to hear more about them and your pursuit of Comares into La Mancha."

Turning, he said, "Barros, you and your lovely wife must stay for dinner, so you can hear it too. You need not travel back this evening. We invite you to spend the night here. Tomorrow, we will show you our gardens where we grow vegetables from the Indies. Mateo was a soldier on a treasure fleet galleon and brought back seeds. We have successfully grown them here. Two vegetables called potato and tomato are available now to include in our dinner. You can try them yourself. They really are tasty and interesting to eat."

Barros listened in amazement and said, "All you have said highly interests me. You are most kind. It would greatly please us to stay."

He looked at his wife, and they smiled weakly at each other, their first smile since the bandit attack on their town.

34. A Troubled Mencía

DINNER THAT NIGHT was enjoyable, considering all the terrible things they had recently experienced. Guillermo's parents Miguel and María were also invited. Mateo and Guillermo told of their pursuit of Comares, their attack on his camp, and about finding the stashed valuables on the way back. Not wanting to upset people, they left out the details of how Guillermo had been wounded during the attack. They also judiciously avoided the mention of Pascual keeping a sack of coins. Domingo and Gabriel listened intently throughout and periodically moaned their disappointment at not having been allowed to go.

"Boys, I could not consent to let you go," Doña Antonia told them firmly. "Your mother would have never spoken to me again, and rightfully so."

The visitors were impressed with the new vegetables. Fresh slices of tomato were available for them to taste, and diced tomatoes were added to a paella dish served for dinner. As an appetizer with wine before dinner, they served segments of a potato tortilla, which the visitors thought was quite tasty. With great curiosity, Barros pulled out a piece of potato from it so he could taste it separately. He chewed it carefully, rolled it around in his mouth, and concluded, "Yes, a pleasant taste and texture, and its mild flavor goes well with the onion and egg."

"They are easy to grow," said Lorenzo. "We will show you tomorrow and will give you some seed to plant this fall."

All in all, dinner was a pleasant break from their recent troubles.

In the morning after breakfast, they all strolled out to the gardens where they met Pedro and Joaquin working. Lorenzo introduced them, and Barros complimented them on their fine-looking garden. As he walked through the garden, Lorenzo pointed out to his guests the potato, tomato, maize, beans, and pepper plants, which were all new to them.

The boys had come along too but were impatient to do some archery practice with Mateo and Mencía. After their tour of the garden was over, Barros expressed his interest in seeing for himself their archery skills. He still thought it incredible that Mencía had fought with the men.

Because of his wound, Guillermo only watched as Mateo, Mencía, and the boys dazzled the visitors with the accuracy and range of their shooting.

"Such archery skill must have been greatly advantageous in your fight with the bandits," noted Barros.

"Comares thought so too," chimed in Domingo.

They all turned to Domingo, who said with embarrassment, "I am sorry, Guillermo. I forgot."

Gabriel smacked him on the shoulder.

Shaking his head with a smile, Mateo explained, "We have previously spared you the details of how Guillermo was shot, but I suppose it is time you should know."

"Yes, I suppose," said Guillermo.

Guillermo's parents and the others listened with concern.

"When we attacked Comares' camp," began Guillermo, "we shot so many of his men down with arrows from a distance, that he accused us of fighting like women. He stood up and challenged someone to fight him like a man with swords. I accepted his challenge and went out to fight him."

They all gasped.

"Guillermo, why should you do such a thing?" exclaimed his father in shock.

"I am sorry, Father, but such challenges must be answered."

"But you were shot, not wounded with a sword?" asked Lorenzo.

"When we faced each other," explained Guillermo, "he talked of what a great honor it was for me to fight him. But I found he was already wounded. When I told him that I would feel no honor in cutting him down, only that I was finishing off a wounded murderer and thief, he became enraged. We stood in the dark, lit only by nearby burning grass. Before I knew it, he had a pistol out, had shot me, and I fell. That is how I received this wound."

The listeners looked at one another with concern and Guillermo's father asked, "How then did you kill Comares?"

"I was in no condition to kill him. It was Mencía. *She* killed him," said Guillermo.

They all looked with astonishment at Mencía. Only Domingo and Gabriel, who knew the story, were not surprised and looked at her with great admiration.

"Mencía, I suppose you should tell them what happened next," suggested Mateo.

Mencía said with some emotion, "I was crouched behind a bush a short distance away. When I saw Guillermo fall, I thought Comares had killed him with his dirty trick. I went into a rage and leapt forward. Comares had taken a step toward Guillermo with his saber, but I had thrown a knife that he suddenly discovered in his side. A second later, I was on him, but he got his saber up just in time to prevent me from cleaving him in two with my cutlass. Still, the force of its impact knocked him backward to the ground."

Her audience listened with great interest, some with astonishment and gaping mouths, as she continued.

"I went to check Guillermo and looked back at Comares as he was picking himself up. I do not know what he was thinking, but he looked at me with wide-eyed horror and turned to run off, still with my knife in his side. Mateo and I got Guillermo up and helped him back to safety."

Most were speechless as they looked about at one another in amazement.

"The villain ran off and was not dead?" asked Barros.

"Not yet," said Mateo. "After throwing more torches into their camp to light them up, we killed several more with our arrows. Finally, we assaulted their camp and killed all there. Comares and two others got away in the dark."

"But they had not counted on our enraged lioness Mencía," said Mateo with pride and a laugh, "who chased after them into the dark."

Again, they looked with shock at Mencía who said, "I caught up with them quickly. Comares was by then collapsed on the ground from loss of blood. I heard the other two bandits up ahead hide in some bushes. When I looked down at Comares on the ground, he looked up at me again in horror and screamed, 'You!' That was only a second before I did then with my cutlass what I intended to do before. He did not survive my second chance at him."

Domingo and Gabriel cheered and shouted, "Well done! Bravo, Mencía!" Everyone began cheering, clapping, and coming forward to congratulate and praise her.

Barros could not help himself. He hugged her like she was his own daughter and told her, "My dear Mencía, I cannot tell you how you have lifted my spirits by telling me how this devil suffered such horrors as you flung him down into hell."

Guillermo's mother Maria was hugging and kissing Mencía on the cheek, saying, "Thank you, dear, for saving my boy."

Even Mateo's mother forgot her normal aversion to blood and gore and was smiling and proudly hugging her.

What Mateo had not mentioned was that he too had gotten a knife into Comares as he was picking himself up. No one had noticed him throw it as he rushed forward in the darkness to help Mencía with Guillermo. He had found his knife later in the camp, where Comares had apparently pulled it out and left it. Not wanting to detract from Mencía's fearless attack that had saved Guillermo, he had told no one about it.

When Barros and Elvira left for home in the early afternoon, they were in far better spirits than when they had arrived. They promised to stay in touch and thanked everyone warmly for their hospitality as well as for the justice administered on the bandits.

Meanwhile, the constable back in town had been working tirelessly to deal with the aftermath of the attack by the bandit horde. When the bandits retreated in defeat from their town, a large number of riderless horses remained nervously racing about at the barricades. When they were rounded up and taken to a stable, the constable noted a very ornate and expensive saddle on one of them. Believing that someone would surely come to claim it, he had safeguarded it separately in a storeroom.

Three days later, a man arrived in a carriage and came to the constable in search of an expensive saddle and two fine black horses.

"Señor Constable, my name is Juan Gallegos. I work in the household of the late Señor Vazquez, a city official in Tierracampo," he said in introduction. "Señor Vazquez and his wife were both killed by the bandits."

"I am very sorry to hear it," replied the constable.

"Yes, a most unfortunate event. I am here because Señor Vazquez had a great interest in horses. He and his wife proudly rode their elaborately decorated horses in city parades. Both of their horses and saddles were missing after the bandits plundered our town."

He laid a flat, cloth-covered object on the table and unwrapped it to reveal a painting of a finely dressed man sitting proudly on an ornate saddle atop a fine black horse.

"I brought this painting of Señor Vazquez on his horse to provide evidence of ownership. The Señora's saddle was found in the wagons brought back. The two horses and the second saddle are still missing, and the family of Señor Vazquez wishes to recover them."

"We have the saddle," replied the constable, "and I recall seeing a fine black horse too. It is most regrettable what happened to your town, and to your Señor and Señora."

"Thank you, they were fine people. It all happened very quickly. When two of the fiends burst in the door of our house, Señor Vazquez became enraged and attacked them with a saber, but the first bandit shot him and he fell, then the second one stabbed him several times. The Señora rushed forward and pushed the man with the knife away. He fell backward and got up very angry. The good Señora was sobbing, repeating her husband's name, and cradling him in her arms when the angry villain stabbed her several times in the back with his knife. She seemed hardly to notice or care as she continued to hold her husband and sob.

"We servants fled out the back and escaped. Inside, the devils had mercilessly killed our Señor and Señora trying to defend their property. Outside, the bandits were absorbed in their plunder and not in killing the fleeing people. Perhaps they were excited at finding a town more prosperous than previous ones in La Mancha. The next day when we returned to the house, we found Señor Vazquez and his good wife dead on the floor, still in an embrace."

"Alas, such an unhappy tale. Again, I say I am sorry to hear it. I will pray for them," said the constable sadly. "Come, let us look at the saddle and see if the black horse is in our stable."

The saddle was clearly the same one as in the painting, so the man loaded it into his carriage. They looked at the captured horses in the stable without finding a fine black one.

After pondering for a bit, the constable said, "Other horses were captured by the party that killed Comares. Perhaps I am thinking of one of them. We can go to the camp of those men in your carriage."

An hour later, they arrived at Pascual's camp. They told him their story and showed him the painting. Sebastian was there too and looked at the painting with a frown.

"Yes, I believe we have it here," said Pascual. "Each of our participants in the exploit was given one of the horses and saddles. I believe you got that one, did you not, Sebastian?"

"Yes," he replied.

"Señor Constable, I believe you have a number of other captured horses?" asked Pascual.

"Yes, and Sebastian can have the pick of them in exchange for this one if he is agreeable."

"I am sure the family of my late señor will be most grateful to get it back and provide you a handsome reward as well."

"That will be fine," said Sebastian with a sigh. "You may take the horse. I knew owning such a fine horse was too good to be true. Besides, my horse and I are old friends, and I probably would only have sold this one."

"That is the spirit, Sebastian," said Pascual, smiling and clapping him on the back.

"Come with us into town, Sebastian, and you can pick out a new one," said the constable with satisfaction. The man shook hands with Sebastian, and they went to get the horse.

When they arrived back in town, the man thanked Sebastian and the constable, and left for Tierracampo. He had successfully recovered two of the saddles and one of the horses. One black horse was still missing but would be found a week later grazing five miles away in some oaks. They conjectured that its bandit rider had been killed, and the horse had afterward wandered off.

While there picking out his horse, the constable told Sebastian the sad story of the killing of the previous owners of the black horse, Señor Vazquez and his wife.

Sebastian considered it for a time and said, "If we had heard that story before pursuing Comares, we would have left him and his men there for the vultures, instead of bringing them back to be buried in Andalusia."

"Yes, they certainly deserved no special favors," replied the constable.

On the way back to Pascual's camp with his new horse, Sebastian stopped to see his friends to tell them what had happened. He found Mateo at the main house and together they went to see Guillermo and Mencía at his home.

Sebastian told them about the man and his painting, and they laughed at his bad luck but commended him for returning the horse.

"This man was a servant of the owners who were killed, you say?" asked Guillermo.

"Yes, the painting was proof enough of ownership and the man appeared to be genuine."

"The constable related to me how they died," added Sebastian with a sigh. He then told them of the sad ending of the owners.

Mencía seemed greatly affected by it and started to cry. The others looked at her with sympathy, and Mateo ran to get her a handkerchief. Guillermo put his arm around her to comfort her, and she put her head on his shoulder.

After a couple minutes, she recovered with some embarrassment and sat upright again.

"I am sorry, Mencía," said Sebastian. "It was not my intent to upset you so."

"The fault is not yours, Sebastian. The story is touching, and I am just being a silly girl. It does happen occasionally."

Not wanting to prolong her embarrassment, Sebastian stood and said, "Well, I should be going. Guillermo, you seem to be recovering well. Ruiz's wounded leg also does well. So farewell, my friends. I will see you again soon."

With that, he got up with Mateo, and the two of them left.

Outside, Sebastian asked, "Is Mencía well?"

"Something appears to bother her since we returned from our pursuit of Comares," replied Mateo. "She avoids talking about it. We can only hope time will help."

A week later, Hector paid them a visit. He had ridden from the estate near La Mancha to check on Guillermo, Ruiz, and the others, as well as bring them fresh materials for their poultices. Mateo, Guillermo, and Mencía were happy to see him again and introduced him to their families, who thanked him earnestly for the excellent medical care he had given Guillermo. Since the wounds had not experienced any infection, they had not felt the need to consult a local doctor about them. Hector too was pleased with the look of Guillermo's wounds. He suggested the bandages be taken off periodically to expose the wounds to air and sun, which would help dry them out and speed the healing.

They gave him a tour of the estate and showed him their gardens. They offered to bring him some seeds of the Indies plants after this year's crop, if Señor Lopez was interested. Hector thanked them for the offer and said he would ask.

Mateo and the boys rode with him to Pascual's camp where he was greeted warmly and treated as an honored guest. He checked and was satisfied with the look of the wounds on Ruiz's leg, Alfonso's shoulder, and Sancho's arm. Wanting to take advantage of the opportunity, Pascual had him look at several others at the camp who had various ailments, such as three who needed teeth pulled, a boy with a broken arm, and a woman with an infected eye. He was busy for so long that they insisted he stay for dinner and spend the night. Being too late to return anyway, he consented. With Hector staying, Mateo and the boys said their goodbyes and returned home.

Hector stopped by the estate the next day on his way home to tell them what a splendid time he had at Pascual's camp. While there, Sebastian's father had repaired the worn heels on his boots. At dinner, they had even provided entertainment for him. One of the men played some small drums and several young girls danced with tambourines. It was quite a treat for him since they didn't often have such entertainment on their remote estate. He thanked Mateo again for the kind hospitality shown to him there and was soon on his way.

Two days later, the town held a dinner, not to celebrate their victory but more to thank its defenders. Tables and chairs were set up in the town plaza in front of the church. A great deal of food and wine was on hand and served. Pascual and his men and their wives attended. Their priest led prayers of thanks. It was an occasion for the mayor and other officials to give speeches in praise of the town's defenders. The constable surprised the crowd with news about a reward for Comares.

Soon after their return with the body of Comares, the constable had sent word to the nearest town to the north in La Mancha saying Comares had been killed and inquiring if any reward might be involved.

In response, several officials from La Mancha had come to inspect the body. They had brought half of the reward with them, although they knew it could not possibly be Comares. He had been the head of a formidable horde of bandits and had successfully evaded and fought them off for many months. Still, it seemed to them that they should go through the necessary motions of coming to verify it was not Comares.

The officials held their handkerchiefs to their noses as the constable lifted the top of the coffin for them to look. They were startled at the sight of the body and grew excited that it might in fact be Comares. One craned forward to look more closely.

"The pointed beard, the scar on the face, the dark mole on the neck! Yes, it is Comares!" he said with astonishment. "How is it possible you have accomplished what we could not?"

"A group of our men, and I might add a woman," explained the constable, "ambushed and killed a good number of the bandits as they pillaged estates around Tierracampo. Then many bandits were killed in their unsuccessful attack on our town. Finally, a group of our men and the woman pursued the remaining bandits and killed the rest. When they attacked his camp, this man declared he was Comares and dared someone to fight him man-to-man with swords, so we know this to be his body."

The official looked again at the body and noting the vicious cut on the neck, said with admiration, "So one of your brave men fought and killed him with his saber. What an exemplary feat of bravery and honor! I am greatly impressed."

"One of our men did answer his challenge and faced him. But this villain lying here had no honor. Our man was almost killed when Comares pulled a pistol and shot him. No, Comares was killed later after they stormed the camp, killed actually by the woman."

They were astounded at hearing this, and finally declared that the constable and the town deserved the highest praise possible for their brave efforts. They handed him the reward money they had brought and promised to bring him the rest of it soon.

The constable related this story to the crowd at the town's dinner and when done, he presented the small sack of coins to Pascual for him to parcel it out to those involved in the killing of Comares. Pascual accepted the sack and held it in the air as everyone applauded. When the second half of the reward was received weeks later, the constable suggested a portion might go to the families of the two men killed during the fighting. But Pascual disagreed and gave it all to them.

The town's dinner broke up in the early evening to get people on the road home before dark. It was a somber yet happy ending to an unhappy experience for the town.

Pascual and his men joined Lorenzo and the others as they rode home from the dinner. When the group reached the drive into Lorenzo's estate, he and Pascual were there together on their horses and leaned in their saddles toward each other to shake hands.

"Thank you again, my friend. I hope we will meet again soon," said Lorenzo.

"It will be my honor to do so, my friend," replied Pascual.

After a chorus of goodbyes and waves between the many people, Pascual, his men, and their wives continued down the road as Lorenzo and the rest started into the drive.

35. At Last

WITH THE TOWN DINNER OVER, Lorenzo and his wife returned their thoughts to traveling south to see how their cousins and their recently found son Reynaldo were doing. The Doña was anxious to check on Luisa as well, although she knew Luisa's parents would take good care of her.

They talked to Mateo and soon plans were being made for the trip. The boys were also eager to return, because they had so much to tell their parents about all that had happened here. When Lorenzo thought about it, he was amazed at how much there was to tell. He hoped it would not detract too much from the main reason for going, which was to celebrate the return of Reynaldo.

In two days, they would be leaving, and it made sense that they would be bringing Luisa and the baby back with them. Still on the mend, Guillermo would not be going. Miguel would run things while they were gone, a time when many of the new vegetables would be coming in. Lorenzo regretted that he would be away, but the trip was important and could not wait.

Mencía would not be traveling south with them either. She had stayed at the estate much longer than initially planned, and she thought it was time to return to her family for a while.

The town in which her family lived had not been threatened by the horde of bandits. When her parents heard about the attack on the local town, they had been worried for their daughter's safety, of course. It didn't ease their worries when they received a message from Lorenzo saying she had fought in the battle there in town, was unhurt, and now had ridden out with the others in pursuit of Comares. His message had caused her parents a great deal more worry.

After returning safely from their pursuit of Comares, she had gotten word to them that she was back, unharmed, and staying at the estate to help care for Guillermo. They had been greatly relieved to hear it and came to visit her. That had been some time ago.

There really had been no need for her to stay to help care for Guillermo for the last two weeks. It had been a difficult time for her, and it pained her to think of leaving him after having almost lost him. She sometimes found herself crying again after thinking about the story of the man and his wife killed by the bandits. Mateo and the others had noticed something was troubling her, and that she no longer smiled. They wanted to help her but did not know how.

She still vividly recalled the moment when she saw Guillermo fall and thought he was dead. He had survived, but the thought of it still bothered her. Now with Guillermo well on his way to recovery, it was time for her to return to her family. After a time, she would then come back to see him again.

Mateo and his family would be leaving soon to travel south, Guillermo would be staying, and she was leaving to go home. It was for some reason very unsettling for her.

Before her planned departure later in the day, she and Guillermo took a walk to look at the gardens one more time. After strolling to the far end, Guillermo was looking at the tall maize plants in front of them when he noticed Mencía was crying.

"Mencía, you are crying?" he said with surprise, putting his arm around her shoulders.

She said nothing as she wiped at her tears.

"Mencía, how can I help you? Something has been bothering you. What is it?"

"I am sorry, Guillermo. I do not know what is wrong. For some reason, I cannot get the thought of the man and his wife killed by the bandits out of my mind."

"The tale is truly a sad one," said Guillermo, "but there have been a great many sad tales lately. Why should that particular one bother you so?"

"When I think of the wife seeing her husband being killed and rushing to him, I am reminded of that night when I thought you were killed and rushed to you. When Comares shot you, I thought you were dead, and I had lost you."

"Mencía, please do not let it trouble you so. Thanks to you, all turned out well. He would have finished me off if you had not attacked him with such force that you knocked him backward to the ground. Mateo told me that he was so shocked and surprised by it that he ran off like a scared rabbit. You saved me once again. I would be such an ungrateful fool if I were ever not to have you with me, by my side."

They stood together for a moment in silence.

"When I think of seeing you fall," said Mencía with emotion, "and of the wife running to her fallen husband, I can only imagine…" she paused, "that she must have loved him as much as I love you."

They looked into each other's eyes, slowly came together, and kissed. Then they tightly embraced, and Guillermo said with emotion, "I love you too, Mencía. I suppose it is high time that I admit it, and we do something about it. Do you not think so?"

"Yes, I do, Guillermo," she said, tearfully hugging him.

They happily kissed again, and Guillermo asked, "Then you will marry me and become my wife?"

"Yes, Guillermo, I will, but we can still be true friends," she said, smiling.

The End

The adventures of Mateo, Guillermo, Mencía, and the others continue in *My Intrepid Brothers*. Cousin Reynaldo has been recently found. Our true friends have just participated in the destruction of a bandit horde and their families are still stunned by the experience. Guillermo and Mencía have finally admitted that they are more than just friends. What more could happen? As stated before, life in late sixteenth century Spain has more adventures in store for our true friends and their families. JRC

List of Characters

North of Cordoba

Mateo, Guillermo & Mencía - the true friends
Luisa & Santiago - Mateo's wife & new son
Don Lorenzo & Doña Antonia - Mateo's father & mother
Santiago & Esteban - Mateo's deceased older brothers

Miguel - Guillermo's father, Don Lorenzo's overseer
María - Guillermo's mother
Rosa – Don Lorenzo's housekeeper
Pedro & Juana - Don Lorenzo's gardener & his wife
Joaquin - morisco gardener

Don Tomás - Retired cavalier friend and mentor
Pascual - local highwayman, Don Lorenzo's friend
Sebastian - one of Pascual's men, the true friends' friend
José - one of Pascual's men

Don Felipe - Don Lorenzo's friend and neighbor
Ana - Don Felipe's daughter
Don Cosme - Don Lorenzo's friend
Bernardino & Lope - Don Cosme's good and bad sons

Comares - leader of morisco bandit horde
Señor Lopez - Overseer of estate near La Mancha
Simón & Hector - Señor Lopez's men

Cordoba
Gonzalo Cruz & Rachel - merchant & his daughter
Pablo - leader of kidnappers
Alonza - woman kidnapped by Pablo
Señor Ramirez - money lender with kidnapped children
Jaime Sanchez - morisco whose sister was kidnapped
Antonio - street person

West of Cordoba
Don Francisco & Doña Isabel - Luisa's father & mother
Domingo & Gabriel - Luisa's younger brothers
Don Carlos & Doña Catalina - Mateo's cousins
Cristóbal & Reynaldo - Don Carlos' missing sons

Near Seville
Don Diego - Mateo's Uncle, Guillermo's natural father
Floriana - Don Diego's love, Guillermo's natural mother
Agustin & Andrés - Don Diego's sons
Beatriz - Rescued girl adopted by Don Diego
Rodrigo - Don Diego's overseer
Martín - Mencía's devotee
Don Hernando - Don Diego's neighbor
Alvaro & Matias - Floriana's late husband & his friend
Bartolomé Gómez - Victimizer of Floriana

Made in United States
Orlando, FL
08 February 2024

43444649R00143